SEYOON AND DEAN, Unscripted

SUJIN WITHERSPOON

UNION
SQUARE
& CO.

NEW YORK

Cover design by Marcie Lawrence
Cover illustration by Sarah Long
Cover type design by Idle Letters

Union Square & Co.
Hachette Book Group
1290 Avenue of the Americas, New York, NY 10104
unionsquareandco.com
@unionsqandco

Union Square & Co. is an imprint of Grand Central Publishing, a division of Hachette Book Group, Inc. The Union Square & Co. name and logo are registered trademarks of Hachette Book Group, Inc.

Print book interior design by Rich Hazelton

Library of Congress Cataloging-in-Publication Data has been applied for.

ISBNs: 978-1-4549-5405-7 (hardcover);
978-1-4549-5407-1 (paperback);
978-1-4549-5406-4 (ebook)

Printed in Canada
MRQ-L
2 4 6 8 10 9 7 5 3 1

For anyone who worries they're too much,
and everyone who feels like not enough.

1

HOW MY COMPLETE LACK OF A BACKBONE LANDED ME ON NATIONAL TV: A TRAGEDY IN TWO PARTS

DEAN

Most people have better things to do on a Friday night than rescue their sister from a first date at Applebee's. I am not most people.

Meredith briefed me on the situation via panicked, typo-riddled texts begging me to bail her out. Apparently, her date spent fifteen minutes complaining about their ex, only to be interrupted by a ping on their phone—which was a text from said ex. So, like the kind twin brother I am, I agreed to brave the horrors of America's most nauseating chain restaurant to save her.

In true white-suburban-town fashion, Applebee's is the crown jewel of Auburn, Massachusetts. Nearly half the population is packed into the maroon booths when I walk in, but it's still easy to spot Meredith's blond curls from across the restaurant. I awkwardly sidle past the hostess, holding my breath so the greasy fumes don't make me queasy. I got food poisoning here a few years ago and haven't been back since. I can still see where I vomited, the stain apparently forever memorialized in the low-pile carpet. I step over it and head to where Meredith's seated in the middle of the restaurant.

Her date, a girl with freckles and short brown hair, stops talking when she notices me approaching. Meredith twists over her shoulder, relief visibly flitting across her hazel eyes. She feigns surprise.

"Dean!" she exclaims. "What are you doing here?"

I cringe as the nearby tables look over to see what the commotion is. I should've changed out of my sweatpants and ratty white shirt. To be fair, Meredith said it was an emergency. Heat singes my ears as a waitress peers over, curious.

"Er," I say. I had come up with an elaborate excuse on the drive over, but with everyone's attention on me, my brain short-circuits. So what I get out is "It's Mom. She's . . . dead."

She's not. Well, I don't know. She hasn't been in our lives for over a decade. A woman at the next booth gasps. Meredith's eye twitches.

"Oh my God," says her date, reaching across the table to lay her hand over Mare's. "I'm so sorry. That's awful."

"Yeah. That *is* awful." Meredith glares at me. I wince.

She throws a few bills on the table, apologizes to her date, and then we hightail it out of there. I keep my eyes trained on the carpet—both to avoid stepping on suspicious stains and so I don't have to see everyone staring at us. Being perceived is one of my least favorite pastimes.

Once in the car, Meredith punches me in the arm.

"Ow!" I swerve into a curb on our way out of the parking lot. We may have similar builds, but she's the only one who got Dad's strength. *My* strengths are more mental than physical. Except for tonight, when I demonstrated neither. "What was that for?"

"For saying our mom's dead in front of a bunch of middle-aged ladies drinking Dollaritas."

"The state of our mother's well-being won't ruin their dollar margaritas, I promise. I got you out of there, didn't I?"

"My hero," Meredith drawls. She slumps back in her seat with a groan. "That was, like, my fourth bad date in a row. Totally not worth sneaking out for. Maybe I should give up and start setting you up on dates instead."

"You don't even know what my type is."

"Let me guess. Someone sweet and bubbly, with a pretty smile, and oh—bigger muscles than you?"

I glare at the road, saying nothing. Damnit. She does know my type.

"Thanks for picking me up," Meredith hums.

"You better be. I'm missing *Forest Feud* reruns for this."

She snorts. Either at my long-standing obsession with reality TV, or at the confirmation that I did, in fact, have nothing better to do than interrupt her date.

I peek over at her as she unfolds the sun visor and wipes something off her pale cheek. On the outside, we're nearly identical: same sharp features, matching dimples, even our laughs sound alike. Somewhere along the way, though, Meredith blossomed into a social butterfly adored by everyone, while I grew into a quiet, nerdy book lover in the shape of her shadow. But I don't mind that she absorbed all the likability in the womb; I'd hate to have the kind of attention on me that she effortlessly attracts. She's still my best friend at the end of the day.

"Speaking of *Forest Feud*," she says, making me perk up. "There was a commercial for it playing on the restaurant's TV. Did you know that they're rebooting the show? The new host is an old contestant. The guy who beat Dad, actually."

My grip on the steering wheel tightens. "Um," I say. "Yeah. I heard something about that."

"I almost feel bad for Dad. Like, man, the guy who betrayed him twenty years ago is gonna host his favorite show of all time. That's gotta hurt." She clicks her tongue. "But that's karma for grounding me for no reason."

"I don't think that karmic scale is very equivalent. Besides, didn't he ground you for sneaking out? Again?"

"No, he grounded me because I said I'm moving to Oregon with you after graduation. The universe is punishing him justly for treating me like a flight risk."

If he weren't my dad, too, I'd think she was exaggerating, but she's not. Dad worries about her. And everything. *All the time.* A trait I unfortunately inherited from him. To say his parenting style is smothering would be phrasing it mildly. It's more like he's simultaneously putting us in a stranglehold and suffocating us with a pillow . . . but with love.

"You shouldn't push his buttons so much," I murmur. "It's what gets you in trouble."

"Easy for you to say. He treats us totally different. Always has. I mean, Dad didn't give you nearly as hard of a time when you said you were moving across the country next year."

I want to argue that it's because we're moving for different reasons. I'm still a junior, but I got an early scholarship to Reed College, so of course I have to go to Portland. Meredith, however, wants to move to the big city for the comforts our small town lacks (i.e., a queer-friendly community and a hangout spot other than Applebee's). I want to tell her *that's* why Dad is giving me more slack than her, but I can't. We both know that's not really the truth.

Meredith sighs and goes on. "I know he breathes down your neck too. Which is why you should stand up to him. He'd listen to *you*."

I'd rather pluck out my own eyeballs and learn to juggle with them. I hum, noncommittal. The rest of the drive home is silent, but I can feel Meredith's frustration roll off her in waves. We park in our driveway, lit only by the brassy glow of a nearby streetlamp. I remove the keys from the ignition, turning them over and over in my hand without getting out yet.

"It won't be like this forever," I say when I eventually find the words. "You won't always have to sneak out of the house. Be stuck in this town. Dad will come around eventually and let you go, too."

Meredith's quiet makes me uneasy. It's a wall in the space between our seats.

"No, he won't," she says.

"He will. He always—"

"No," she interrupts harshly. I look at her. "Dad said he won't help me. If I can't pay for the move myself, I can't go to Portland."

My jaw falls. "What?"

Our family's fortunate enough that we've never had to worry about the roof over our heads or if there'd be food on the table. My scholarship covers my expenses, but if they didn't, I know Dad would help in a heartbeat. He's good like that. So for him to not help Meredith—his favorite child?

Guilt churns my stomach. *I* was the one who wanted to leave Massachusetts first. Well, after Mom, that is. I remember telling Dad about the scholarship, about Reed's amazing literature program—and then breaking the news that it's all the way in Portland. His silence lingered a little too long before he said in a gentle, almost sad tone, "You really are like your mother."

I have to take his word for it. Everything I know about her is filtered through him. Sometimes, when he tells me I remind him of her, I hear in his voice how much he misses her. I hear what he really means to say: *"I'm going to miss you too."*

It's clear Dad's not angry at her for leaving. Just confused. I think he didn't always understand her. Maybe it's why she left. Maybe it's why I want to leave too.

My throat tightens. It's not my fault Dad treats me and Meredith differently, but I do feel guilty for leaving her no choice but to be the one who stays for him.

"Mare . . ." I start.

"Hey, what can you do?" She smiles, but it doesn't touch her eyes. "Let's go inside."

We avoid the front door. Dad's probably asleep in the living room, and I don't want him to realize we've been gone, so I guide us around back where there's a sliding-glass door that leads directly to my room. I slide the door open carefully.

Sitting there, on my bed, is Dad. My heart drops. Meredith and I lock terrified eyes with each other.

"I can explain," I blurt.

"You better," Dad says.

He stands, crosses the space between us—and then wraps me in a hug. "Why didn't you tell me right away?"

Through my confusion, I notice two things: One, he's wearing his old, three-sizes-too-small *Forest Feud* camp shirt. And two, my laptop is open on the bed, with the life-changing email I received this morning still on the screen. My blood runs cold.

"What's going on?" Meredith asks, looking between the two of us.

"Dean's going to be on TV!" he exclaims, too giddy to remember she's supposed to be grounded.

"You went through my email?" I wheeze.

Dad smiles sheepishly behind his thick, dark goatee. "I wasn't trying to snoop again, I promise. I came to check on you because I thought it was strange you skipped out on TV night, and your laptop was open so . . ."

Meredith picks my laptop up to see for herself. I've read the email so many times, I practically have it memorized.

> Mr. Dean Parker:
>
> On behalf of TSW Studios, we are thrilled to invite you to be a contestant on the reboot of *Forest Feud*, the #1 game show in television history.
>
> As you probably are aware, *Forest Feud* is a beloved reality show where twelve teens compete in high-stakes games and challenges in the Pacific Northwest wilderness for a chance to win one million dollars. This season, each player is a relative of an iconic contestant: six relatives of former winners and six relatives of former losers.
>
> We would be delighted to have you, Vince Parker's son, join us for filming this summer.

> Attached is a media kit and documents for you and your legal guardian to review and sign. Please let us know your decision as soon as possible.

Meredith whips her head at me. "How could you not tell me?"

I grimace, dropping my eyes with shame. We never keep secrets from each other.

Dad throws an arm around my shoulder, pulling me in close. I accidentally inhale decades-old dust embedded in the threads of his shirt. His green eyes are sparkling.

"Can you believe it? The show we watched every week for years. The one your old man almost won." Pride spills into his words. "You're going to be on *Forest Feud*."

Fuck. *Fuck*. This is exactly why I didn't tell them.

I open my mouth. I can't get the words out. Dad pats my back, then the words expel themselves like puke on an Applebee's carpet.

"I'm not accepting it," I blurt.

Their jaws fall. Meredith picks hers up faster. "Why the hell not?"

"I . . . I'm not fast enough, or interesting enough. I'm not the kind of person who should be on TV. I don't—I'm not like you. Or you." I look at Dad, then avert my gaze.

You may be thinking, *Geez, this guy's self-esteem sucks*. And yes, there's some truth there, but it's objectively factual that I'd lose. Sure, I'm smart, and I've seen enough game shows that I know the winning strategies well enough. But I don't have the physical strength necessary to get me very far. Or the charm. I get sweaty on picture day—what the hell would I do in front of a hundred cameras? The truth is I'm weak. If I went on the show, I'd just be letting Dad down. Proving that we're nothing alike.

It hurts to admit. To acknowledge that I've always been good enough, but not great. I'm not the kind of guy who lights up a room when I walk into it. I'm a follower, a floater content with my quiet life and handful of friends from the Lit Happens book club. The opposite of the man Dad was during his time on the show, or the person Meredith is now.

They're both watching me. I want to scratch the sensation of their eyes off my skin. Dad blinks. He drops his arm and steps back, tugging down his ridiculously tight shirt. Something settles heavily on his shoulders. Disappointment.

"You don't have to make a decision right away. You might change your mind," he tries.

"Dad, I really—"

Meredith laughs. "If Dean doesn't want to do it, I will. A million-dollar prize would be more than enough to fund a move to Portland. Then, you'd have to let me go, right?"

Dad's thick brows pinch. "Well . . . did you receive an offer email?"

She pulls her phone out and frantically scrolls. The hope in her face fades. "No. No. Why not? I'm your kid, too. Why didn't they send me an offer?" Bitterness crests her words. "It's not fair."

I stiffen.

The air is thick with tension. Dad clears his throat. "It's late. How about we all head to bed, and we can discuss this more in the morning?"

There's nothing more to discuss, but I nod. Meredith purses her lips. Dad leaves awkwardly—thankfully forgetting to be mad at us for sneaking out.

Meredith sucks her teeth. "Thanks. For coming to get me. And for showing me how to sneak in through the back door." A frail smile twists her mouth. "I think I'll be using that trick for a while."

And then she leaves too.

I sink to the carpet with a groan. I was so preoccupied with how much I didn't want to be on the show that I didn't consider whether they'd asked Meredith: the much-more-qualified, much-more-TV-friendly version of the two of us. She's right. Why wouldn't they reach out to her too? Despite being twins, nothing about our lives has been equal.

Turning back to the email on my laptop, I pick at the skin around my nails and think. It's not fair, I know it's not, it never is. I wish I could change that. I'm already leaving her behind. And leaving her with no choice.

. . . But maybe I can leave her with *something*.

✧✧

It's midnight when I creep downstairs. I'm a night owl. Dad is too. One of the few things we have in common.

The TV is playing quietly from the living room. It's the only source of light in the otherwise-dark house. I hover near the wall behind where Dad's sitting in his recliner. The finale of the fifteenth season of *Forest Feud* is playing. The season he almost won.

The teenage version of my father runs across the screen. A girl with black hair darts after him. Jungeun Kim. The other member of Dad's alliance. Finally, Garrett Moxley—the third member of the famous Final Three, and *Forest Feud*'s new host—appears. He's slow. It never made sense why the two of them didn't drop him from their alliance. I would've asked why, but Garrett Moxley is a sore subject in this household.

Dad turns the TV off when the three of them get to the last fork in the obstacle course race. Right before Garrett betrayed them and convinced them to go down the left path, when he somehow knew the one on the right was the one that led straight to the finish line.

He never rewatches this part. We both know how the finale ends.

I clear my throat.

"Christ!" Dad jumps, looking back at me. "You almost gave me a heart attack. Why are you up?"

I take a seat on the sofa. "I'm sorry I didn't tell you about the invitation."

There's a long pause. "I haven't told you something either." He takes a deep breath. "The producers of *Forest Feud* reached out to me about the reboot a few months back. I told them about you, but they couldn't guarantee you'd be selected, so I kept my mouth shut until I—"

My jaw drops. "You signed me up? What—why didn't you tell them about Meredith instead?"

"Because this show is *our* thing."

I stiffen at the vulnerability in Dad's strained voice. I'm grateful for the dark so I don't have to meet his eyes.

Dad sighs. "I shouldn't have done it without asking you. I know—I'm sorry. But it just got me excited, imagining you doing the same thing I did at your age. I . . ." He laughs lightly, awkwardly. "I had this vision of when you go off to college, and we can't have our weekly reality show nights anymore, that I could turn on the TV and see you there. That way, it'd almost be like you're still around."

His words hit me so hard that my gut turns in on itself. It hurts to leave somebody who doesn't want to be left alone. I want to give Dad something, too. I turn my eyes to the ceiling when they start to sting. I picture Meredith upstairs, snoring loudly in the childhood bedroom she outgrew a long time ago.

"I wanted to talk to you about Mare," I say.

The recliner squeaks as Dad shifts uncomfortably. He knows what I'm going to say. "A big city like Portland is dangerous, it's no place for a young girl on her own. I'm just looking out for her."

Meredith is more than capable of looking out for herself. More than I am, frankly. It's not fair how differently he treats us, just because one twin came out as a girl. *I should tell him that.*

But the words get stuck in my throat, as they always do.

In truth, I don't have the courage to break the safe, comfortable dynamic between me and Dad. We don't have a lot. He and Meredith? They share nearly everything: their love for sports, their taste in food, their effortless charm. But me and Dad? We have trashy reality TV, conversations about Mom, and an unspoken understanding that I'm his easy child. I'm not the one who pushes his buttons. If I ruin that, what will we have left? Mom's long gone, and pretty soon, he'll be watching reruns by himself.

So, instead, I say, "I'll go on *Forest Feud*."

He pauses. "Really?"

"But only if you let Meredith move to Portland with me. You told her she has to fund the move herself, right? Well, if I win, I'll use the money to get a place for the both of us out there. What do you say?"

Dad doesn't respond for so long that I wonder if he got up and left without me noticing. I'm about to reach out blindly and feel around when his recliner squeaks and two meaty arms wrap me in a bear hug.

"Is—" I cough into his shoulder. "Is that a yes?"

He lets go. My vision adjusts enough to make out that he's smiling. I smile, too, relief washing over me.

"How could I say no? *My* son. On *Forest Feud*." He sniffles. "Wait, hold on, I have something for you."

He hurries out and is back a few minutes later. Dad flicks on the light and I shield my eyes, blinking until they stop burning. But when I catch sight of the hideous, battered, *neon-orange* suitcase he's wheeled in, they start to hurt again.

"This is the exact suitcase I brought to the show. I want you to have it."

Dad puts the handle of it in my palm and folds my fingers over it like it's a treasured family heirloom. The handle is oily for some reason.

"It's, uh . . ." I clear my throat. "Nice? Thanks, Dad."

He ruffles my hair, and this time, I don't really mind that he's frizzing up the curls.

"I'm so proud of you, Dean." Dad smiles. "I know you won't let us down."

"I won't," I reply.

I can't.

2

I GOT ROBBED AT A NATIONAL PARK AND I DIDN'T EVEN GET A LOUSY T-SHIRT

SEYOON

America's favorite reality show is not only back . . . but better than ever!

What's that sweet sound? Nostalgia? Better. It's me, Garrett Moxley, your new host of Forest Feud*—returning twenty years after the epic finale. But don't think this is some lame reboot. No, we're ramping things up. I'm talking high-stakes challenges and competition like never before.*

So tune in next summer for the brand-new season of Forest Feud, *where twelve brave teens will battle each other and the elements for a chance at one mill—*

Jesus, not this guy again. How much advertising budget could one washed-up ex-star really have?

I reach over and click the radio off with more force than necessary. Umma, her hands stiff on the steering wheel, frowns at the highway.

"I was listening to that," she complains mildly.

"I've had enough of Garrett's nasally voice. I'll be hearing it every day here pretty soon," I complain, but I turn the radio back on, flipping to another station. A Christian jazz choir? Sure, fine, I'll take anything that isn't the *Forest Feud* commercial.

"Maybe *I* want to hear his voice. Have you thought about that?" Umma teases, sparing a glance away from the road to give me a shit-eating grin. "It's been a long time since I've heard it. He sounds as handsome as he did when we were on the show together."

I burst into laughter. "Umma! Gross!"

"What? I'm a single woman now."

My laughter dies down. Right, she's single now. The rattling of her busted car engine that we can't afford to get checked out makes it impossible to forget how the ink on the divorce papers is still wet. And there's also the fact that Umma—the most nervous driver in the state of Oregon—is driving me up to the set of *Forest Feud* herself.

When Appa was still in the picture, she never drove. The only thing I could reliably count on him for was driving me to and from school while she worked. Drives with him were always silent, though, no matter how many times I tried to start a conversation. He thought my "chatter" was distracting. But Umma doesn't. Even though her knee's bouncing with nerves, she's still managed to crack jokes with me the whole ride.

At the thought, I look over at her and smile. "Fine, tell you what: When I win Garrett's stupid show and that million dollars, I'll give him your number." *And buy you a new car you feel safer driving.*

"Oh God, Seyoon. Please don't. He seems like such a . . ."

"Shithead?"

"야. Language."[1]

---

1. Hey.

"Didn't he betray you when you guys were allies? Is that *not* the definition of a shithead?"

She huffs. "Fine, he was a bit of a shithead."

I snort, and out of the corner of my eye I see her relax in her seat.

It's barely dawn, so there's no line before we reach the entrance of the mountain. Excitement sparks in me once I spot the wooden MOUNT RAINIER NATIONAL PARK sign. I still can't believe I'm going to compete in the very same game Umma did when she was my age. We both freaked out when the network reached out to us with the offer. It was a no-brainer to agree to. Not only for the prize money but for the opportunity to avenge Umma's legacy.

Because if Garrett Moxley hadn't cheated her over, she would have won.

We roll to a stop at the park ranger's booth. There's a woman in shades leaning against the open window, chewing on gum lazily. "Do you have a pass?"

"No, I'm just dropping off my daughter," Umma says. "She's going to be in the reality show they're filming here."

"You still need a day pass to enter. It's thirty dollars."

"Thirty dollars?" I blurt, leaning over Umma to gawk at the woman. "What's up there? Gold?"

"시끄러워,"[2] Umma hisses, shoving her hand over my mouth.

"This is highway robbery. The state of Washington is robbing us blind," I say behind her palm.

The park ranger pops her gum. "This is a national park. So it's the federal government that's robbing you, not the state."

---

2. You're too loud.

I take that as my sign to shut up. Umma gives the park ranger an apologetic smile, then reaches back for her purse and angles her body, as if shielding it from view. She rifles around in it for a moment. Two.

Quietly, Umma turns back to the ranger and mumbles, "Do you take credit cards?"

We get our pass and are back on the steep road heading up to the main visitor center, where guardians were instructed to drop us off. The air is heavy with the unspoken. I know Umma's doing the math in her head to see if she can get back down to Portland without having to gas up again. Thirty dollars is a lot these days. Guilt turns my stomach. She's sacrificed so much for me to get here. I won't let it be for nothing.

I press my forehead against the window, watching the tall evergreens lined along the road blur into one thick, dense wall of umber brown and deep green, broken by slivers of sunlight that manage to peek around each trunk. When the road is less treacherous, I ask in my most casual tone, "Does Appa know?"

Umma doesn't answer right away, and I half hope she didn't hear me.

"I texted him when you got accepted," she eventually says.

That was about a month ago, right after my junior year of high school wrapped up. "He didn't respond, did he?"

". . . I'm sure he's excited to see how well you do."

I shake my head. Appa has been waiting sixteen years to see me do something well. None of my state medals or district trophies for track, volleyball, and swim are impressive enough to him, apparently. "Yeah, he'll see," I say. "See what an idiot he was for leaving when I bring back a million big ones."

Eventually, we pass the sign for the visitor center and pull into the parking lot like the producers instructed us to. I'm out of the car before she's turned off the ignition, any bitterness on my tongue gone at the first inhale of crisp, woodsy air. The needles of the spruce trees surrounding the lot are so dense, they scatter the sunshine in a million flickering, dancing spots around me as the foliage shifts in the warm breeze. Despite how early it is, there's still a few dedicated hikers nearby unloading gear and picnic baskets, as several trailheads start here. I'll be hiking one myself to camp, so this is where Umma and I have to say goodbye.

Umma comes to my side as I pull my duffel bag from the car. She wraps me in a hug and rocks us side to side. She feels small for the first time, with the way she's holding me like she's afraid to let go. I hear her sniffle.

"왜 울어?"[3] I ask with a chuckle. "I'm about to win the biggest game show of all time. You should be excited."

"Because I'll miss you."

My smile falls. An image suddenly pops in my head of her all alone in our new dingy apartment. She grew up in Busan with a big family and married Appa when she was young; she's never been alone before. Not like the jackass was great company, but he was *something*. Then when he left this year, we always had each other. She always had me.

But not anymore.

---

3. Why are you crying?

I hug her back, squishing my cheek against the top of her head and swallowing past the lump in my throat.

"Umma will be okay. Don't worry," she says. She has a sixth sense for what goes on in my mind. Or maybe my poker face is terrible.

"You'll be better than okay when I come back with the cash prize," I promise. Because when I come back, it'll be with enough money for her to pay off the debt Appa racked up in her name *and* for her to quit her back-breaking, minimum-wage jobs. She can finally live the comfortable, easy life she deserves.

Umma pulls back. There's a furrow in her brow like I said something wrong. She fixes my bangs with pursed lips. "Have fun while you're here, okay? Try to make friends."

The implication makes my throat feel weird and tight, so I chuckle to loosen it. "Of course I'll make friends. How could I not? I'm so lovable. Besides, I *have* friends."

"I know you have your teammates, but none of them are like Amelia. It would be nice for you to meet someone you can be that close to again."

Oh, I see where this is going, and I am *not* interested. A big fat no thank you. Talking about my ex-best friend when I'm about to embark on the coolest adventure of my life is the last thing I want to do. "Let's just focus on what really matters, which is me winning. Any last-minute advice?" I ask.

Umma looks me straight in the eye. "Winning isn't everything, Seyoon."

I can't help it. I laugh.

She wouldn't be saying that if Garrett Moxley hadn't screwed over her and the other guy in their alliance at the last second. Seriously, like, twenty yards away from the finish line. Because if he hadn't, she would've won. Without a doubt.

I know people don't think of her as a winner. Umma's a tiny, gentle-spoken Korean woman with an affinity for smiling and making small talk with clerks at the grocery store. They'd never believe she almost won the most cutthroat season of *Forest Feud*. She hardly got any airtime on the show despite being in the finale, and the scenes they did include never fully portrayed how awesome she was.

But people don't know Jungeun Shin like I do. They don't know that she's so brave, she immigrated to a different continent when she was just a child. They have no clue how tough she is, taking care of a kid *and* a deadbeat husband on her own. Even if I told them all that, they still wouldn't realize the full extent of Umma's strength. Not like I know.

Umma's always been a winner; I get it from her, and I'll do it for her.

I give her another long, tight hug, say my final goodbyes, and watch until she's back in her car and driving safely (and slowly) down the mountain. My chest pangs when she's fully out of sight. But then I slap myself out of it, plaster on a smile, grab my bag, and march past the trailhead post the producers told us to find, the one that says CAMP CLEARWATER–0.5 MILES.

I have no complaints about having to trek to set. I love nature. The sweet smell of grass, the way the sun warms the top of my head, the birds chirping and the ambiguous rumbling in the distance—all of it. Good stuff. Great stuff. Besides, half a mile is nothing. Our warm-ups in track are longer than this.

If I don't win, we won't be able to afford the extracurricular fees for track this year, the small voice of anxiety says in the back of my head. *Or volleyball. Or swim. Or—*

Snap out of it, Seyoon. What am I wasting my time worrying about that for?

"Of course I'm going to win," I tell myself.

Then I stop, my brain catching up to my senses. In particular, to the ambiguous rumbling that seems to be growing less distant by the second. Ambiguous rumbling isn't usually a good sign.

It's the last thought I have before a giant, hideous, neon-orange suitcase comes bouncing down the path and barrels into me.

3

THIS SUITCASE IS GOING TO GET ME A MANSLAUGHTER CHARGE

DEAN

I've been humbled plenty of times in my life. But trying to figure out how to escape the SeaTac airport? That was a particularly demeaning experience.

The day's only just started, and I'm already exhausted. The producers wanted us on set by 8 a.m., which means I had to take a red-eye flight from Boston to make it on time and have been running on critically low sleep since. I mistakenly thought the worst was behind me when an Uber driver picked me up and we were on our way to Mount Rainier, but I was swiftly proven wrong when, no matter how many times I tried to explain the situation, the driver refused to take me to the parking lot the producers specified.

"No, no, no," the man told me. "I'm not going *into* the park. Do you have any clue how expensive those day passes are?"

So he dropped me off at the park's entrance instead—about two and half miles away from the set. At least the ranger at the gate felt bad for me and gave me a map.

I'm man enough to admit my weaknesses. My cardiovascular system, to name one. A two-mile hike is tough enough on its own, but a two-mile hike while wearing a backpack, in seventy-degree heat, up an incline, on the side of a road, all while toting the world's ugliest, heaviest, neon-orange suitcase?

Admittedly tougher.

Sweat drips down my hair and soaks the collar of my hoodie. An hour later, and I'm sure my arms are going to fall off. Not even the crisp mountain air makes me feel better, and I'm too exhausted to appreciate what I'm sure is a beautiful view around me. Time loses meaning by the time I finally make it on the trail to Camp Clearwater and begin up a particularly steep hill.

I'm starting to consider believing in God just so I have someone to blame for my misery when I hear it: dozens of voices. They babble over each other, distant but there.

Camp.

The realization is so euphoric that I loosen my hold on the greasy handle of my suitcase.

Well. The euphoria is mostly responsible. My weak grip strength is probably partially to blame as well.

I watch in horror as my suitcase rockets down the hill.

"Fuck, fuck, fuck, fuck," I mutter, hurrying after it.

A vision of it sliding all the way down the mountainside flashes through my mind. But even worse, somebody turns around the bend in the path at the exact wrong moment, and my neon weapon of destruction knocks them over with a heavy *THUNK*. My heart sinks.

I'm a murderer. I'll live the rest of my life behind bars.

I run the rest of the way and scramble to my knees next to the person. It's a girl my age lying flat on her back. I shove the suitcase off her. "Shit. Please don't be dead?"

After a moment, she cracks her eyes open to my relief. "I'm alive," she groans. "I refuse to die an embarrassing death."

The girl gingerly sits up. I examine her face for signs of a concussion. Her irises are dark, nearly black, which makes it difficult to tell if her pupils are dilated or not, plus her thick, straight eyelashes hide them. There aren't any cuts or bruises on her face, which is good. My eyes trace over her soft, round cheeks, catching on the mole below her lips, and the long strands of black hair falling elegantly over her face.

My mouth dries. I swallow.

"Are you okay?" I ask.

"Yeah. Help me up, though."

I stand and offer her a hand, which she takes with a wince. Once on her feet, the girl looks at me, then at the incriminating suitcase, then back to me. She raises a brow.

The idea of being yelled at by a pretty stranger is terrifying enough that I blurt out an unconvincing, "I have no idea where that came from."

"No?"

What is wrong with you, Dean? "I meant—I have no idea how I *dropped* that. But, uh, yeah, that's mine. I'm so sorry, it was an accident. I was on my way to the set when—"

"Set? The *Forest Feud* set?" she interrupts, lighting up. "You must be a contestant, too. That, or a really overpacked hiker."

"I am. To the first thing. Technically both."

She grins. "Don't tell me you rolled that fugly ten-ton suitcase into me on purpose. 'Knock your opponent off their feet, then their game' kind of thing?"

I balk, not sure if she's serious, until she laughs.

"I'm joking!" Then she thinks about it a second longer, and her brows pinch. "It *was* just an accident . . . right?"

"Of course," I squeak.

That satisfies her. She slings her duffel bag that got knocked to the ground over her shoulder. Her tanned bicep flexes with the motion. I forcefully avert my gaze. "Okay, good. Well, since you weren't intentionally trying to take my kneecaps out, let's walk the rest of the way together."

She begins her ascent up the hill, a spring in her step despite getting the wind knocked out of her. I pick my suitcase up off the ground and hurry to wheel it over the rocks and uneven dips in the ground.

"I really am sorry," I say, catching up. "I'm glad you're okay."

Apparently unruffled by my maybe-sabotage attempt, she goes on. "No harm done. Accidents happen. It's playing dirty I don't like." She clenches her fist in front of her, as if strangling some imaginary cheater. Or me, had she not believed I was telling the truth. She drops her hand. "So, are you excited to be on the show?"

Making conversation with new people has never been my biggest strength. I usually find myself floundering. Or sticking my foot in my mouth. See exhibit A: that time I blurted "My mom's dead" in the middle of Applebee's. The intensity of this girl's eyes on me as she waits for an answer only makes my throat tighten. "Kinda?" I say.

God. That was pretty bad. Meredith would kick me if she were here.

My dry response and ensuing silence make her furrow her brows. "Oh?"

Except now I'm thinking about Meredith. And Dad. And how, once we get to the top of this hill, I'm going to be surrounded by a million cameras. I'm going to be on TV. For some reason, my brain is finding it a good time to spiral over that fact now.

She waves her hand in front of my face. "Hey, you okay?"

I've been unintentionally ignoring her for nearly a minute. Feeling like a jerk, I mutter, "Yeah. Sorry."

Silence settles in the space between us, but I don't know what to say. She glances over a few more times, opening her mouth as if to try and start a conversation again, but then shuts it, seeming disappointed. Another minute passes. I should say something so she doesn't think I'm a complete asshole.

"I'm Dean," I say.

Wow. Creative.

"Seyoon," she replies with a small smile. "I'm glad we ran into each other. I was hoping to meet some people before the show got started. Although, it's kinda hard to get buddy-buddy when you're in competition. I've been there before. *Not* fun."

Then, as casually as if she were commenting on the weather, Seyoon says, "Even though I'm going to win, I hope we can still become friends."

The gears in my head whir to a confused stop.

Is she . . . taunting me?

Nothing about her tone or expression indicates she's anything but serious. Her smile is too sweet to be hiding viciousness. But who says that kind of thing out loud? Who *assumes* they're going to win without even a single doubt?

I glance down at myself, feeling suddenly bare despite my jeans and hoodie. What does she see that makes her so sure she's going to beat me? How does she already know that I'm weak?

A mixture of embarrassment and irritation rubs against my side, but I don't have time to figure out what to do with it before she calls out, "Hey look, we're here!"

She jogs the rest of the way. I shake my head. I'm sure I was just overthinking things again.

I hurry my steps, crest the hill, and there it is, painted onto a wooden entrance arch: CAMP CLEARWATER.

The grassy clearing is about the size of a little league field, with five log cabins encircling a bonfire pit, and surrounded by towering evergreens on every side. Down a short knoll from camp is an enormous lake—Summit Lake—spreading for miles in every direction. For the first time, I'm actually taken aback by the beauty of my surroundings. It's so awe-inspiring, it makes me aware of my five senses in a way I've never been before. The birds chirping over each other in the trees; the hot, muggy air clinging to my skin; the subtle taste of sweet pine on my tongue with every inhale. And the *colors.* I've never seen shades of green this vibrant or water so blue before. The term *crystal clear* finally makes sense as I gaze upon the reflection of Mount Rainier's snowy peak in the rippling lake.

"This is the exact view my mom had twenty years ago," Seyoon mumbles, apparently equally blown away.

The sound of chatter returns to my ears, and my attention turns to the crowd of people all around. There are *so* many of them. My stomach dips.

I turn to see what else is around—and run face-first into a video camera.

"*Hurgh,*" escapes from my lips like a fork in the garbage disposal.

"Please try not to look directly into the camera," the operator says.

The camera and the man behind it step back enough for an older white woman to step in the space between us. Despite the out-of-place prim shirt and crisp jeans, I recognize her instantly.

Blake Perry: the former host of *Forest Feud.*

My eyes pop open. Oh my God, it's *the* Blake Perry. In the flesh. The only person who'd share my excitement about meeting her is Dad, so I stifle the embarrassing urge to ask for her autograph. Despite two decades having passed since she was on TV, her age doesn't show except in the silver of her slicked-back bun and the crow's feet next to her gray eyes.

"Seyoon Shin and Dean Parker arriving at the same time? What a happy coincidence," Blake says, all smiles. Her every word is enunciated with the crispness of a TV anchor.

She tucks her clipboard under her arm and shakes each of our hands. "Blake Perry. I'm not offended if you don't recognize me without the camp counselor getup I used to wear. I'm the executive producer and director now. It's good to have you here."

I blink, taken aback by the woman's neat, tidy aura. *This* isn't the Blake Perry I grew up watching. *That* Blake spent fifteen seasons delighting in stirring up drama between contestants and feeding on the ensuing chaos—the best kind of reality show host to watch. Maybe I shouldn't have expected her television persona to be her real personality.

Blake checks her watch. "Oh—we need to get you both to wardrobe and makeup. One of the techs will point you in the right direction."

Before leaving, Blake turns back and winks. "Hey, don't tell the other contestants, but you two are the ones I'm most excited about."

I'm given no time to bask in the realization that *Blake Perry knows who I am* before a frazzled-looking assistant whisks both me and Seyoon into a canopy tent pitched near the entrance. There, a stylist asks to see what clothes I've brought, then frowns at each plain white T-shirt I pull out.

"You can keep the hoodies and shorts, but white washes you out. Here, take these," the stylist says, handing me a stack of T-shirts colored emerald green, earthy brown, and dark purple. As soon as I finish changing into a hoodie that's not soaked with sweat, a different crew member flits by, blotting my face and pressing powder beneath my eyes. Once they're done, yet another tech steps into their place and clips a mic to the collar of my shirt, like an assembly line of workers.

"Keep this on you at all times," they explain, slipping the transmitter pack into my pants pocket and weaving the thin wire connecting it under my shirt. "You can only turn it off when filming hours are over, or when you're in the bathroom. Just click that little switch on the mic here."

Right when I think they'll finally free us, one of the techs blocks the entrance, his palm out. "Your phones, please."

"We can't keep them?" I ask.

The tech just wags his fingers, raising a single brow.

Suppressing a sigh, I fish it out and hand it over, already mourning the loss. Seyoon is lingering, looking at something on her phone, her thumbs hovering over the screen. I catch a glimpse without meaning to. She has a message thread open to somebody named Amelia. She chews on her bottom lip before shutting it off and handing it to the man.

Finally, they shoo us out with instructions to stay close. Seyoon floats toward the center of camp and, to my surprise, beckons for me to come. With nowhere else to go, I follow. The whole campsite is swarming with people, some carrying microphones, others lugging around cameras, and even more scurrying around with clipboards and looking like they're about to cry. I rub my chest to soothe the uncomfortable squeezing around my lungs and carefully weave my giant suitcase through the crowd.

We take a seat on one of the logs around the empty bonfire pit. Seyoon drops her bag on the ground and massages her hands. They're torn and bloodied.

She notices me looking. "I guess I took that fall harder than I thought."

Guilt stabs me straight in the stomach. "You should see the medic, that looks seri—" I start to say, but she's already wiping the blood off on her leggings. She looks up at me with wide, deer-in-headlight eyes.

"Whoops," she chuckles.

Unhygienic. "I brought a first-aid kit with me. Here."

I unzip the orange suitcase that got me into this mess in the first place and rummage around until I find the travel kit. I throw one leg over the log, straddling it to face her, then put out my hand—an offer. Seyoon glances at it, then at me. Her hesitation makes my body go cold. *Does she think this is weird? Wait, is it weird? I'm being weird, aren't I?* I'm no good at social cues. I should put my hand down, pretend I was just stretching or something.

But then she presents me with both her palms, and my nervous system stops trying to eat itself.

"Thanks," she says with a shy grin. There's a gap between her front teeth that suits her.

I get to work picking out the dirt and splinters from her palm, all while paying a normal amount of attention to how much smaller her hands are than mine.

At some point, a camera operator and sound technician creep up behind us, filming our interaction like they're wildlife photographers. Or vultures, circling, waiting for a potential meal to present itself. Sweat beads on my forehead. Fuck. That's going to be hard to get used to. Seyoon either doesn't notice or isn't bothered. She hisses when I swipe her hands with an alcohol wipe.

"Sorry," I say. I blow on her palms to help.

"It's okay."

I glance up. Her voice is rougher than I would have expected from such a delicate face. Well, delicate in the roundness of her pink cheeks and smiling mouth. Her eyes, on the other hand, are intense as they roam over me. I usually hate being looked at. I feel people's gazes like fingers digging into my skin. But the sensation isn't *totally* unpleasant when it's from her.

Wait, she's watching me expectantly. Did she ask something?

"What?" I say like an idiot.

"I said, was it one of your parents who was on the show, or a different relative?" she repeats. "Given we're all nepo babies here."

I snort as I uncap the jar of petroleum jelly. "I don't know if there's much nepotism to be taken advantage of if you're related to someone who lost. It was my dad, though. He was on the fifteenth season."

"No way! My mom was in the same season. Jungeun Kim?"

My fingers freeze midway through unwrapping a roll of bandage. "That's your mom?"

"Why do you sound so surprised?"

I should probably *not* answer that, right? I barely know this girl, and I don't know her mom at all besides what I've seen of her on TV, but just from first impressions . . . "It's nothing."

"Come on," Seyoon urges. "Now I'm curious. Tell me."

She's not going to let it drop. I squirm. "Well, your mom was . . ."

Oh God, the camera operator has found a friend. There's two of them now, positioned behind me and Seyoon respectively. It's hard to focus on the right thing to say when I'm reminding myself not to look into the camera, and trying to recall how I saw them clean a wound on *Aliver*, and thinking about how long my silence has dragged on and—Jesus, just speak.

"Kind of forgettable?"

That was bad. *Very* bad. I shut myself up.

A singular eyebrow raises on Seyoon's face. "Forgettable? She got third place."

"Wait, that's not what I meant." The camera pulls in. I accidentally glance at it and stutter over my own tongue. "It's just that, you know, you're really talkative and have this big personality, and in comparison your mom seemed kind of quiet, so I didn't see the connection right away. But I'm sure she's great too and—"

"A big personality?" Seyoon repeats, incredulous.

I don't mean it as a bad thing. I wish I was half as sure of myself as she is. But what I think doesn't usually correlate with what everyone else around me is thinking. I open my mouth to hopefully salvage this interaction before I offend her *and* her mom more, but Seyoon beats me to it.

"So that's why you kept ignoring me back there," she says bitterly. "Sorry I was *too much* for you."

My stomach flops. I wasn't ignoring her attempts at conversation; I was just failing spectacularly to form a response. "I—"

"Clearly you don't want to be friends, that's fine, but don't make my confidence sound like a bad thing. It makes *you* seem insecure."

Her words pierce the weak point in my chest. The sting of irritation she sparked in me earlier ignites into a flare now. She *was* goading me back then.

"Confidence?" I repeat, my voice quiet but steady. "Confidence is one thing. But *cockiness* is declaring you're going to beat someone five minutes into meeting them."

Redness colors her face and she blinks, as if just now realizing what she'd said earlier. She stands, ripping her hands from my grip. I stand too. In my periphery, I notice the cameras move in closer, but the roiling anger in my gut is too overwhelming for me to care right now.

"I'm not going to apologize for believing in myself," she says.

"And you're probably not going to apologize for the arrogance either, right?"

"Okay, jackass. You're a hypocrite, you know that? Calling me arrogant when you were the one sticking your nose up at everything I said, like you're too good to talk to me. If what I said bothered you, why didn't you speak up?"

Speak up. I've heard that my whole life, since I was a little kid who was too shy to talk to the grocery clerks, let alone the other kids at school. I bite my tongue until I taste iron.

At some point, one—or maybe both—of us must have taken a step forward, because the roll of bandage is on the ground and there's only a few inches of space between our faces. She's taller than average, but still shorter than me, coming up to my nose. She makes up for the distance by craning her neck up, giving me a good look at her lips pulled in a sneer. She has a perfect cupid's bow. I can smell her shampoo from this close too: sweet, like honeycomb. *Focus.*

"Because unlike you, I act before I speak," I grit out. "Which is why I'll gloat *after* I beat you, not beforehand."

"I'd love to see you try."

Two hands clap our shoulders and pull us apart.

"Ooh, a little friendly rivalry?" says an unfortunately familiar voice. "At least wait until I get here so I can make some witty commentary."

4

STUART LITTLE MUST DIE

SEYOON

My first instinct is to bite the hand of whoever is currently holding me back from tearing a new one into the six-foot-bag-of-dicks who made the dumb decision to disrespect me *and* Umma in the same breath. But then I whip my head around and see who stepped between us.

Garrett Moxley.

"Seyoon Shin and Dean Parker! I'm right, aren't I? Don't answer that, I know I am."

I should've recognized the smug voice from all those commercials. He obviously looks older than he did when he was on *Forest Feud*, but still shockingly similar after twenty years. He's kind of like an aged Shaggy from *Scooby Doo*, with salt-and-pepper hair, a fake tan, and a five o'clock shadow. He flashes me and Dean what he must think is a disarming smile. It's insulting, but what's more offensive is the Hawaiian-patterned, three-piece suit he's wearing. It's so ugly, I temporarily forget my anger and just gawk in disgust at his blazer.

Garrett's eyes flicker back and forth between me and Dean until realization flashes across his face. He throws his head back and laughs. He laughs like he has money. You know what I'm talking about: that rich, white man *Ha! Ha! Ha!* that comes from deep in their chest.

"Hold on, this is too good. History loves to rhyme, doesn't it?" Garrett says. He points between us. "Have you guys made the connection already?"

"What connection?" I ask. Dean grimaces, so I think he has.

"The connection between your parents," Garrett responds. "You don't recognize the son of Vince Parker? The guy that beat your mom for second place?"

My jaw falls as the gears in my head turn. Dean shrugs under my accusatory stare, as if to say, *Well, you never asked* me *who* I *was related to.*

"Vince, your mom, and I were all allies, you know?" Garrett says, straightening the lapels of his blazer with pride.

"Allies until you tricked both of them into going down the wrong path in the final obstacle course race."

"Yup!" He pops the *p*. "Hey, that's showbiz, kid. No hard feelings. How are your folks doing, by the way?"

"None of your business," I spit at the same time Dean says, "Fine."

"Hey, enough about the past." He claps his hands and turns to the crowd at large. Loudly, he calls, "Let's focus on the future! All contestants, meet me at the front of camp!"

He turns to face the team of camera operators to our left, who have been filming us the whole time, I realize belatedly. "How was that, Kim? You need another take?"

One of the women scratches her chin. "Yeah, you had your back to us for part of that. Can you repeat your line?"

"No problem." Garrett shuffles around, tilting his face to get his jawline in the shot this time. "Let's focus on the future! All contestants, meet me at the front of camp!"

Kim shoots him a thumbs-up, and Garrett finally saunters—yes, saunters—away, leaving me and Dean to ourselves. Well, ourselves, plus the crew of camera techs and the boom mic operator, who are still focused on us. I chew the inside of my cheek so I won't sink my teeth into Dean's arm while the cameras are rolling. Usually, I have no problem being the center of attention. You can't be shy when you're the only one doing flips on the gymnastics mats or giving your teammates pregame pep talks. But I realize now how inconvenient it might be to have cameras trained on me twenty-four-seven, capturing everything I say or do.

Okay, maybe I got a *little* heated back there. He started it, though, implying I'm loud and too much—things Appa has criticized me for plenty of times before. Although I guess I did tell Dean to his face that I was going to beat him. I didn't mean it in a rude way; it's just what was on my mind. Although, if someone said that to *me* . . .

He shouldn't have insulted Umma, though.

That brings the fire right back into my blood. Yeah, you know what? Fuck that guy. And especially fuck his perfect curly hair and his dumb gentle hands. I snatch my duffel bag off the ground, intent on beating Dean to the front.

"Hey, take this."

I look over my shoulder in time to see Dean tossing the roll of bandage he never got to finish wrapping around my hands. On instinct I catch it, then yelp at the sting in my palms. He smirks. I want to knock all the teeth out of that smile with the way it transforms his sad, pretty, mousy face into something wicked.

Ugh. He's like if Stuart Little were hot. And an asshole. And human, I guess.

I throw the wad of gauze back and take great satisfaction when it bonks his forehead.

"Jackass," I mumble under my breath as I stomp across camp, weaving around the millions of production assistants and barely dodging a light stand. And to think I wanted to be friends. That's what I get for trying to befriend somebody I'm in competition with. Have I learned nothing from The Agonizing Amelia Accident of Junior Year? Adrenaline and rivalry don't make a great combo for lasting friendships. That's why we're not on speaking terms anymore.

. . . Mostly why.

I scowl. I don't *need* to fill the hole in my heart Amelia used to occupy with somebody else. But Umma asked me to make friends, so I will. Because I *can*. Just because the first attempt didn't work out doesn't mean none of them will. Right?

My face warms and I cringe as I recall how hard I tried to get a conversation going with Dean on the trek to camp. God. How humiliating. He was giving me the cold shoulder the whole time, biting out short replies if not ignoring me completely, and yet I kept blabbering on. I want to bang my skull against the nearest tree just thinking about it. *And* he rammed that butt-ugly suitcase into me. Seriously, how do you let go of a suitcase with handles—

Aha! I knew it. It *was* an intentional sabotage attempt—oh, that bastard. He tried to physically incapacitate me, and when that didn't work (because of my hardy head and incredible safe-falling techniques), he went for the sweet-nerd angle to lower my defenses.

I take it back, he's not like Stuart Little. He's like Jerry, that tricky mouse motherfucker. And he's not going to fool me again.

There are ten other teens lined up beneath the CAMP CLEARWATER entrance sign, all carrying their luggage. An array of crew members position their cameras, microphones, and light stands around us. I get in line, accidentally knocking my duffel bag into the guy next to me. He drops whatever he was fiddling with.

"Oops, sorry. Let me get that for you." I bend down to grab it, but he snatches it first.

I give him a cautious look. His strawberry-blond hair blends in with a sunburn that's already developing on his suspicious face. How is that possible? We're in the shade. My gaze falls to the object he's clutching against his chest like he thinks I'll take it from him. It's a gold-plated multitool, the kind that folds out with a knife, bolt cutter, and other gadgets. He shoves it into his pocket.

"Fancy," I comment.

He scrunches his face into a condescending smile. "Gift from my uncle."

Garrett arrives then, swinging a megaphone at his side. Blake approaches him, running down a list on her clipboard with him, prepping him with talking points. Once they're done, she retreats to her spot next to one of the cameras.

"Cameras, you set? Sound team, all good? Great. Ready when you are, Garrett."

He clears his throat and launches right into it.

> Campers! I am thrilled to welcome all twelve of you to the reboot of America's favorite reality show. Welcome to *Forest Feud*.

". . . Huh. Was expecting more of a rambunctious applause there," Garrett says, breaking his announcer voice. "That's okay. We can edit that in post. Anyway—"

> I'm your gracious host, Garrett Moxley, winner of the last season of *Forest Feud*. I bring that up *not* because I'm still holding on to my claim to fame from twenty years ago—despite what the Internet likes to say—but because it's relevant to all of you, as six of you here are related to someone who won like I did, while the other six are related to someone who lost. Talk about tension.

I glare at Garrett hard enough that my eyes strain, but if he notices, he doesn't let it show.

> Just like your family members, the twelve of you will compete in thrilling challenges, plus obstacle courses in places and elevations we've never gone to before, with an all-new elimination system to really turn up the heat. Excited yet?

A girl somewhere down the line lets out an enthusiastic, "Whoo!" Garrett finger guns at her.

> Now that's more like it! Let me introduce the rules.
>
> You will compete in six high-stakes challenges to earn points that will determine your ranking. The player with the fewest points after each challenge goes home and kisses their shot at the million-dollar

grand prize goodbye. However, there are also a few challenges where *more* than one player will get the boot. Anxious yet? Good!

Any questions?

"Yeah," says another contestant, raising their hand. "Where do we, like, sleep?"

"And when can we put our bags away?" somebody else pipes up. "I'm sick of dragging this thing around."

You'll be happy to hear that we have *excellent* accommodations arranged for you. And by excellent, I mean eight twin-size bunks in that cozy cabin over there, probably without bedbugs.

I see some gears turning in your heads. "But Garrett, there are twelve of us?"

Not for long!

Players, get ready for your very first challenge, Mountain Marathon: a race through the woods to determine which of you gets to claim one of those beds and which of you are going home today without even unpacking your things. The top eight players get to stay, and the last four are going bye-bye. Isn't this exciting? Who's excited?

"Yeah!" I shout, uncaring that I'm the only one who answered. The guy I bumped into gives me a sideways look, but I hardly register it over my exhilaration.

The others in line groan and complain about how they weren't warned, this isn't fair, "I'm wearing brand-new Jordans!" But I've never been more eager. I placed in the top three at state for the 400m and 100m last fall, and got first in the 200m.

I start stretching immediately. Will the race start here? Makes sense we'd begin at camp. But, to my surprise, all the crew members start packing up their equipment.

The boy on the other side of Sunburn notices, too. "What's going on?"

Blake steps forward. "Field-trip time. We only have permits to lodge and film on the grounds, so all of our challenges have to be on private property."

"But isn't this just a race?" I ask. "You don't need a permit to take a jog."

The woman grins, a sparkle of excitement in her gray eyes. "Oh. It's a *little* more than that."

Adrenaline rushes through me. I lean backward to see past the row of people and spot Dean at the end, looking like he's about to shit himself. He glances my way. He's not grinning anymore. Good. I stick my tongue out at him, and he turns a satisfying berry red.

He's going down.

5

EITHER EVERYONE HERE IS AN IDIOT, OR I NEED TO GIVE MYSELF MORE CREDIT

DEAN

Yeah. I'm going down.

Okay, let's try framing that more positively. I'm *not* going down. As the #1 bestseller in self-help books for teens—*Help! I'm Sweating More Than I Used To: Surviving Puberty*—says, "Act as if you are not afraid, and gradually you won't be." Although I think they stole that quote from Teddy Roosevelt.

But I can't tame my worries as we hike back down the trail to the parking lot, where us contestants are ushered into one sleek black bus, and the camera crew pack themselves into three others. Just my luck that the first challenge relies on speed, something I don't have. How can I make up for my points through the strategy-based games when the slowest four people are going home right now? I could beat a first grader in a race on a good day, maybe a third grader on a very good day, but *today*? Any energy I had left after my flight I exhausted trying to get up this goddamn mountain and then arguing with a beautiful, annoying girl.

I wonder for half a second what Garrett and Blake are thinking, throwing us headfirst into a marathon after what must have been a long morning of travel for everyone, until it clicks: They want to push us to our limits, physically and mentally. Everyone knows the best outbursts on reality TV come when the contestants are too exhausted to filter themselves.

Or maybe they're just evil.

It's a long, bumpy road down the mountain to wherever the set of our challenge will be. Once the bus turns off the highway, we stop passing cars and start cruising alongside the Nisqually River. I watch the muddy, brown water run on the other side of the road, waiting for a sign of a nearby town to appear, but after we drive through Elbe, there are only markers for the speed limit. An hour later, the bus takes a turn onto a gravel road that leads into the woods. One of the crew members hops out and opens the gate blocking the path, knocking down the PRIVATE PROPERTY: DO NOT ENTER sign in the process.

We drive until the trees get so dense they block out the sunlight. Eventually, the bus groans to a stop in a clearing, and we step out. It's hotter here than on the mountain, muggy without the crisp breeze from the snowcaps. The sound of babbling water nearby and birds tweeting in the trees mixes with the clatter of equipment as the crew members unload their luggage.

One of the contestants, a tall girl with thin braids to her waist, puts her hand on her hip as she scrutinizes our surroundings. "This forest is almost identical to the one at camp," she says. "Why'd we have to come all the way out here?"

Garrett, who is apparently an omnipresent figure ready to barge into any conversation, sidles up next to her. "Because we own *these* trees and can do anything we'd like to them. But if we so much as snap a branch on the ones on Mount Rainier, our lovely friends at the ranger station will slap a hefty fine and a federal misdemeanor on us," he says, not a trace of shame in his tone. "With the challenges we have in store for you guys, we can't exactly 'leave no trace.'"

He walks away then, whistling to himself. The girl watches him go with her mouth pulled back in a disgusted sneer. "Just because you can *legally* damage this land doesn't mean you should."

She put to word the feelings I didn't have the guts to say out loud, especially not with the cameras up and rolling again. It's not like I should be surprised that a game show playing with people's emotions for views has no moral qualms about buying out a forest to do whatever they'd like with it. Money-hungry network executives aren't exactly saints.

I take a moment to size up the competition and quickly realize I'm out of my league when it comes to physicality. My only strategy is to keep up as best I can and hope there's a component of this race that's better suited to my strengths. The first challenge is important for so many reasons—it sets the tone for the rest of the season, and both the viewers and producers will use this moment to gauge your character moving forward. But for me, I know I have to go above and beyond if I want to earn any shred of my dignity back after that embarrassing fight with Seyoon.

Once all the camera operators have stationed up in the woods, we're led a few paces away to an opening in the wall of trees: a flattened, dirt hiking trail. Garrett paces in front of us with his hands behind his back like a drill sergeant. I squint to see him against the backdrop of a million lighting umbrellas.

"Now, contestants, this isn't going to be any regular old race. I don't want to spoil anything, but prepare for a few obstacles in your way. There are plenty of cameras placed in the trees and along the route, so smile. The only rule is you can't cut through the woods, but besides that, hey, get creative." Garrett pulls a whistle out of his blazer pocket and brings it to his lips. "On your marks . . ."

I look down the line to where Seyoon is. She digs her heels into the dirt, then glances my way when she feels me looking. The corner of her mouth quirks up. Like she already knows she has this in the bag. My stomach flips.

"Get set . . ."

Floodlights set up in the trees explode with life, illuminating a stark path down the mountain trail.

The whistle screeches, and everyone takes off in a flurry of stomping feet.

I get jostled in a sea of shoulders and elbows. Seyoon moves out in front, taking the lead in just three long, quick strides. It's not long after until her and the others are lost to the forest ahead of me. I'm behind. Already. *Fuck.* I scramble to catch up.

Forget that corny quote about overcoming your fears—Teddy Roosevelt would stone me to death himself, I think as my feet pound the earth, shins twinging at every heavy step. *Shit. Don't panic. You can't give up yet. The race has just started. Something will—*

"Woah!"

There's a shout from up ahead. Then a second confused yell, and the rustle of foliage. I pick up the pace, round a corner in the path, and follow the flags lining the trail until it opens into a large clearing.

A handful of the others are here, but they're not running like I expected. Instead, they're milling around the open area, eyes on their feet, jumping at every snap of a twig like they're worried the ground is going to open up and—

"AAAH!" A girl at the far end of the clearing disappears into a pitfall trap, neatly concealed by foliage and branches. A moment later, her hand shoots up above the earth. "I'm okay."

Somebody else falls into another hole that was hidden by moss, and now I get why they had to buy a plot of forest for this show. Can't exactly get away with digging trenches on government-protected land. I take a step back, wary of the dirt beneath my feet. I'm glad I wasn't the first person to stumble upon this.

. . . Wait. It's actually a *good* thing I'm last. I can use this.

Despite the itch that tells me to hurry, I wait and analyze where the contestants ahead of me place their steps. A girl with a short black bob leaps over a suspicious lump of grass and makes it to the other side safely. A boy to her left doesn't have such luck. Someone else inches across slowly like it's a minefield (and makes it across in one piece) while another person zigzags like they're outrunning a crocodile. (That strategy is a myth, I'm pretty sure. They trip in a hole anyway.) Six people fall in, and the rest make it across. The camera operators stick as far to the outskirts as they can, looking at their own feet anxiously.

I follow the path of safety the others laid out and spare a quick glance into one of the pitfalls. They're shallow, and those that have fallen in are already scrabbling up the dirt walls and climbing out. It's not much, but it does buy me some time.

I run for several minutes, avoiding looking at the cameras positioned every fifty feet or so and the ones hiding in the tree branches, before I'm stopped by the path ending abruptly again.

The dirt crumbles into a steep crag about five or ten feet above a creek. Carefully, I inch toward the edge and gaze at the water and rocks below.

"Is Garrett trying to kill us on national television?" I ask aloud.

> *TSW Studios would like to remind viewers at home that all* Forest Feud *challenges and courses are quality tested to ensure contestants' safety. TSW Studios is not liable for any harm or injury that may come upon contestants during their time on the show, and individuals waive their right to sue* Forest Feud *or its affiliated company for damages, injury, or death.*

The only way across is over the bridge, if you can call it that. It's a long, skinny wooden board just wider than my shoe. Three people who beat me here are trying to cross it, wobbling and holding their arms out as they carefully place one foot in front of the other. I watch them in a mix of confusion and awe and make no move to join them. I have brain cells to preserve, after all.

"Why would they *all* try to go across at once?" I mutter aloud.

Whoever's in front puts their foot down a little too hard, wobbling the board and sending everyone overboard. My heart drops—until their heads immediately bob back up. The water's deep but slow.

"Gah!" yells one contestant as the creek drifts him lazily downstream. "Fuck you . . . uh, what was your name?"

"Sid—" Another person, the guilty party, gargles as water washes over his face. "Sorry. Siddharth."

"Oh, yeah. Fuck you, Siddharth!"

Speakers from somewhere in the trees crackle to life. Garrett's voice fills the forest.

> Contestants! Even if you fall in the water or one of the pitfalls, don't give up. You're not out of the race yet!

That's my sign to get a move on. Doing my best to ignore what sounds like rapidly approaching footsteps behind me, and those in the water already swimming toward shore, I swallow down my fear and force myself onto the bridge.

You can do this. Be brave, Dean. Or at least, pretend that you are for the next ten seconds.

My foot slips, and I barely manage to regain my balance. My half-hearted optimism is not helping. What *does* get me all the way across the creek—albeit slowly and unsteadily—is the memory of Seyoon sighing and saying, *Even though I'm going to win, I hope we can become friends.*

Like hell.

Once I'm on solid ground, my breath returns to me more steadily than it has all morning. I glance over my shoulder, stunned to see the distance between me and the others.

Huh. I may not be the fastest, or the strongest, but I can think on my feet. It's the one thing I'm confident about.

Or maybe I just have more common sense than everyone else here.

My earlier impending sense of doom dissipates. It's happening. A two-bedroom apartment in Portland with my and Meredith's names on the lease. Something for Dad to remember me by when

I leave, something that'll ease the sting when he laments the distance between us. I'm doing it. I'm going to make them both proud. Because I *can* win. And nobody is going to get in my way, no matter how infuriatingly beautiful or athletic or annoying they are.

Without wasting another second, I take off down the path, adrenaline licking at my heels and fire burning in my lungs as I chase after Seyoon.

6

THIS SIGN CAN'T STOP ME 'CAUSE I HAVE DYSLEXIA

SEYOON

Pitfalls? I eat those for breakfast. A suspended bridge over the water? Balance beam was my favorite event in gymnastics. I was right. I have this race in the bag.

. . . Okay, I did fall in one of those holes, but I got out faster than anybody, so I still have every right to be confident.

"*Cocky*," I spit, remembering Dean's taunt. "I'll show that mousy prick what cocky really looks like when I'm waiting for him at the finish line. That rodent-looking . . . blond . . . little . . ." Ugh, forget it. I'll come up with a good insult later.

My feet hit the dirt of the hiking trail in a quick, rhythmic pattern. I revel in the reverberations through my legs and the humid, summer air filling my lungs with every breath. I've found my perfect rhythm. Nothing can break it, not even the sight of camera operators slinking out behind bushes to follow me. There's no one else ahead of me, and only the boy with the sunburn was anywhere close to being on my tail.

I've hardly broken a sweat when the path suddenly diverges into three. A wide tree sits squat in the middle of the fork, and when I get closer, I realize there's a wooden sign nailed to it. What is this?

I squint to make out the faintly engraved words.

TO FIND THE QUICKEST PATH TO FLEE,
ANSWER THE TREE THESE QUESTIONS THREE:
1. THE WINDIEST ROADS DON'T OFTEN LEAD TO—

Oh, fuck me. It's a riddle. I hate these.

It's a herculean task getting through the whole thing. I use my full concentration, swearing when I mistake a *d* for a *b* and when I finally get through a sentence only to realize I didn't understand any of it. The letters seem to jump, so I do what Appa drilled into me and hold a finger below each squirming word, but it still doesn't help.

"Shit, shit, shit, come on," I mutter, staring harder at the sign like sheer willpower can cure my dyslexia. Maybe it will. Appa certainly thought so. Why the hell would we have to *read* in the middle of a race, anyway? Okay, focus, damnit. I'm suddenly aware of a boom mic subtly shimmying over my head. When did that operator get here?

What's the point? Even if you could understand it, it doesn't mean you're smart enough to solve it. Forget it.

That's the first thought I've had in the last five minutes that doesn't hurt my brain.

"Screw this," I say, stepping back. I wasted too much time trying to figure out the puzzle when I should've just picked a path and counted on my speed to get me there before anyone else. If I'd ignored the sign and still gone the wrong way, at least it wouldn't be because I couldn't solve the riddle. Now, people will see that I *tried*, which is worse. It's better to not try at all than to try and fail.

I shut one eye, lick my thumb, and hold it out to the wind. Eeeny, meeny, miny . . . yeah, let's go with that one.

Veering to the farthest right path, I take off as fast as my legs will go. Unfortunately, even with me at a dead sprint, the path seems to go on endlessly into the woods. Shit. Definitely chose the wrong road. My ears warm. That's fine, Seyoon, just keep running, one foot in front of the other, don't trip over the pebbles, ignore the camera peeking out behind a tree trunk, watch that turn there—

Finally, I break out of the path and onto a grassy bluff. High above me is an elevated wooden platform. A dozen cables extend from it and disappear into the foliage of the woods below. They're like zip lines, I realize, but not the kind with harnesses. Instead of being strapped into a seat, you hold on to a rope and stand on a circular disk that rings around the bottom.

My excitement is dampened when I spot Stuart Little's human counterpart climbing the ladder up to the platform.

"You beat me here?" I yell, making Dean startle and look down at me. His eyebrows jump like he's just as surprised as I am. I hurry to clamber up the ladder and catch him, but he beats me to the launch platform.

I pull myself up and pause at the row of zip line cables. There's a wooden sign in the middle with a big red WARNING, but like hell I'm going to try and read the rest of it now. Which one am I supposed to take? It might be like the fork in the road, where they all lead to the same place, but through different routes. Dean runs to the one in the center. How does he know which one is right? Was it included in the riddle? Fuck.

He puts one foot on the mini circular disk at the bottom of his rope and glances back at me, still frozen with indecision. He cocks his head.

"You got the riddle wrong, didn't you? Or else you wouldn't be looking so confused," he says.

I grit my teeth and run to the cable on the left. No . . . maybe the one next to it? "Shut up. I didn't even *read* the riddle, so there."

The corner of his lips turn up, a glimmer of mischief flickering in hazel eyes that have been stoic up until now. I glare at his rope. That *must* be the right one.

I need to get on that one.

Dean grips his line and taunts, "Guess you won't be beating me after all."

He shifts his other foot onto the disk, and—without thinking—I leap at him and cling to his rope.

My stomach shoots into my throat as we soar over the bluff.

"What the hell!" he screams as the disk swings wildly under our combined weight. "Why would you get on this one?"

"I don't know!" I shout back, clutching to the rope for dear life. "I figured you'd choose the right one!"

"Well, get off!"

"I can't now, genius!"

The cable above our heads ducks below the line of foliage. We glide through a cleared row between the trees, hovering a few feet above the ground as the wind whizzes past us. My guess was right; I can see where the other cables twist and turn in longer paths before becoming parallel with ours again. This was the most direct route.

Because of how narrow the disk is, Dean and I are nose to nose, stepping on each other's toes to stay on. I hold myself closer to the rope, wincing when my palms sting. Dean's hands are practically on top of mine, gripping so tight that his knuckles turn white. The line swings, and I bump against his chest.

"Shit," he gasps.

He falls back. Before I can think, my hand shoots forward to fist in the fabric of his hoodie and pull him back on. The gash on my palm tears open at the movement, but I hardly notice, distracted by Dean's wide-eyed look of shock. My face burns. I wrap my fingers around the rope again, focusing on the path ahead.

I see it now, a few hundred yards away: the end of the race. Camera crew, Garrett, and Blake cheer and holler behind a checkered banner. In front of them is a low platform where all twelve cable lines brake, and then a short dash to the finish line. Glee bubbles up my throat and escapes as laughter. No matter how much better at riddles or reading instructions or any of that boring stuff Dean is, I'm faster.

I'm going to win.

Then the cable above us snaps.

We scream as our line gives out. It's a short drop, but the air still punches out of my lungs as my back smacks the forest floor. Dean is flung farther, rolling and tumbling to a stop ahead of me.

Through the ringing in my ears—did I actually hit my head this time? Damnit—the metallic whizzing of a hanger gliding down the neighboring cable makes me twist up from the ground to see who it is.

It's Sunburn.

As he zips down and passes me, he smirks. Something in his hand flashes.

It's the gold utility tool he had back at camp. A beam of sunlight glints on a sharp edge.

The realization of what happened helps me suck in a gasp of air, enough for me to put my hands in the dirt and push myself up to stand. Ahead of me, Sunburn hops gracefully off his rope and trots across the finish line.

Fuck! I can still get second, at least, if—

Where the hell did Dean go?

Instead of wasting time like me, Dean's already up and racing toward the finish. A symphony of metallic whirring and whizzing surrounds me as the other contestants catch up, some zooming ahead, others shouting in complaint as their cables lead them through long, winding detours. Several others zip to the finish line now.

Fuck fuck fuck.

I kick up clouds of dirt. The straight shot path is like any hundred-meter dash I've run a million times before, but now it feels as if I'm sprinting through water. My breath escapes in uneven, jagged gasps. My tailbone and back twinge in pain every time my right foot hits the ground. Two more people fly past me on their cables, and I barely dodge getting rammed into by another coming in hot from behind. Everyone's ahead of me—but there's still a chance. Twenty feet ahead. Fifteen.

I've never had this view before. I've never been this far behind.

I can't lose. I can't be a *loser.*

Adrenaline screams through every vein, every muscle, every joint in my body, and I push myself faster than I ever have. I hurry past three people who are slow hopping off their zip lines. *Come on. What if Appa sees this? You have to prove him wrong.*

Mere feet away from the finish line, I catch up to somebody who's running hard, but not as hard as me. Because I want it more. I *need* it more.

I lean forward on my very last stride and cross the finish line just in time. Seconds later, a few people run after me. I glance around and count. *Two . . . Five . . . Seven . . .*

My knees nearly give out as relief washes over me. I came in eighth. I made it.

Shame licks at my sides like hot oil. I tried so hard, yet I barely made it.

I may as well have lost.

7

YOU WANT ME TO HAVE YOUR BACK? THE THING THAT GOT JULIUS CAESAR KILLED?

DEAN

I watch Seyoon out of the corner of my eye, examining her splotchy flush and her exhausted stance, bent over and gripping her knees. Her gaze is fixed on the dirt between her shoes. She's so stiff, I'm not even sure she's breathing. I've never seen anyone run that fast.

More unfathomable than me placing second in a race is *her* scraping to make the cut at all. If I wasn't still trying to calm my heartbeat, I'd rub it in her face. With class, of course. Not like she would.

Garrett blows his whistle in a happy tune. "Campers, I'm impressed! I—wait, wait, wait, hold on." He straightens his blazer and turns so the closest camera gets his good side. He starts again.

> Campers, I'm impressed! You all demonstrated some serious skill and agility. Well, those of you who didn't fall in the pit holes, get washed down the creek, or fall off your zip lines. The rest of you? Nice work. We're in for a seriously cutthroat season.
>
> Unfortunately for those who came in last, this was your last hurrah with us. An assistant will show the four of you to the Loser Limo; your bags are already inside. That's right, get out of here. Shoo!

One of the people who didn't make it in time, a girl with dyed purple hair and watery eyes, sniffs. "Like, now?"

"No," Garrett concedes. "We still have to film a going-away outro for you guys when we're back at camp. Stick around for now. Just . . . maybe out of my shot."

> For the remaining eight of you, congratulations! You've made it through your first challenge. Now, for the exciting part: How many points have you earned? Let's turn to the handy-dandy tally board that my buddy Luke has put together for us in real time.

A blond, lanky man who must be an executive assistant of some kind and doesn't seem pleased about earning the title of Garrett's "buddy" picks up a large board. The left side is numbered with places from first to eighth, while the right side has the points column. In between are tiny pieces of wood with our names carved on them, slotted into place.

1ST	CARTER MOXLEY	10 PTS
2ND	DEAN PARKER	9 PTS
3RD	VENDREDI TENGKU	8 PTS
4TH	SIDDHARTH PATEL	7 PTS
5TH	ADIN ZAVARY	6 PTS
6TH	BECK MCLAUGHLIN	5 PTS
7TH	AENEAS HUDSON	4 PTS
8TH	SEYOON SHIN	3 PTS

Nine points. Seeing my name so high on the leaderboard makes pride balloon in my chest. I wish Meredith and Dad could see this.

They will, I remind myself. I scan the rest of the contestants' names, catching on the one in first place.

Wait. Is that—?

"Moxley?" Seyoon says, broken from her stupor. People move out of her way as she approaches the board. Her jaw falls. She swivels around and points her finger at the guy who came in first. "You're Garrett's kid?"

Garrett ruffles the boy's strawberry-blond hair. "This is Carter, my nephew. Winning must run in our genes."

"You call that winning?" Seyoon continues, completely oblivious to the way all five cameras have been trained on her since her voice started rising in volume. "He cut our cable. I saw your tool, you *tool.*"

Carter crosses his arms and shrugs. He's Seyoon's height but has perfected the art of looking down on someone, even with his stature. "I had it on me. It's not cheating to use the resources available to you."

"And was one of those resources having your uncle as the host? I'm *sure* you were as caught off guard by this challenge as the rest of us, and that it was a total coincidence you had a bolt cutter on you."

To my horror, Seyoon seeks me out in the crowd. "Back me up, Dean. He could have killed us!"

Everyone and the cameras turn to me. The blood drains from my face. I don't know what happened to the zip line. All I knew was there wasn't any time to waste, so I didn't stop to think about it. With all these eyes on me, I can't think anything at all. "Uh . . ."

My silence punctuates the air. Seyoon glares, shaking her head.

Shame crawls down my spine.

"That's the nature of the game," Garrett says to her. "And I explicitly said the only rules are you can't cut through the woods. So, no, Carter didn't technically cheat."

"Winning on technicalities instead of merit, yeah, okay. That definitely does run in your family, you sleazy—"

She seems to finally notice the cameras surrounding her and snaps her jaw shut. Blake, next to one of the camera operators, looks disappointed that she didn't finish her scathing line of thought. Insulting the host would make great TV.

When it's clear Seyoon's done, Blake steps in and clears her throat. "Alright, everyone. We need to get back to camp and film contestant introductions before the sun sets, so everyone head back to the buses, please. Sound good?"

Her crisp, clear tone leaves no room for argument. The rest of the contestants murmur and cast Seyoon, Carter, and me glances on their way back to camp. My skin burns. As Carter passes, he crinkles his nose in disgust. I didn't even *say* anything to him. Damn Seyoon for dragging me into this.

And then it's just me, her, and a single camera and mic operator. My earlier plan of rubbing in the fact that she didn't end up beating me seems moot now.

"Did you actually see Carter cut our zip line?" I ask.

"No, I accused the nephew of the host in front of everyone for shits and giggles. You seriously don't believe me? *Yes*, I saw. He played dirty *and* had an unfair advantage. How could you not back me up there?"

The thought of Carter, the nephew of the guy who cheated Dad over, doing the same to me makes my face flush with a mixture of humiliation and resentment. But I swallow it down. I know better than to cause a scene while being filmed. I'd rather die than have a public outburst. "There was no point."

She barks out a laugh. "That's pathetic."

My breath stutters. Anger is quick to fill my lungs instead. "I'm not pathetic because I don't let emotions get the best of me. I use my head. That's the kind of player I am."

"Don't bullshit me. You were just scared to speak up."

A bit too close to home. "And *you're* too full of yourself to accept why you lost. We both fell off that zip line, but I didn't stall. You did."

Seyoon pauses, biting her tongue. I can see the gears turning in her head as she replays the last moments of the race. Regret crumples her expression. "Whatever."

She sniffs indignantly, rubbing her nose and smearing something red on her face. My eyes drop to her hands. They're bloodier than before; she opened her cuts back up at some point. Probably in the fall.

I rub my chest, suddenly tight, and notice there's half of a bloodied handprint on the front of my shirt. A memory of her grabbing it to keep me from falling off the zip line pops into my mind.

Shit.

Seyoon starts to storm away.

"Wait," I say, reaching out to her but stopping midair. My tongue is thick in my mouth, making the words difficult to get out. "Uh. Thank you. For saving me from falling off."

It's obvious she barely remembers. Like it was a reflex to help me instead of a decision. Seyoon flexes her hand, grimacing. "Well," she spits. "That's the kind of player *I* am."

Something ugly scratches at my insides as she walks away.

Our fight replays in my head as I head to the bus, trying to pretend like I don't see the camera operator in my periphery. *Fight* is an uncomfortable word. It implies letting my feelings take over—which they did. They never do. At least, I never let it show when they do.

A pressure headache grows behind my temples as I think back further, to the ugly sensation of everyone's eyes on me. The bulge in my throat I couldn't speak past. The shame that stuck to my skin when Seyoon leveled me with a look of disgust.

I should've spoken up about Carter cheating. Dad and Meredith would have. They would have said something smart, something tough. They would've stood up for what's right.

The show's just started, and I'm already letting them down.

8

TO DEFEAT MY ENEMY, I MUST KNOW MY ENEMY, THEN MEMORIZE MY ENEMY'S FUN FACTS, THEN SIT WITH MY ENEMY AT DINNER, THEN . . .

SEYOON

It's a long, torturous drive back to Mount Rainier with the four contestants who lost sniffling in the back of the bus. Either it wasn't in the budget to rent a separate car for them, or Garrett's just an asshole. Probably the latter. I definitely don't spend the entire hour thinking about how close I came to being one of them.

When we arrive at camp, we get a brief tour of the place right as dusk starts to mark the horizon line. There are five cabins: the Communal House, where we can eat, hang out, and spend what little free time we have between challenges and filming; another large cabin for the crew; a bathroom and shower building; and our cabin.

Instead of letting us in to take a break, Garrett leads us around the back of the cabin, where there's a small wooden shed a few paces away from the woods. Blake is waiting there for us.

Blake pats the side of the shed. "This is the confession booth. While you can expect anything you do or say to be recorded with the exception of off hours between one and six a.m., this is a dedicated spot for you to talk one-on-one with the camera and let the viewers in on what you're thinking at any given moment. Get your side of a story out, make a funny quip, confess something you need to get off your chest—it's all welcome."

She opens the door to the shed. It's cramped inside, with only a small bench, a pair of side lights, and a camera hooked up on the opposite wall. She smiles disarmingly. "Who wants to go first?"

I'm the only one to raise my hand. She gestures for me to come up, and I take a seat on the rickety bench inside the shed. It smells like someone's grandpa in here.

"What do I say?" I ask.

Blake leans against the wall outside, drumming her fingers on her clipboard. "Set the scene for viewers. Tell us how you felt when you first got to camp. What were you thinking? What brought you here?"

Humming, I try to recall. "I thought it was really cool to be in the same place my mom was twenty years ago, and—"

She cuts me off. "Speak in the present tense, as if you're having these thoughts for the first time and just happen to be letting the camera in on them. For viewers watching this, these confession tapes will be edited in mid-scene, so it'll make sense to them."

Blake reaches in to squeeze my arm encouragingly. "Try again. I'll ask some questions to help get you started, but remember that my lines are going to be edited out. So focus on giving a cohesive answer." Blake nods at the camera. "And look there. It makes the audience feel like you're letting them in on a secret."

Something about that makes me squirm in my seat. But still, I face the camera and try to remember everything she's just asked of me. I put myself back in the headspace I was in when I first crested the hill and saw Mount Rainier's snowy cap peeking out from behind camp. My throat tightens.

CONFESSION TAPE—Seyoon Shin, Contestant

> My mom was on the last-ever season of *Forest Feud*. She got third place, but she should've won. If she had, our whole lives would have been different.
>
> So, being here now, playing on the same show she did, seeing the same view she saw . . . it feels very full circle. Every time I look at that mountain, these trees, I remember why I'm here. Who I'm doing this for.
>
> I'm here to win for her. And I'm not leaving this mountain unless the prize money comes with me.

Blake cackles. "That's *perfect*. Oh, I knew I'd like you."

She asks me a few more questions, coaching me into talking more about who I am, my life back home, that kind of thing. It's kind of fun, actually, and really cathartic, until she asks, "Tell us how you feel about narrowly managing to escape elimination in the first challenge. For context, we're probably going to splice this in right after you crossed the finish line."

CONFESSION TAPE—Seyoon Shin, Contestant

Um, uh . . . I . . .

"You know," I say, turning away and hopping out of the booth, "I think I've been in here long enough."

Blake's perfectly thin eyebrows rise, but before she can argue with me, I escape into the group of other contestants waiting for their turns nearby. She sighs, then looks at her clipboard.

"Alright. Dean, come on up."

I purposefully look bored as Dean gets into the booth, but I eavesdrop on every hesitant, awkward answer he gives. Guy does *not* like being in front of the camera. After a while, I can't hide my interest, especially when all the others have their turns. Is it because I'm nosy? That's none of your business.

Okay, fine, maybe I am. But these are my competitors; it's important to hear all about their strengths, weaknesses, and hobbies. Especially if I want to befriend any of them—I mean, crush them in competition. I'm reminded of how I used to pore over the stat sheets of the rival team before each and every track meet. Thank you for always enabling my digital stalking habit, Athletic.net.

I start picturing little stat cards in my head for each person, internalizing the barrage of information in the only way my brain will accept.

Dean Parker

Personality: A jerk who uses his boyish charm and stupid good looks to get away with crimes against humanity (me).

Strengths: Nothing!!!

Weaknesses: Doesn't know how to hold on to a suitcase handle.

Relative: Vince Parker, dad. Allies with Umma and Garrett (ugh).

Fun Fact: I hate him, he's seen every season of *Forest Feud* (nerd), and oh yeah—I hate him.

Notes: I must defeat him in a way that is so humiliating he spends every day agonizing over how he insulted me and ignored my attempt at friendship.

Carter Moxley

Personality: Snobby nepo baby.

Strengths: Probably knows a lot about reality-TV tactics because of his uncle. Kind of athletic, *I guess.*

Weaknesses: He's an entitled asshole. Doesn't use sunscreen.

Relative: Garrett Moxley, uncle. "Won" the last season. Don't make me repeat this.

Fun Fact: He has sleep apnea and preemptively told the rest of us to "deal with it."

Notes: I must destroy him, too.

Siddharth Patel

Personality: Class (camp?) clown.

Strengths: As resilient as a rock.

Weaknesses: Had to be informed what *resilient* means.

Relative: Anvi Patel, sister. Won the fourteenth season. He wants to win too so that his sister doesn't have one up on him.

Fun Fact: Thinks Bigfoot is real and is deathly scared of him.

Notes: Laughs too hard at his own jokes and spoils the punch line.

Vendredi Tengku

Personality: Fueled by spite and sunshine.

Strengths: Athletic. Bubbly. A literal social butterfly because she's both social and beautiful like one. Good thing these notes are just for me.

Weaknesses: Says she's really competitive like it's a bad thing, but I think that's a strength.

Relative: Mariah Dillworth, mom. Won the twelfth season, but Vendredi didn't mention much else about her.

Fun Fact: She wants to be an actor.

Notes: I think we'd make good friends.

Beck McLaughlin

Personality: Unassuming, but with entirely too many talents and niche hobbies.

Strengths: I don't even know where to start. Math whiz, plays every wind instrument, speaks three languages.

Weaknesses: Not very physically strong. Loses her train of thought easily.

Relative: Her mom *and* dad were both previous contestants. Her mom won the eleventh season, and her dad lost the same one.

Fun Fact: She's already been on a reality show before. She almost won *Phantom Pursuers,* a ghost-hunting show, but accidentally exorcised the spirit instead of catching it. She hopes to win *Forest Feud* to redeem herself.

Notes: Ask her how one catches a phantom.

Adin Zavary

Personality: A confusing mix between a frat boy–type and a loser. So maybe not that confusing after all.

Strengths: Good with people. Athletic.

Weaknesses: Makes enemies as easily as friends.

Relative: Bilal Malik, uncle. Lost the same season that Siddharth's sister won.

Fun Fact: Wants to win to make sure he gets elected as student body president and wrestling captain next year . . . wait, that's it?

Notes: Has already started bonding with Siddharth, which seems like a headache in the making.

Aeneas Hudson

Personality: Has the anxiety levels of somebody being hunted for sport.

Strengths: Kind, easy to get along with, logical.

Weaknesses: I don't think they crumble under pressure, per se. More like pressure beats them with a mallet.

Relative: Courtney Grill, grandmother. Lost the seventh season.

Fun Fact: They accidentally signed up for a lifetime membership at their local hot dog–eating league.

Notes: Uses they/them pronouns and really, *really* doesn't want to be here.

After what feels like forever, we finally wrap up and break for a very belated dinner. I grab my ambiguous brown slop and survey the cafeteria with a mission: I *will* make friends today, goddamnit.

There are two girls sitting together in the corner: Beck and Vendredi. Perfect.

I round their table with my tray in hand, waiting so I don't interrupt their conversation. Beck, a girl with shocking green eyes that pop against her pale skin, talks a mile a minute, gesticulating so much that it makes her black bob flip this way and that. Vendredi is listening intently, nodding like she's fascinated. She's one of the prettiest girls I've ever seen, with her square, dark-brown face and perfect smile.

"—So while the Whaley House claims to be the most haunted house in America, based on my investigation on *Phantom Pursuers*, I think it only lands as the sixth or fifth most haunted, right under—" Beck notices me then. "Oh, hello."

"Hi." I smile. "Are you talking about ghosts?"

"Yeah." Beck perks up. "Why? Are you a truthseeker, too?"

"Um . . . maybe? I like all sorts of stuff. I thought it sounded interesting when you were talking about it in the confession booth," I say. "Can I join you gu—"

"No," interrupts Vendredi, sounding panicked. Her eyes widen, and she hurries to finish. "Um, sorry. It's just that, uh . . . we're saving those seats. I'm sorry, really."

Beck shoots her a confused look, and my ears warm.

Oh.

"That's okay. Actually, I just remembered I have an appointment," I blurt. My skin gets hotter. I notice the camera operator at the neighboring table now, tracking us. "I mean meeting. I mean—"

Alright, leaving now.

I turn on my heel, ignoring the brief crumpled expression of regret on Vendredi's face. Okay. So the first and second attempt to make friends didn't work out. That's fine. You know what they say about the third time.

I look around the rest of the cafeteria, at the several camera people milling about, capturing all our interactions. The positive and the painful ones. How many failures of mine have already been documented today? Do I really need another?

. . . Maybe I'll wait to try again.

I toss my dinner into the trash on my way out, not that hungry anymore.

9

TWO RIVALS, ONE BUNK BED

DEAN

Garrett and Blake are there after dinner to personally escort us to our cabin so we can begin assigning bunks, a team of cameras close behind them. Even after just one day with those glassy, all-seeing screens following me around, my senses are chafed.

The cabin itself is quaint but charming. The dark oak logs of the walls have been decorated with warm, homey string lights. I scan along the ceiling, my suspicions confirmed when I spot cameras tucked into the corners of the room. It seems like a lawsuit waiting to happen, but reality TV is known for its blatant disregard for privacy. I'm not surprised, but I'm not thrilled, either.

More concerning are the bunk beds. There are double-decker bunks along each wall of the room, with a dresser on either side of each bed. Our luggage sits next to the door, waiting to be collected.

Adin, trailing in behind me, hacks and pounds on his broad chest. "Has this place not been aired out since our folks were staying here?"

"Think of it as inhaling a piece of history. A souvenir you get to keep in your lungs forever," Garrett says. "Now then. Carter gets first dibs on beds, then Dean, then down the ranks, depending on how you placed."

Carter picks the bottom bunk in the farthest corner, so I pick the one on the opposite wall. It goes down the line until people start pairing up one by one, leaving only the last contestant.

Damnit.

"Don't look so excited," Seyoon grumbles at me as she flings her duffel bag on the ground next to my bunk. She hesitates, glancing at the empty loft bed. "Could I maybe have the bottom bunk?"

"That defeats the purpose of picking based on ranks," I reply.

She crosses her arms and glares. "I move around a lot in my sleep, okay? So if I roll off the top bunk, fall, and break every bone in my body, it'll be your fault. Can your conscience handle that?"

Probably, but I'd like to avoid hearing springs squeaking above me all night, so I haul myself up and onto the loft bed. Seyoon gives me a tight-lipped smile, probably her version of a thank-you.

Chatter flits through the cabin as everyone settles in. I stay where I am, frowning up at the oak ceiling. I wish I had my phone to tinker with as an excuse to not socialize. Even if I wanted to, I have no idea how I'd insert myself into any of these conversations. I'm oil on water. Bleach in vinegar. Similar to the side effects of chlorine gas that is produced when you mix those, my attempts at socializing cause breathing difficulties, watery eyes, nausea, and headaches for all those involved.

Garrett sidles up to one of the bunk beds and knocks on the post, getting our attention. "Glad to see you're all getting cozy! Before ol' Blakey and I head out and let you get some rest, I just have one more parting piece of advice for you all. Remember earlier today, when I said there'd be an opportunity to win points outside of challenges?"

Seyoon's mattress creaks below mine as she sits up. "You did?"

"Does no one listen to me?"

"Well, what is it?" asks Beck.

Garrett ambles to the center of the room, hands crossed behind his back as he turns in a slow circle, eyeing us with amusement.

"As you know, *Forest Feud* is the name, but *family* is the game. We and the studio network aren't shying away from the whole legacy shtick, and neither should you," he says. "You're all here because of your past connections, so now we want to encourage you to make a few of your own."

Aeneas, in the bunk closest to him, raises their hand hesitantly. "Um, sorry, what does that—"

Garrett holds his hand up. "Wait. Let the silence sit. Dramatic pause."

The pause is more awkward than dramatic as a camera operator swivels around to get all of our baited reactions.

"Alright," Garrett continues. "What that means is: We want you to form alliances with each other. The audience will eat that stuff up, especially if relatives of past rivals start working together."

He peers around the room, lighting up when he spots his victims. "Seyoon, Dean, and Carter—the perfect example. How about a follow-up to one of TV's greatest alliances? Eh?"

None of us reply. Blake steps around Garrett.

"Perhaps it'll change your mind to hear that those in an alliance will get three bonus points for every challenge they continue working together," she says. That *is* tempting.

A sharp scoff from the bed opposite mine. "I don't care. I'm not taking them under my wing," Carter says.

"I'd never want to work with you anyway," Seyoon snaps, standing up from her bunk. "And you better not go crying to Uncle when I beat you in the next challenge."

Someone makes an obnoxious cat noise from across the room. Carter sits up.

"Big talk for a girl who hardly made the cut—just like your mom barely made the final three." He turns and locks eyes with me next. "And you. Don't get comfortable in second place. Your dad may have done it, but you don't seem like half the man he was." Carter lies back down. "There's no competition here, and certainly no chance for an alliance. I'm going to beat both of you just like my uncle beat your parents."

The cabin erupts into excited hoots and calls for a fight. Garrett's riotous laughter bounces off the walls. "He's definitely my nephew!" he says. Blake tries to quiet everyone, but there's no quelling a room of teens sensing tension brewing.

No, that's not the only thing that's brewing. My blood boils hot under my skin, scalding where my pulse hammers.

Carter's good. It's smart to make a strong first impression; there was always one person who made a big show like this on every season of *Forest Feud*. It's a surefire way to be remembered as a tough player. If the rowdy crowd wasn't interrupting every thought in my head, I'd think it through and realize that taunting me isn't personal. In all likelihood, Carter probably doesn't give two shits about me, let alone how I measure up as a man against my dad.

But for once, I'm not able to think it through. Because the pressure building in me hasn't had a chance to cool all day. Because

I came here to do right by Dad and Meredith, not embarrass the Parker name and come home empty-handed.

In the ruckus, I glance at Seyoon. She's silent, shockingly. Her back is turned away from me, so I can't make out her expression, but by the way her clenched fists shake at her sides, I know she's not letting this one go, either.

That Moxley is going to pay.

Afterward, everyone is too exhausted to do much more than collapse in bed. Once they call lights out, the only sound in the dark cabin is the occasional snore or sleepy murmur. But I can't sleep. I toss and turn for hours, staring blankly into the dark.

In the middle of the night, shuffling below catches my attention. I lie still as the mattress creaks and feet softly hit the floorboards. The door to the cabin squeaks opens, letting in a sliver of moonlight before it's shut just as quickly.

I last only a few minutes before curiosity and restlessness get the best of me. I toss the blankets off, hop down, throw on my hoodie, and head outside.

The sky is a shade of heavy, inky black, suffocating in a way that could swallow you whole. But it's the stars—*millions* of them—that compress the air from my lungs.

I thought I'd seen stars before. You can spy Ursa Major from my bedroom window on a good night. But this? *These* are stars. Bright, crisp pinpricks stand in contrast on a sea of emptiness, spanning each corner of my periphery. The sky feels less like a roof over my head and more like a hole in the ozone. I'm reminded of how small I am, of the gravity keeping my feet on the dewy grass.

I understand for the first time why people go out in nature.

A cool breeze whistles through the forest, sobering me from my trance. I drag myself back to Earth, to the stillness of an empty campsite. Only the wind and my stuttered inhale interrupt the quiet.

Well. That, and the muffled, angry ranting coming from the shed next to the cabin.

10

SHARED SPITE IS A DOUBLE SPITE, OR HOWEVER THE PROVERB GOES

SEYOON

CONFESSION TAPE—Seyoon Shin, Contestant

Let me set the record straight: I am *not* a sore loser. That would imply being a loser, which I'm not either. I just can't stand injustice, which is what happened here today. I'm not going to apologize for calling Carter out on what he did. Even if I'm the only one who will.

Who the hell does he think he is anyway, insulting my mom? She would have won if Garrett hadn't tricked her, you know. Ugh, those Moxleys disgust me. It's going to feel *so* good when I beat Carter. I'll show him.

[quieter]

Going to show my sorry excuse of a dad, too.

[several moments of silence, then, muttering]

. . . Fuck. I'm such an idiot. Why did I *stall*? Why didn't I get up and run like Dean? Standing around like a moron while everyone passed me . . . you're a goddamn idiot, Seyoon. Just like he said: You can't do anything right. You always—*AH!*

The door to the shed opens. I scream before I can stop myself, belatedly slapping a hand over my mouth. The moon backlights the figure, concealing them in shadow.

"You know," the person says. "You shouldn't take the confession booth so literally."

It's Dean. His voice is groggy. Did I wake him up?

"Were you eavesdropping? This is a private conversation."

"No, it isn't. That's what I mean. This isn't a place to air out your frustrations. This is going to be edited straight into the episode. You should think about what you're comfortable sharing with the cameras—with the world."

I blink, glancing at the camera in the corner of the shed. "I was just trying to explain my side of things . . ." Although maybe I did overshare there at the end. Shit. I've never been good at holding back.

Dean steps away, and I exit the confession booth. No one else has stepped out of the cabin, so he's the only one who caught that embarrassing slip. I give him a once-over, standing barefoot in just a hoodie and some pajama pants.

"How much did you hear?" I ask.

"Would it make you feel better if I lied?"

Huffing, I walk away toward the bonfire pit. Dean follows, taking a seat on the log next to me. "It might have," I grumble.

He's quiet. Then, "I never said you can't do anything right."

"What?"

"In the confession booth, I heard you say 'Just like he said: You can't do anything right.'"

"Oh." The blood drains from my face. "No, I wasn't talking about you. It was . . . someone else who told me that."

Luckily, he doesn't pry further. Not so luckily, it means quiet hangs over us instead, so smothering that it itches. God, I hate awkward silences. And silence in general. I usually try to fill it, but I'd rather make small talk with the crickets yammering around us than with Dean. I scratch at my palms, focusing on the sting as a distraction.

"Stop that, you're making it worse," he chastises.

I make eye contact with him and scratch harder. When I don't quit it, he separates my wrists. His fingers are thin and elegant like an artist's, and his skin is hot where it touches mine. I watch as he holds my wrists in one hand, his other reaching into the pocket of his hoodie and pulling out the roll of bandage from earlier.

"Oh, *now* you want to finish the job?" I say.

"Yeah, I do. That okay with you?"

There's a sarcastic bite to his question, but he waits for permission. Slowly, I nod. Dean begins wrapping the bandage around my palms, clumsily weaving it between my fingers. Twice, he pauses before undoing his work and trying again.

"Are you nervous, or just bad at this?" I ask.

"Hey."

Still. It's an unexpected kindness. I look off into the forest, pursing my lips. He finishes up without a word, dropping my wrist once he's done.

Umma didn't raise an ungrateful daughter. "Thank you," I say. "And thanks for interrupting me in the confession booth. I probably would've said something I regret."

"Call us even. You did save me from falling off the zip line."

"Are we really even if you're the reason my hands are busted in the first place?"

"I apologized for that already."

"But you didn't say sorry for not backing me up. Or for insulting me and my mom."

"You first. I think you goaded me within five minutes of meeting and then called me pathetic?"

We both glare at each other. Dean's hazel eyes are pitch-black in the night, drilling into mine. A moment passes. Another. Then his back slouches, and my shoulders loosen. We both shift on the log. I'm tired, and I think he is, too. An unspoken truce settles in the space between us for now.

I inspect his handiwork, flexing my fingers. It's not the neatest job in the world, but I hardly mind. My hands do feel better, I guess.

"I should've let you finish patching me up earlier. Would've made the challenge easier. It's cool you know how to do this," I say, the closest thing to an apology I'll give him right now.

"My sister got really into rock climbing for a while, and I'd help patch up her callouses," he explains. "Anyway, I'm surprised you played as well as you did with both your hands like that." Dean stiffens, as if he didn't mean to let that slip.

"Was that a compliment?" I ask excitedly.

"No."

"Aw, thanks, I'll take it."

He groans and I laugh, momentarily forgetting it's the middle of the night and I'm still ticked off at him. After a moment of deliberation, I say, "You did pretty good in the race, too. You caught up super quick and solved that riddle so fast." I don't mention how I tried but failed to do the same.

For a long, awkward moment, I don't think he's going to reply. Then, "I got lucky that there was a strategy component. The rest of it wasn't in my favor."

"Just take the compliment, dude."

He huffs. "Thank you." Begrudgingly, he adds, "If it wasn't for Carter cutting our line, you probably would've won."

"Ugh. Whatever. I'll beat him next time."

"If he doesn't pull some nepotism strings again, that is."

I scowl at the grass. "With that sleazeball Garrett on his side, he has an advantage over all of us. No way his uncle will play fair." I dig my shoe into the ground. "It's almost funny. Garrett screwed your dad and my mom over, and now he's helping his nephew do the same to us."

"We have different definitions of *funny*. But agreed. I don't think any of us on our own stand a chance against Carter *and* Garrett."

There's a sharp, bitter edge to Dean's usual monotone voice that has me turning his way. He glares at the cabin like he's trying to pierce Carter through its walls.

On our own.

He's right. Carter's fast, strong, and he has game show knowledge on his side as Garrett's nephew. I have him beat in the first two categories, but the third? I just gave my daddy issues away in a confession booth—that should show how little I know what I'm doing when it comes to TV etiquette. Good thing Dean interrupted me. He probably has an edge over Carter when it comes to understanding how to play the game; he's seen every season of *Forest Feud,* after all. Wish I could borrow some of that.

Huh.

I have an idea.

"What if we *weren't* on our own?" I ask carefully.

"What?"

"Don't let it get to your big head, but you are kind of smart. Plus, you understand how reality TV works better than I do." Dean flusters at the compliment, tugging on the string of his hoodie. I grin. "And as we both know, I'm fast, and strong, and athletic, and—"

"And humble."

"Exactly right, thank you. Garrett did say we should play to the whole 'family legacy' thing, follow in our parents' footsteps, so . . ."

"Spit it out. You're making me nervous."

I shift around on the log so I'm facing him fully. "What if we worked together?"

Dean blinks at me. I blink back.

"You and me?"

"Yeah."

"Teaming up?"

"That's the idea."

"So . . . like an alliance?"

I snap my fingers. "That's the word." I lean forward. Dean stiffens at the closeness but doesn't move away. "We have complementary strengths. You're a better strategist, and I'm a better athlete. We could get each other to the finale, even if Garrett helps Carter out. Plus, the alliance bonus points wouldn't hurt."

Still, Dean's eyebrows are knitted, and he doesn't seem sold on the idea. I try again. "We can't let a *Moxley* get away with beating us."

That gets him. "Are you sure?"

"Of course I'm sure. It was my idea."

"I know, I'm just . . . surprised that you'd want to team up with *me*."

And suddenly, the fidgeting, the long, silent pauses, the one-word responses—they make a little more sense now as Dean's voice trails off and I watch him hunch in on himself almost subconsciously, like he's not even aware he's doing it.

I think of soft, timid Joy Lata on the JV volleyball team last year, who was too shy to call the ball and would get yelled at by the other girls until I stepped in. Then I think of when *I* was a newbie JV player that the varsity girls snickered at because I called the ball too often and too loudly. Amelia was captain my freshman year and the only one who patted me on the back and told me I was doing great. That was before we let rivalry get in the way of things.

I wonder if Dean ever had an Amelia.

I stick my bandaged hand out between us. "I'm sure."

Dean considers the offer a second longer. Then he meets my eye and reaches for my hand, his lips turning up. Huh. He has dimples. I didn't notice them until now. He should smile more.

"Let's do this. Carter is going down."

"Ow, my hand!"

"Oops, sorry."

11

ONE BAD PUN WAS PLENTY, THANKS

SEYOON

Forming an alliance with Dean does not make us friends.

He's stubborn and has the emotional capacity of a brick wall, but, I don't know, I thought that since we're teaming up, we might at least sit together at breakfast to have a conversation about the game. But the next morning, which we have off, Dean makes it his mission to be scarce, popping by the cafeteria only long enough to grab food before he disappears. Fine. Dean's free to spend his time however he likes. I take the opportunity to go for a swim in Summit Lake. Not because I'm avoiding making friends after yesterday's disaster. But because . . . it's hot.

Come noon, when the sun crests in the center of the intensely blue sky, Garrett and Blake call us all to gather around the empty bonfire pit—noticeably, without the usual camera crew flanking them.

I spot Dean sitting on one of the logs. He looks up. "Hi."

"Hey." I glance at the empty spot next to him, and Dean pats the log in a wordless invitation before I can ask. I sit, silently relieved. "What were you up to earlier?"

"Nothing much. Just reading."

"How come you didn't hang out with everybody else?"

He crosses his arms defensively. "How come *you* didn't?"

"How—how did you know?"

"Saw you swimming by yourself."

"Okay, creep. I thought you were reading, not stalking?"

"I was reading by the lake."

"You were at the lake? Why didn't you join me? We could have raced. Whoever wins gets to choose our alliance name."

"I'll definitely take you up on that offer."

I sit up. "Really?"

"No."

I slouch, disappointed.

Blake clears her throat, and all of us around the firepit stop talking. She's as polished as ever, in another equally nice blazer and pantsuit. Garrett standing next to her, on the other hand, is dressed like a camp counselor. Or a zookeeper, more accurately.

"Thank you, campers." She smiles. "As you know, tomorrow kicks off your next challenge, which will be—"

"Survival of the Skillest!" Garrett interrupts, throwing out jazz hands.

Silence.

"That's not even close to being grammatically correct," Carter says.

"Yes, well, we left the creative naming to the host," Blake says, pushing Garrett's hands down.

He's not deterred. "I don't want to spoil too much, but your task tomorrow will be in-*tents*."

"Are you trying to say *intense*?" asks Siddharth. "Why are you putting so much emphasis on it?"

"I'm saying in-*tents*."

"Dude, I think he has a lisp, lay off," whispers Adin.

"*Oh*, my bad, Mr. Moxley."

"No, ugh—" Garrett groans. "It will be in-*tents*. Like, inside of tents. As in, you're all going to build a tent and camp in it and show off your survival skills. God, children, I can't . . . just laugh when I say it on camera tomorrow, alright?"

CONFESSION TAPE—Vendredi Tengku, Contestant

You know how some celebrities look better on TV than they do in real life? Well Garrett is kinda like that, where he seems funnier on TV than he actually is. He also looks worse in real life, too.

. . . Do you guys show him these tapes?

CONFESSION TAPE—Beck McLaughlin, Contestant

I still don't get the joke. That was supposed to be a joke, right?

"Anyhow," Blake says. "We wanted to check in ahead of time and see if any of you have considered teaming up. We'd love to see unions form, especially those that would excite viewers and longtime fans of the show. Remember—alliances earn three bonus points."

Me and Dean raise our hands. So do Vendredi and Beck, and Siddharth and Adin.

Blake's face creases as she glances over at Carter. She points a neatly manicured nail between us and him. "*Just* Seyoon and Dean? I can't convince you to do me a solid and replicate everyone's favorite Final Three?" She drops her voice like she's joking, but the anxious lilt to her voice kind of ruins the bit. "The network would really love to see it."

I scoff. "It's not happening."

"No," Carter says plainly.

Dean curls up like a stink bug, trying to shield his face from view. Helpful, as always.

Blake looks less than pleased, lips pursed thin, but ultimately stands down. "Alright. Well, our three alliances, let me drop the other shoe that our host forgot to mention yesterday. Teams must *split* any points they win or lose."

That changes things. Siddharth and Adin take one look at each other, then unanimously nod and scoot away subtly.

"Maybe we're better off on our own," Siddharth says, scratching his neck. "No hard feelings, bro?"

"No, no," Adin's quick to say, waving his hands in the air. "No hard feelings for *you*, bro."

"None here, bro."

"Brother, I'm telling you? None here either."

Aeneas, on the other side of Adin, leans away even as the boy keeps scooting into their personal bubble.

CONFESSION TAPE—Aeneas Hudson, Contestant

How did I end up here, like on the show? Well . . . sometimes I have trouble stepping outside of my comfort zone. So my therapist gave me a challenge: For one week, instead of turning down new and uncomfortable opportunities, I have to say yes. To all of them.

I got the email asking me to be a contestant during that week.

[strained]

On day *six* of that week.

I look over at Dean, who swallows thickly, his Adam's apple bobbing. I hold my fist between us, knuckles out.

"We can do it," I reassure him. "We'll win so many points together it doesn't matter that we have to split them."

Dean's honey eyes widen in surprise. I nod at him, certain, and watch as some confidence bleeds into his expression. He smiles back, albeit hesitantly, and bumps his fist against mine. "We will," he agrees.

"Don't speak so soon," Carter drawls. I ignore him.

"That's the spirit!" Garrett says.

Beck and Vendredi, sitting on the adjacent log, exchange whispers, then Vendredi straightens. "We're still going to form an alliance, too," she says. I glance over and accidentally catch her eye. I turn away first, pretending I was just stretching.

After that, we're excused to go to lunch. Once everyone else leaves, Dean pulls me aside.

"So, about the challenge tomorrow," he says, scratching his neck. "Would this be a bad time to tell you I don't know the first thing when it comes to survival skills?"

This mother—

12

STICKS AND STONES WILL BREAK MY BONES, AND WORDS WILL ALSO DEFINITELY HURT ME, TOO

DEAN

"—fucker. What do you mean you don't know anything? I thought you've seen every survival show known to man? Were you watching them with your eyes closed?"

I glare at the back of Seyoon's head as she walks ahead of me, trekking through the woods at a faster pace than necessary. When I let her know the slight disadvantage working against us (the disadvantage being my total lack of outdoor ability), she insisted we have a practice run ahead of tomorrow's survival skills challenge. Which is how I ended up here, hiking yet again through the forest, a pack of supplies on my back and the afternoon sun beating down on my head.

And, awkwardly, with a small team of camera and sound operators following behind us and doing a bad job of blending in.

"Watching it on TV doesn't mean I magically absorbed the skills by osmosis." I huff. "I understand the technical aspect of things, I just haven't put it to practical application . . . per se."

"Feels like the kind of thing you tell somebody before you form an alliance with them is all I'm saying."

"It was your idea to team up, remember?"

Seyoon mumbles something about a mouse, but I don't catch it.

I push a branch out of the way. "How much longer do we need to hike, anyway? Can we even be out this far?"

She turns around to wait for me to catch up. "Aw, Goody Two-shoes, aren't you cute? If it's the rules you want, listen up, nerd, because here's the first rule of camping: Get off the beaten path."

My face is warm with a blush, although I'm not sure if I should care more that she called me cute or a nerd. Seyoon unfolds the map Garrett gave us before we set out. "However, with that said, Blake told us we need to stay within the show's zone permits. There's another campsite a little bit away where no one should disturb us."

I kindly refrain from telling her that we're not going to run into anybody anyway because no one in their right mind would be out in this blistering heat when they could stay back at camp, relaxing in an air-conditioned cabin. Also, because the idea of just the two of us—minus the crew—out here makes my gut churn. A skill I've cultivated over the years is making sure I'm never left alone with someone so as to prevent the horrible situation where I'm anyone's only option for social interaction. Unfortunately, it looks like that'll be unavoidable today.

We continue marching along until we reach the campsite. There's not much to it besides a firepit and some flattened land. Seyoon sniffs around, then stops so abruptly that I almost topple her over.

"Perfect," she whispers.

I survey the area in front of us. "What's different about *this* patch of dirt?"

"It's flat, and these trees will help block the wind. Plus, look, there's enough pine needles on the ground to keep us comfy."

"Whatever you say," I oblige.

"Go on, lie down, you'll see what I mean."

Skeptical, I set down my bag and stretch out across the dirt, cringing at the pine needles surely getting tangled in my hair. I look up at Seyoon.

"What am I supposed to be getting from this?"

"Nothing." She shrugs with a grin. "I just wanted to see if you'd do what I said."

She laughs as I scurry up. "Okay, enough of that. Do you even know what you're doing, or are you just pretending to be better than me again?"

"Hey, hotshot, I'm not pretending, I *am* better." She slips off her bag and tosses it against the tree trunk. "I go camping all the time. Plus, I used to be a Girl Scout."

So was Meredith. An image of a young Seyoon with pigtails in that dorky Scout outfit flashes in my mind. I roll my eyes. "Well, now what, Scoutmaster Shin?"

"Good to see you putting a little respect on my name for once. How about we start with something easy, like setting up a shelter?"

It turns out setting up a shelter is not easy.

"Have you never built a blanket fort as a kid?" she asks incredulously as the fourth attempt at propping up a basic lean-to collapses under my clumsy touch.

"This is a little different," I say with a grunt, not mentioning how it was Meredith who built our forts. I was always on snack-retrieval duty.

Seyoon sighs, wiping sweat from her brow. "That's okay. Uh . . . let's try another skill then. Tying knots?"

An hour of unsuccessful knot-tying attempts later—with plenty of rope burn to show for it—and it's clear I'm failing at this, too.

"But," Seyoon says with a tinge of hysterics in her voice, watching my shaking fingers try to loop the rope the way she did. "Your shoelaces have knots. How did you put them on this morning if you can't tie one?"

The camera operator steps on a branch as they circle around me to zoom in on my hands, and the *crunch!* makes me jump. "Hold on. Just let me . . ."

But no matter which way I fold and loop and tuck, it's useless. I throw the rope down, collapsing against the dirt in frustration.

"Are they permanently laced up?" she mutters. "That must be it. So you can just slip your feet in without having to tie a knot every—"

"Seyoon?"

"Yeah?"

"Shut up."

"No, *you* shut up. Ugh. Let's just move on," she says in the same kind of weary tone that Dad gets when I still don't understand the difference between a 2-4-5 defense and a 3-3-5 defense in football, no matter how many times he tries to explain it. My hands twitch in the dirt.

"Maybe you're better suited to other things, like foraging," Seyoon says.

Except I can't tell a chanterelle from a poisonous lookalike, and Seyoon smacks my hand when I go to pluck it because 1: That's a jack-o'-lantern mushroom, do you really want to shit yourself on national television? And 2: Did you not hear me when I said,

"Leave no trace"? But I'm not suited to purifying water, either, apparently, because every time I try and dig a pit for a solar still, the walls cave in. I *am* able to hang a bear bag on a rope, but I fail tirelessly at hoisting the bag up on a tree branch. Finally, we get to the very last of the day's tasks and Seyoon's patience.

"Why would you save the hardest thing to do for last?" I ask. Between us in the firepit is our tinder nest of dry grass, leaves, and bark: the optimistic start of a campfire. Seyoon sits across from me with her legs folded beneath her, her bangs stuck to her forehead with sweat. I'm in no better shape, covered in dirt and splinters. Even the crew members look exhausted. The sunlight glints off the camera's lens, blinding me every time the operator hurries around to record my pathetic, despaired reactions.

"Because I was hoping you'd be able to get some of the easier tasks right and build up to this," she snaps. Although the temperature is finally starting to drop as it nears evening, it's clear the sun beating down on us all day has sapped her composure. "If you can't do it, it's fine, at least then we can head back and take a shower."

My nostrils flare. Seyoon reclines on her elbows, head lolling to the side. Her eyes are half-lidded in disinterest; she's already given up on me. She knows I'm going to fail.

She knows I'm going to let her down.

I glare down at the piece of wood in front of my lap. The fireboard, I think she called it. Trying to recall the instructions she went over a million times, I cut a V-shaped notch into it with the jagged edge of a rock. I blearily search for a stick—the spindle?—and jam it into the notch. Seyoon's eyelids have fully shut now. Even the camera operator yawns. Frustration pools in my gut, and I wish I could transfer some of that heat into the wood as I start rolling the spindle between my hands, praying for sparks.

"You're not rolling fast enough," Seyoon drawls. She's not even looking. Maybe she can do this in her sleep. Or maybe she just expects me to mess up. Grunting, I try to speed up, but my hands are clumsy, slow.

"You'll go faster if you run your palms up and down while you roll."

"*Okay,*" I grit out, the warmth in my gut ebbing into shame.

"Are you putting enough pressure on the bo—"

"I'm trying!" I snap. *That* gets the camera operator's attention. They swivel their camera directly at me. Damnit.

She sits up. "What are you getting mad at me for? I'm helping you."

I keep grinding the spindle into the board, glaring daggers at the stick instead of at that awful camera that's the window to a million eyes who'll watch this and see just how inept I am. "Maybe if you gave me more than two seconds, I'd be able to get it right."

"More than two seconds? We've been out here *all* day."

"And you"—The spindle slips and I grunt, repositioning it—"have been on my case all day."

Seyoon scoots over and shoulders me out of the way, snatching the fireboard and spindle from my hands. She stabs the stick into the notch I made and rolls the spindle between her palms with so much force that the veins in her hands bulge. Within a minute, smoke billows out from where the spindle meets the plank. My heart sinks into the ground.

She keeps going until the smoke is a plume, then taps the ember onto a waiting piece of bark, transferring it carefully to the nest of tinder we—*she*—prepared. Crouching now, Seyoon blows until sparks catch and ignite the dry leaves. Before long, a roaring fire sits at our feet. The flames are nothing in comparison to the pure heat licking at my insides. I stare into the fire, digging my nails into my palms as the *shame shame shame* seethes along my skin.

There's another crunch, and the crew member operating the boom mic curses under her breath as she nearly trips over a rock. My gaze flicks over to the camera. The sun's practically set now, and without its light glinting off the screen, I can see my own reflection in the dark glass. My face is heavy. My eyes dull. For the first time, I think, *I look like Dad.* At least, how he did when I first told him I didn't want to be on *Forest Feud.* Disappointment had settled into the creases of his face like it does on mine, now.

Why am I so upset?

I know why: because I said this would happen. I never wanted to be here. I knew I didn't have what it takes. Now, so does Seyoon, and once this airs, so will everyone.

Seyoon's glare is a physical sensation on my turned cheek, a hot iron against my skin. "Should I explain how I did that, or would I just be getting on your case again?" she says.

I know if I speak, I'll just make this worse. Seyoon doesn't take my silence well.

"Ignoring me again. Great. Why would you listen to me, anyway? I couldn't *possibly* know better than you." She laughs bitterly. "Fine. If you don't need me, we should just end things here."

Seyoon stands and kicks dirt at the fire until it fizzles out. The action douses my anger, too. All at once, embarrassment and remorse floods through me, sobering me up.

"Fuck . . ." I mutter as I stand. It's not her I'm upset with; it's myself. "Seyoon, I'm sorry. I didn't mean to ignore you. Or your advice. I'm just . . ."

I lose my train of thought watching her expression morph. Her face is as cold as the last of the sun's dying light setting around us. Even though I stood up, I feel tiny beneath her gaze.

"Just so you know," she says, voice hard and steady. "It doesn't matter that you can't build a shelter or start a fire or any of that stuff. I don't care about that. What I do care about is having a teammate who will actually work *with* me."

Then she leaves. I want to follow or call out with another apology, but my shame keeps me silent and rooted in place. By the time I've gathered the courage to say what needs to be said, Seyoon's out of earshot.

I messed up.

13

BREAKING THE ICE (I LIED. IT'S WATER)

SEYOON

The water is freezing this early in the morning, but I'm committed to swimming three laps around Summit Lake before today's Survival of the Skillest challenge. Swimming's always been an outlet for me. Stressed? Do some crawl strokes until you're too tired to think. Angry? Scream under the water until the lifeguard tells you to *quit that, what's wrong with you?*

So I keep pushing, driving my arms over my head and into the water, kicking my legs hard enough to ward off the numbing cold. Swim season is in the winter, which means shivering through laps is muscle memory. But before coming here, I hadn't swum since state championships in February—which happened to be the last sporting event Appa drove me to.

Umma had picked up an extra shift that evening and wasn't able to come, so when he dropped me off, I did something I never had before: I asked him to stay and watch. He paused for a long time before eventually agreeing, telling me to go on ahead and he'd find parking first. The aquatic center was huge, with unending rows of bleachers high above the pools, so I couldn't spot him through my dark-tinted goggles when I was down in the lanes. I got second place in the 800m.

He was waiting by the front entrance for me when I finished. On the drive back, the only thing he mentioned was that the girl in lane five beat me by a single stroke.

But the way the morning sun is rising over Mount Rainier's silhouette doesn't remind me of state champs. It reminds me of learning to swim in the Willamette River as a kid. The water was just as icy then, and the sky a similar shade of slate blue. Umma would take me every morning during my summer break before she had to go to work, so we went really early, when it was still dark and cold. But we went every day.

Not for the first time since getting here, I think of Umma. I wonder if she's lonely. I hope she's eating okay. I miss her.

On the last leg of my second lap, I glide by the docks and hear a splash, then a muffled "Fuck!" while under the water.

I pause and look back. Hanging onto the dock for dear life is Dean: shirtless and shivering like a drowning poodle.

"H-hi," he says between chattering teeth. "Wanna race?"

"What?"

Wincing, he slowly lowers the rest of his body into the water and swims toward me. Or tries to. He can stay afloat at least, which is . . . something.

"Do you want to race?" he asks again when he's a foot in front of me, like I couldn't hear him the first time. Instead of answering, I cross my arms and glare at him. He watches me tread water just by kicking my legs. "Wow. That's impressive."

"You're ruining my relaxing morning swim," I say.

"How could this possibly be relaxing? The water's freezing."

"Then, get out."

I start kicking myself backward, still crossing my arms and glaring at him. Dean pouts—*pouts*, God, he actually *is* a wet puppy—and follows after me at a slower pace.

"You said you wanted to race. Winner can choose our alliance name, right?" Dean stops, letting me swim farther away. A smile lights up his face. "Look—you win."

I scoff. "That was when I still wanted to team up with you. Besides, don't *give* me a win. It's only worth something if you actually try."

"But we both know you'd crush me, so I'd rather not drown trying to prove it."

I finally stop floating away. Dean paddles over. His blond curls are fully matted to his head, and he pushes them up and out of his face. A shy, fluttering smile forms. It's a while before he can meet my eyes. "Um. Hi."

My gaze darts to his dimples, then back. "What are you doing here?"

"Trying to make amends?"

"Is that a question?"

"No? I mean . . ."

Dean sighs, averting his gaze. The few birds awake at this hour chirp lazily in the surrounding trees. The waves of the lake slosh against the shore. Besides that, camp is asleep. It's probably not six yet; filming hours haven't started. The rare moment of privacy feels too intimate for that reason. I wait for him to speak, exhausting my kiddie-sized pool of patience.

He finally does: "You know, my sister Meredith was a Girl Scout, too."

"This apology is ass."

Dean gives me a look that says *I'm getting there.* "She loved it. She was amazing, obviously, because she's amazing at everything she does. My dad was so excited about it that he immediately signed me up for Boy Scouts, too."

My eyebrows raise. "Then, how come you can't tie a knot?"

"Because I quit after a week."

"That still doesn't explain the shoelaces."

He rolls his eyes, but he's smiling. "My dad let me quit. He said it was okay, but I could tell he was disappointed. So, even though I hated it, I asked Meredith to show me a few skills she learned. I thought I could surprise him. Make him happy."

"Your poor sister," I mutter. "How'd that go?"

"She said I was a lost cause and gave up after a day." Dean finally looks up from the water to meet my eyes then. "I hate to admit it, but I . . . I suck at this. This rugged, outdoors, survival stuff, and . . ." He runs both his hands across his face, sighing into his palms. "And you don't. You're smart, and you're better at this than me, but instead of being grateful that you tried to teach me, I was a jerk. I was ashamed and frustrated, and I took that frustration out on you. I'm sorry. I don't deserve it, but will you give me another chance? *Please?*"

No one's ever called me smart before.

Looking at him, I imagine Dean as a kid, his clumsy fingers smaller and even more uncoordinated, being the only one in his troop to struggle knotting a rope. What did he fill his time with when his sister was at Girl Scouts? Did he have to sit in the car while his dad dropped her off for trips? Was he quiet on the rides home, so that maybe his dad could pretend he had dropped off both of them?

The girl in lane five who beat me at swim championships was in track, too, I found out. She ran the 200m just like me. This spring at districts, we ended up in the same heat, and I crushed her by four and half seconds. I got gold, but Appa had already left us by that point. He didn't stay and watch. I never got second chances with him. Umma didn't either. Neither of us are the kind of people that life gives endless opportunities to—that's why I have to get things right the first time. That's why I have to win.

"Alright. It's cold," I eventually say. "Let's head back."

I purposefully paddle slower so that Dean can keep up, trying not to make it obvious, but when we reach the dock and pull ourselves up, he shoots me a shy, grateful smile as we dry off on the edge.

"I hate being bad at things, too," I say, not as eloquent as I wanted, but there it is. "Failing sucks. Realizing you're not good enough is the worst. I've been there."

"I can't imagine you not being good enough," Dean says offhandedly as he scrunches lake water from his curls.

"You'd be the only one," I reply. Tucking a wet strand of hair behind my ear, I mutter, "I'm sorry I gave up on you so easily yesterday. You're not a lost cause."

I don't dare look over, but I hear a smile in the lilt of his voice when Dean says, "Thanks."

I pull my knees up to my chest, resting my chin on them as I gaze below. The water is so clear that I can see the multicolored rocks layered across the lake bed, distorted only by the rippling waves on the surface. I think about begging Appa to watch my swim meet. I think about how long Dean must have waited for me to circle the lake before he could join.

I've failed plenty of times, more than I'd like to admit and more than Dean could probably guess. It's nice to be thought of as good enough for once.

"Seydean," I test out.

"Yeah?" he replies.

"No, not *say, Dean*. Sey-Dean. Like our names. Team Seydean. Has a nice ring to it, yeah?"

He gets a look on his face like he's trying not to laugh, but he successfully holds it in. "You won naming rights, fair and square. Does that mean . . . ?"

I hold a fist out between us. "It means I'm giving you another chance to prove you want to work *together*. And I'm only offering this because I'm the kindest, most patient person on this mountain, but I don't do third chances. Got it?"

Dean grins, maybe the first unabashed one I've seen from him. He knocks his knuckles against mine. "Yes, ma'am, Scoutmaster Shin."

14

THIS EPISODE IS SPONSORED BY YOUR LOCAL FARMERS' MARKET

DEAN

Welcome, campers, it's good to see you all! Well, those of you who survived the first challenge, that is. Natural selection took four of your fellow competitors out last episode—womp womp—but are *you* strong enough to face Mother Nature today?

It's my pleasure to introduce you to the second challenge: Survival of the Skillest.

For this adventure, you'll set off into the woods and demonstrate your wilderness survival skills to earn points and see which of you will make it to the next round, and which of you will be—

"Alright, alright, cut," Garrett interrupts himself. "My voice cracked. We have to start over."

The other contestants and I groan as Garrett restarts his spiel for what must be the twelfth time, trying again for the perfect take. It's apparently not the next one, or the one after that either, as he stops again with a shake of his head. One of the assistants manning the tall fill light sidles over to the left two inches, which pleases him. I knew that reality television was more scripted than they showed, but seeing it for myself is removing some of the magic. Growing up sucks. So does having Garrett as a host.

We're back on the studio's private plot of forest for today's challenge, in a clearing about a mile away from where the buses parked. The area is nearly the same size as camp and suspiciously tidy, absent of any overgrown brush or shrubs.

Seyoon, standing next to me, notices as well. She gestures for me to bend down so she can whisper in my ear, pointing at the neatly clipped blades of grass beneath our feet. "Look at this. They had somebody come by with a lawnmower. I can't believe them. They have no respect for nature."

After Garrett's blasé response last time, it's clear he and the network have no ethical qualms about damaging the forest for a sixty-minute episode. I eye one of the nearby trees, where a camera has been jammed into a hollow in the trunk, likely evicting some poor squirrel from their home. My stomach sinks.

Yeah. Less magical by the second.

I'm about to reply, when my attention catches on Siddharth a few yards away, who's looking at me and Seyoon. I wonder if I mistook his perfectly windswept black hair for movement, but nope; he was waving. As soon as our eyes meet, Siddharth points at me and Seyoon, then turns around and wraps his arms around himself, rubbing his hands up and down his back in a crude making-out gesture. Adin, next to him, waggles his thick brows and gives an exaggerated thumbs-up.

I purse my lips and look away, face burning. Nice. Classy. I'm glad Seyoon didn't notice.

Garrett finally wraps up, so we move on to filming the next scene, where we repeat the conversation from yesterday about teaming up.

Like before, Seyoon and I raise our hands. Afterward, a production assistant comes around and hands each of us a pack with supplies inside—except for me and Seyoon, and Vendredi and Beck, who each share one.

Since we've already heard Garrett explain today's objectives in his many takes, Blake spares us and tells us we can start. This challenge is a nice change of pace from Mountain Marathon. I think the idea is to set us all loose in the same area and see what happens. It's like the infinite monkey theorem: Eight teenagers doing mildly dangerous activities for what feels like an eternity will almost surely produce something entertaining, right?

Seyoon picks a spot for us in the open clearing to set up camp, with about fifteen feet between us and the next camper. She dumps out the bag of supplies: a rope, tarp, compass, headlamp, roll of bandage, weather blanket, utility knife, some protein bars, and water. There's also a list of tasks and the number of points we can earn for each one, from first aid, whittling, knot-tying, and water purification, all the way to foraging, building a shelter, and starting a fire.

"Perfect, I know how to do all of this," Seyoon says, skimming the list.

"Where should we start, Scoutmaster?" I reply. She eyes me over the top of the list, and I smile. See? I'm ready to be a team player.

Surprisingly, she wants to forage first, while the others are scrambling to build a shelter.

"We'll get all the good stuff before they can," she explains as she leads us out of the clearing and to one of the other film zones. The producers want to make us look more spread out than we really are, like we've actually been dropped into the middle of the woods with nothing but a pack to survive. In reality, the team of cameras and crew positioned behind trees form a clear boundary of where we can and can't go. Plus, we've passed four fire extinguishers already. It's relieving to know that no matter how bad I screw up, I won't set the whole forest on fire.

The second film zone is an untarnished plot of land, not carefully cultivated like the main clearing. Mossy vegetation covers most of the ground. Slivers of reddish-brown mulch are visible through tangles of flora, twisting over roots and up trunks. The foliage above blankets us in shade, but all the trees keep the air moist and my forehead beaded with sweat.

"Remind me where we should be looking?" I ask.

Seyoon crouches down next to an overgrowth of plants and starts sifting through it, pushing the leaves to the side. "Mushrooms grow best in dark, shady spots on the forest floor. Usually near . . . Oh! I see some. Hand me the knife, would you?"

I fish it out of our pack and pass it over, kneeling beside her to get a better look. Golden mushroom gills peek out underneath a chunk of moss, surprisingly clean from debris. Seyoon unsheathes the utility knife and goes to grab the cap of the mushroom—only for it to slip easily out of the ground. We both blink. She swipes some dirt away in the same area, revealing three more chanterelles buried in a loose bunch, stems cut neatly and laying on their sides.

"Is that normal?" I ask.

She gives me a flat look. "Sure. In the produce aisle of a grocery store."

"Ah."

Even though everything we're foraging today has been neatly planted by some underpaid intern who made a run to the closest farmers' market, we still give it our all, spending a good part of the afternoon pilfering through bushes and dirt for hidden pockets of berries and mushrooms. It's three points for every handful of berries and five for mushrooms, so we gather as much as we can hold and bring it back to the clearing. Then it's on to knot-tying and whittling. We earn the points without struggle because Seyoon's leading us and I'm not fighting her every step of the way. Even when I slip the rope into the wrong loop for the third time, she explains the steps in detail again without a hint of frustration or exhaustion in her voice. I steal a glance at her while we begin setting up our shelter, quietly grateful.

"Did you really learn this stuff in Girl Scouts?" I ask. "Because Meredith didn't know *all* of this."

"Some of it, sure," she hums. "But I also just spent a lot of time outdoors camping with my family. We're from Portland, after all."

I start unfolding the other end of the tarp. "Your dad taught you, then?"

She laughs bitterly. "Nope. My mom and aunts, when they would come to visit. My dad never wanted to join us."

Seyoon messes with the tarp more aggressively now, glaring at the creases as if enough ruffling will flatten them out. I watch her, fiddling with my knuckles.

"Explains how your mom got third in *Forest Feud*," I say. "Can't get that far in the game unless you really know what you're doing out here."

That eases the vein bulging in her neck. Some of my anxiety unfurls, too.

"Yeah," says Seyoon. "She sure does. But she's amazing at everything."

"You must take after her."

Seyoon stiffens, clenching the tarp and undoing her precious work of smoothing it out. Oh God. Her bewildered, flustered stare makes me want to rip the tarp from her hands and wrap it around my face until I pass out. But I don't. I look away, then back up for as long as I can stand it, offering a small smile.

"Is that *another* compliment, Dean?" she asks once she's shaken off her surprise, a teasing lilt to her voice.

"Don't think too hard about it."

"Who knew Mr. Brick Wall could be so sweet?" A smile plays at the corner of her mouth. "Hand me one of those rocks so I can stake this corner of the tarp down. Unless you want to go on about how wonderful and smart I am?"

I roll my eyes. "Maybe another time."

But I forgot the first rule of reality television: When the going is good, the producers will throw something in to fuck it all up.

In this case, that something is Carter. I see Blake whisper something to him, and then he's crossing the glade to approach us.

"I'm glad I skipped out on this '*team*.'" Carter says, inspecting our setup. "Looks like only one of you is doing the heavy lifting here. Didn't take you for a pillow princess, Dean."

CONFESSION TAPE—Beck McLaughlin, Contestant

> What's a pillow princess? Someone who naps a lot? Sounds nice.

Heat creeps up my neck. Vendredi and Beck are set up maybe fifteen feet away—close enough to overhear, apparently, because they start giggling. I glance over at Blake. She's directing three camera techs not-so-subtly positioned in the surrounding trees to get a better angle of us.

My brain scrambles for some kind of retort that will make for a good sound bite, but the familiar sensation of Seyoon's eyes on me reminds me I've yet to earn the second chance I was given.

"Seyoon's been a great guide," I say, plainly and honestly. "I'm lucky she's willing to help me out so much."

Carter's eyebrow quirks up, his perpetually sleepy gaze now mildly interested. He seems surprised I didn't take the bait. I'm shocked I didn't either.

Then a pine cone smacks him in his forehead.

"My hand slipped," Seyoon says. "I was aiming for your mouth."

Carter's face turns pink. "You—" He closes his eyes and takes a deep breath. Neutral again, Carter lifts his nose and says, "You'd think with two heads, you would have gotten a fire started by now. Maybe Seyoon's not as good of a wilderness guide as you thought."

Both Seyoon and I look over to Carter's area, where there's a crackling fire. He's the only person to get one going so far.

She stands up and steps over me to get in Carter's face. "Quit talking about me like I'm not here. But since you came for a pissing contest, Dean here is just about to get our fire started. On his own."

"Is he?" Carter deadpans.

Am I?!

Seyoon gives me a pointed look over her shoulder, one that clearly says *Play along and don't let this asswipe make a fool of us.* I learned my lesson the last time I didn't back her up against Carter.

I stand, towering over him. "Yeah, I am."

From where she is, Vendredi throws the two stones she had been banging against each other to try and form a spark. "Well, shit, if you're giving a demonstration, I want to watch."

"Me too," Beck's quick to say.

That's apparently Adin and Siddharth's invitation to fully approach. Even Aeneas, who had been lingering at the farthest edge of the clearing, comes to join the group gathering around our campsite.

Seyoon, who thrives in social situations that would kill a lesser being (me), singsongs, "Come one, come all! Witness the incredibly talented Dean Parker start a fire with his own bare hands in *just* under a minute—"

"Stop that," I hiss at her.

"Alright, no time constraints, but he will do it." She turns to me with an affirming smile on her face. "You *can*."

The only thing I *can* is no *can* do.

15

SEE, I TOLD YOU PEER PRESSURE WORKS. RIGHT? SAY IT WORKS. DO IT. COME ON, EVERYONE'S SAYING IT

SEYOON

Dean looks like he wants to kill me. Harsh. He'll thank me later, though. This is good for him, I promise. As volleyball captain, I know one thing kicks asses into gear better than anything else: peer pressure. All great things are created under pressure, after all. Diamonds, the hit Queen song. Other things, probably.

I step back into the semicircle of contestants, camera operators, and other crew members that has formed around Dean. Even Blake and Garrett idle along the sides. Garrett turns to one of the cameras near him and stage-whispers like he's the Crocodile Hunter.

> What we see here is a fundamental component of the teenage hierarchy system at work: social pressure. Dean, a member of the lower tier, an *underdog,* some may say, is being forced to participate in a humiliation ritual in front of his peers; a common demonstration of the powers that be dominating—

"I can hear you," Dean grits out. Garrett lowers his voice and steps farther away.

"Ignore him," I say. "You know what to do."

He gives me one last pleading look. I shoot him two thumbs-up. I wouldn't be putting him on the spot if I didn't think he could do it. Alright—if I wasn't 85 percent sure he could do it.

Dean sighs in front of the tinder pile we collected earlier. His shoulders are tense, his movements stiff, as he hesitates with where to start. But then he grabs the fireboard and holds it in place with one foot. His eyes dart to mine. I nod subtly, and he gets back to work, more confident.

It's dead silent as Dean positions the spindle into the notch of the board. Soon, the only sound filling the clearing is the grating of the spindle as he twists it against the wood. Shit. He's still not doing it fast enough. I open my mouth—

Then shut it. *Give him a chance, Seyoon.*

The others aren't as patient as I am, though.

"I've never seen it done at this . . . speed before," Aeneas says.

"They're going to have to make this an extended episode," Vendredi whispers.

Dean, abruptly, drops the wood and sits back on his heels. My heart falls.

But he's not giving up. He's just pushing the sleeves of his crewneck sweater up, drawing my attention to his lean but surprisingly defined forearms. With elegant fingers, he pushes his hair out of his flushed face. A bead of sweat drips from his temple, across his sharp jawline, and runs down his throat before disappearing under the collar of his sweater—

Oh.

CONFESSION TAPE—Beck McLaughlin, Contestant

Oh!

CONFESSION TAPE—Adin Zavary, Contestant

Oh.

CONFESSION TAPE—Carter Moxley, Contestant

Ugh.

I swallow, rubbing the side of my neck. Dean gets back to it, more aggressively than before. Another minute passes. Then two. Then it becomes too painful to keep counting them. I look up and spot Blake wincing, writing something down on her clipboard. A note to trim this part in the episode, I hope.

Carter huffs in amusement, because of course he can't even be bothered to laugh all the way. "Like I thought. Not even half the man your dad was."

And it's there, in the split second between when those words leave Carter's mouth and the muscle in Dean's jaw tenses, that I realize: The best way to inspire Dean into action *isn't* through peer pressure. It's through spite.

We're more similar than I thought.

Dean rolls the spindle between his palms faster, harder, *angrier* than before. And smoke starts billowing from the fireboard.

I watch, transfixed, as he follows what I did yesterday step by step, transferring the ember onto the tinder, blowing carefully until it ignites into a flame. Soon, before all of us and the cameras, there's a roaring bonfire.

“I did it,” Dean mumbles in disbelief.

“He did it?” Carter repeats, equally shocked.

The first thing Dean does is look at me, his eyes gleaming with excitement. The same feeling that expanded in my chest when I heard Joy Lata call the volleyball out loud for the first time balloons in me now. Pride.

“You did it!” I yell.

I tackle him. It’s a habit my less enthusiastic teammates have tried to train out of me, but I can’t help it. We both go flying in the dirt. I roll backward and am up on my knees to punch him in the shoulder, laughing in equal parts surprise and relief. “I knew you could! Well, you had me a little nervous there for a second, but you—sorry, sorry, forget all that. You did it!”

Dean’s laughing too, a breathy, soft sound I haven’t heard from him before. “Okay, okay, ow, thank you. I get it, Seyoon.”

There’s twigs and leaves in his curls. He’s blushing from exertion and smiling so hard I can barely see his eyes.

He’s beautiful.

And then somebody clears their throat.

We sit up. Everyone’s watching us, their faces ranging from amused to shock, with the exception of Carter, who looks constipated. All at once, the cameras and mics and fill lights surrounding us are too much. I have to glance down to make sure I haven’t had a wardrobe malfunction or anything with how naked I feel.

I scramble up to my feet. Dean quickly follows. There’s about three milliseconds of opportunity for me to prevent an awkward conversation here, and I pounce on it.

"It's starting to get cold," I say, nodding to the dimming sunlight. "Since none of you could get a fire started yourself, you're all welcome to sit by ours and warm up."

Beck gasps. "We can tell ghost stories around the fire."

Adin sighs. "If only we had marshmallows."

"We have those protein bars," Aeneas offers.

And that's enough to distract them from poking fun at whatever . . . that was. The others hurry to grab their food and weather blankets, and in the moment of solitude we have, I turn back to Dean, still conscious of Cameras A and B capturing every second.

"You did great," I say.

"Well, I had an okay teacher." He scratches the back of his head, and a leaf comes loose. "Thanks for believing in me."

He must be aware of the cameras, too, but he sounds sincere.

My small, reserved smile stretches wider. "You gave me a good reason to."

The others are returning now, and something settles in the air that feels like we're wrapping up for the night. Dean and I have completed everything on our list, and it's getting too dark for the others to catch up. I'm confident we're in the lead, which means I can finally relax. I take a spot in front of the fire, patting the dirt next to me for Dean to sit.

"Know any good ghost stories?" I ask.

"I don't believe in that stuff."

"You're no fun."

I've always wanted to go to a slumber party.

I imagine they're like this: loud, with multiple conversations overlapping one another, only interrupted by laughter. I don't really get invited to those, though. You need a group of friends for that—*close* friends, who you trust won't judge your tiny apartment, or be weirded out by your unwelcoming dad, or mind sleeping on the ground because you only have a tiny twin-size mattress.

I have my teammates, of course, but they're not all the "hanging out after practice" type. Besides the weekly coffee runs the gymnastics girls do, but Mallory said her car only fits five, unfortunately. Which I get. And the post–track meet arcade nights, but the one time I went, I got a bit too excited about beating Danny Bluth at air hockey, and I think they forgot to tell me about any team-bonding activities after that. There's a lot of people in track, so it's easy to lose count. I understand.

While I've never been to a slumber party, I've had plenty of sleepovers. With just one person: Amelia. Because Amelia thought our apartment was cozy, not cramped, and if Appa's passive-aggressive comments were too much and we didn't feel like squeezing into my tiny bed, she'd just invite me to spend the night at hers.

Even though I'm having fun now, sitting cross-legged in front of the fire, with the stars above our heads and the flickering firelight illuminating everyone's faces, I feel a pang of nostalgia for all the slumber parties I missed out on, and grief for the sleepovers with Amelia I'll never have again.

I'm toasting one of the mushrooms Dean and I "foraged" today over the fire, when somebody sits at my side. Vendredi.

She's smiling, albeit hesitantly. "Hey," she starts, her voice barely above a whisper. Beck and Adin are arguing about Bigfoot's origins too loudly for anyone to hear us, and even if they could, Siddharth's nervous pleas for them to stop are too distracting. But there's a camera a few feet away trained on us that I think she's wary of. "Um, I wanted to apologize."

"Huh?"

"About the other day. When you wanted to sit with me and Beck, but I iced you out."

The pang in my chest turns into a hole. I feel my heart caving into it like a plane cabin depressurizing. "Oh, that?" I say, straining my voice to sound normal to her and the clip-on mic below my chin. "Pfft. No apology necessary. I hardly remember it."

I remember it.

Vendredi holds her knees up to her chest, tucking one braid behind her ear. "Still, it was really rude of me, and I wanted to explain."

My mushroom's burning in the fire. I keep rotating it over the flames so I have something to do with my hands. "Seriously. All good. You don't need to justify not wanting me to sit with you guys, I—"

"I was trying to convince Beck to be in an alliance with me," Vendredi says, "and I was worried you were going to swoop in and snatch her up before I could. *That's* why I brushed you off."

I sit back. "What?"

"Beck has two parents who are former contestants, *and* she's been on reality TV before. I needed her on my team, bad."

My stomach stops trying to eat itself. It wasn't about me. "Oh. *Oh.*"

"I'm really sorry. I can get pretty competitive, but I shouldn't have been so cold to you."

I touch her shoulder to cut her off. She doesn't move away. "Hey, I get it. Thanks for explaining," I say. "For the record, I just wanted to talk to you guys about ghosts."

Vendredi clutches my forearm and collapses against my side in dramatic fashion. "Oh my *God,* that girl can go on about ghosts. I haven't told her I don't believe in them. I think it'd ruin our alliance."

"What, not even a little bit? How can you be sure they're not real?"

Vendredi's more than happy to indulge me in a debate about the existence of the paranormal. We argue about it, and the tingle of adrenaline from going back and forth with someone who's just as combative as I am is nearly euphoric, even if I don't *really* care about what does or doesn't go bump in the night. She ultimately gives up when I won't budge on orbs.

"Ugh. You're as bad as Beck," Vendredi teases. We've scooted out farther away from the circle by this point and can talk a bit more freely. She bumps my shoulder with hers. "You should join us for breakfast tomorrow. Dean, too, if he wants."

I swallow my grin so it doesn't scare her off. "Cool, that sounds nice."

It's not long before the day's events start wearing on us all, and everybody heads back to their shelters. Soon, it's just me, Dean, and the dwindling embers of our fire.

"Uh," Dean says. He tugs on the collar of his sweater. "I guess teaming up means sharing a shelter, too."

This is not how I pictured my first-ever sleepover with someone besides Amelia.

"We'll make it work." My voice is higher than usual. "We'll just . . . yeah."

It's not very roomy inside the shelter, and with the stick in the center supporting it, it leaves even less room for us to arrange our bodies. We line the ground with pine needles, both to help insulate our body heat and to prolong the inevitable. But, eventually, we have to go to bed.

"There's no way you'll fit—"

"Get your *foot* out of my *face*—"

"Your face is on my foot!"

"Just—" I sigh and sit up, nearly hitting my head on the tarp roof. "Okay. Lie down like this, along this wall, and I'll lie next to the other one."

But with only one weather blanket between us and the temperature rapidly dropping, I find myself closer to Dean than I would have liked. We're packed like sardines, stiff on our back, with our hands folded on top of our stomachs to avoid grazing each other. This is too intimate for comfort. A thought occurs to me then.

"You don't have a girlfriend, do you?" I blurt.

There's silence in the dark tent. Then, "Are you calling me a virgin, or is that a genuine question?"

"I'm asking for real, dickweed. What if your girlfriend isn't comfortable with you sharing a bed with someone else?" I start sitting up. "Maybe we should—"

Dean fumbles in the pitch-black and grabs my shoulder, pushing me back down. "First off, the pine needles digging into my back hardly qualify as a bed. Second off, it's *fine,* just lie down."

"I don't want to be rude—"

"Seyoon?" Dean says, voice strained. "I don't have a girlfriend. Or a boyfriend. Or anybody who would throw a fit about me sleeping under the same tarp as you. Satisfied?"

I relax. "Okay. Just checking."

"Why? Do you have a boyfriend or something?"

Emmanuel Wiley, the captain of the boy's swim team, and I dated for three and a half months last year, but that was more because we could carpool to the aquatic center together than kismet. And there was that one awkward double date that Amelia begged me to go on with her. But besides that, no.

I roll over and give Dean a shit-eating grin even though I know he can't see. "Wouldn't *you* like to know, lover boy."

"Oh God, shut up. There's my answer."

Dean shuffles around. But I can't go to sleep. The ground is hard and cold, and I'm not used to sleeping with someone. Next to someone. I can't even see the night sky with the tarp blocking the view.

"I wish we could stargaze right now," I say, just to say something. "I love stargazing."

"Just picture a black sky with little specks in your mind."

I twiddle my thumb and let the silence sit for almost a full minute before more word vomit spews up. "I think we're in good shape, points-wise. We foraged more than anyone, and besides us, only Carter was able to get a fire going."

"Yeah." Dean hums. "Still can't believe I made a fire."

"I knew you could."

A pause. "Did you really?"

"Yeah. You're smart. And you had an excellent, knowledgeable teacher."

"Watching you really did help," Dean says quietly. "Thank you for still wanting to team up with me after I was an asshole."

The tent feels, somehow, even smaller. "I'm an asshole, too, sometimes."

"Well, yes."

"Hey."

Dean snickers, and I relax. "We make a better team than I thought we would."

"Couple of assholes."

"That could be our team name. Would be better than Seydean."

I kick his calf, and Dean curses. Enough time passes that I think he's fallen asleep, but then he asks an unexpected question.

"You said you're from Portland, right?"

"Born and raised."

"Do you like it there?"

"Love it. Fingers crossed I get to stay in the area for college."

He rolls to face me unexpectedly. I turn my head, blinking until my eyes can distinguish his darkened silhouette from the rest of the shadows. I swallow a gasp when I realize how close he's settled. Only inches separate our noses. The gentle heat radiating from his body, nearly touching mine, feels like sitting in the sun on a bright day. Has it always been so hot in here?

"What school?" he says.

"University of Oregon. They have the best track team, plus in-state tuition is cheaper. Why do you ask?"

"I have a scholarship to Reed College," he says. "If I win, I'm going to move out there with my sister. Was wondering if it's a nice place to live."

I laugh through an exhale. "It's great. Tell you what—when *I* win, I'll fly you and your sister out to come visit and see for yourself."

I can hear Dean shake his head rather than see it. He rolls away to face the wall, and I'm suddenly ten degrees colder. "Cocky."

"I think you mean confident."

"Go to sleep, Seyoon."

16

THIS COULD RUIN MY REPUTATION. IF I HAD ONE, I MEAN

DEAN

Seyoon has mentioned a myriad of things in the few days I've known her. It'd be impossible to try and remember them all. One crucial detail I wish I had stored in the memory palace, though?

She said she moves a lot in her sleep.

The sun in my face wakes me up. It's a searing pain even behind my closed lids, so overwhelming I can't focus on the input from my other senses. But then, slowly, I become more aware. The sound of birds chittering. A heavy weight over my chest, constricting my movement. Why is the sun so bright? Where's the tarp?

I realize then that it's not birds I'm hearing. It's muffled snickers and giggles. I crack an eyelid open, and instead of the underside of the tarp greeting me, there are at least five people, three cameras, two boom mics, and one Garrett standing above me. All but the partridge in the pear tree.

"What?" I try to sit up but am held down by the weight on my chest.

The weight is Seyoon, who's currently passed out on me like a snoring koala bear. I swallow thickly, and the movement makes my Adam's apple bob and brush against her lips. Oh God. She grumbles and tucks her head farther into the crook of my neck. All of the atoms in my body are going to dissolve.

"How embarrassing. I wish I had a camera," Carter says around a smirk.

Garrett rifles in his back pocket. "I got my phone on me. Here."

The flash disturbs Seyoon. With her whole body curled up around mine, I can feel exactly when she wakes up and her breathing pattern changes. Her fingers curl in the fabric at my shoulder before she tries to wipe her eyes, accidentally hitting me in the jaw.

"What's . . ." Her eyelashes flutter against my skin as she wakes up. "Oh my fucking God." Seyoon shoots up, the fallen tarp sliding off her legs. She must have kicked the central beam in the middle of the night while she was tossing. Sure, that's possible—but we also *nailed down* the tarp. How hard can one girl thrash?

With her off, I sit up and scramble away, but the damage is already done.

"Totally called it," Adin says to Siddharth. "I told you they'd hook up before the third challenge. You owe me your dessert for the rest of the week."

"*Ugh.* Couldn't you guys have kept it in your pants for another challenge?"

Vendredi peeks her head over. "I didn't know it was like *that* between you two."

"It's not!" both of us respond at the same time. We whip our heads around to glare at each other, and I can't help but wince. Seyoon's hair looks like the pile of kindling from last night. I'm sure I don't look much better. Despite the early-morning chill in the air, I'm hot and sweaty from sleeping under a weighted human blanket. This does not look good.

Oh God. This is on *camera*.

There's three short claps from the center of the clearing. Blake. If she has an opinion on the mess, she's too professional to let it show.

"Now that everyone's awake, we'll trek back to camp so Garrett can distribute the points and announce the new standings."

She says it so clinically, it's easy to miss the real message: One of us is going home.

The others disperse, leaving us to our pile of limbs and humiliation. I kick Seyoon in the thigh.

"Ow, what was that for?" she says, untangling her legs from the tarp still trapping us.

"I should be asking *you* that. You're the one who was clinging to me. And you took down the shelter!"

She scratches her neck. "I told you I move around a lot."

"You also drooled on me."

"Did not!"

I don't bother arguing anymore, wiping my collarbone in an attempt to salvage some sense of my dignity. The action makes me remember the way her lips brushed against the skin there. My stomach flips.

"How do you think *I* feel?" Seyoon grumbles. "Now the whole world will think I'm sleeping around. Ugh. Oh no, my mom's going to *freak*. She's already has so much to worry about."

"They'll think we're both sleeping around." I'm getting a headache just envisioning how much shit Meredith will give me when she sees this. No, worse—Dad's going to give me The Talk. *Again*.

"It's different for you," she snaps. "It's not cool when a girl does it."

Even though I'm still mad about her taking down the shelter, I bite my tongue, because, well . . . she's right. It's worse for her.

Begrudgingly, we get to work cleaning up and gathering our supplies. I run through my mental list of everything we had in our pack, looking around for the missing bandage roll.

"Have you seen the gauze?" I ask.

"Siddharth asked if he could borrow it last night," she says. "He wanted to wrap Adin up like a mummy. He probably still has it—I think I saw him head into the second film zone."

Sighing, I trek through the woods to find him. Honestly, I don't really care about the roll too much, but it's a nice excuse to break away from Seyoon and get some air. As I'm nearing the area where we went foraging yesterday, I hear them before I see them: Siddharth and Adin, whispering to each other. Curious, I stay hidden in the line of trees.

"Shit, man," Siddharth says. "I think their alliance is for real."

They're talking about us, I realize.

"We don't gotta worry," Adin replies. "Seyoon's still the weak link. She'll drag both of them down when they have to split points."

"What? You think *Seyoon's* the weak link? It's obviously Dean."

My stomach drops. I dig my nails into the bark of the tree, frozen.

"She got dead last in the first challenge!" Adin whisper-argues.

"Yeah, but she was in the lead for most of it. She's way faster than he is, and a whole lot better at survival skills."

There's a beat of silence. "So, what, you think Seyoon's the bigger threat to worry about?"

Siddharth grunts. "No, man, that's the problem. They're working together *and* sleeping together. She's not going to drop him, and he won't drop her. We need to worry about them both."

I chance a peek around the trunk. They're standing close, heads nearly knocking together as they think.

Adin scratches the side of his face. "Okay, they're stronger together. Should we try to sabotage them in the next challenge or something?"

"No, idiot," Siddharth punctuates with a flick to Adin's forehead. "Haven't you seen *Alivers*? Or any of the earlier seasons of *Forest Feud*? They always pick off the weak ones first, duh. It's easier."

"Oh, you are *good*, man. *Real* good."

"Yeah, I know."

"No, really, like, you're the smartest person I've met, bro."

Alright, it looks like they're devolving into another one of their brotherhood moments, so I take the opportunity to slip away before they catch me, or before I barf.

"There you are," Seyoon says when I'm back. "What took so long?"

"I'll tell you later," I say, eyeing the lingering camera crew and contestants. Not the time or place.

Soon, all us campers and the crew are trekking down to the buses. Seyoon and I awkwardly hold the tarp and all our foraged items in it between us, even more awkwardly not saying a word and avoiding eye contact. My chest is still warm from where she was sleeping on it. But my heart sinks when I repeat Siddharth's and Adin's words in my head.

They think *I'm* the weak one. At least, if I were on my own.

Maybe it's not so bad if everyone thinks Seyoon and I are together.

17

THE WORST PERSON I KNOW JUST MADE A GREAT POINT

DEAN

Back at camp, we're ordered to shower and get presentable while the crew stage the bonfire pit to film the point distribution and elimination scene. An assistant ushers me to the hair and makeup tent afterward. I grin and bear it until the makeup artist tries dabbing my cheeks with a pink powder.

"Why blush?" I ask, leaning away.

"Director's request. She wants you to look flushed from this morning."

My cheeks heat. The artist cries in delight, "Oh, perfect, you're doing my job for me."

When I'm done, I go to wait with the others by the bonfire. There's one empty seat left at the end next to Aeneas, but when I try to sit, Garrett's assistant, Luke, steps in.

"Actually, let's move things around. Ms. McLaughlin, let's have you here next to Ms. Tengku. Then Mr. Parker can sit next to Ms. Shin."

Begrudgingly, I sit on the log next to Seyoon, who looks just as stiff and uncomfortable as I feel. I do my best not to think about how awkward this is, but it's hard when everyone around us is glancing over and snickering.

Vendredi leans over and wags her finger between us. "So . . . you two."

"It's not what it—"

"No, there was a—"

She laughs at us tripping over our words. "Okay, this is clearly new, I won't pry. For now." She bumps Seyoon's shoulder with a teasing smile, who pushes her away in a surprisingly familiar fashion. I ignore the sting of jealousy in my chest. Of course Seyoon would befriend someone after a single conversation around a campfire. She could charm a snail out of its shell.

Finally, Garrett's done getting his nose powdered. He strolls back to us, rubbing his hands together like a delighted raccoon. Blake gets into position next to the camera operator. She signals a countdown on her hands, then a nearby assistant slaps the clapboard. The fill lights surrounding the firepit ignite. Garrett steps forward.

> Campers, glad to see you all survived the elements. After a long night of putting your wilderness abilities to the test, we're about to find out who among you is the Skillest of Them All.
>
> We have before us the fruits of your labor. Literally. From foraging, making tools with the resources available to you, demonstrating your handy knot-tying skills and more, the number of tasks you completed—and completed well—will determine how many points you'll receive. Me and a team of unbiased wilderness experts have tallied up the numbers. Here they are.

Garrett presents his open, waiting palm to the air, and an intern runs up and hands him a folded note. He opens it, clears his throat, and reads the results.

> Our first contestant, Aeneas. Buddy, what happened? No fire, your tent barely stayed up, and you foraged poisonous mushrooms. Did you eat those? No? Okay, thank God. We can't handle another lawsuit.

Aeneas pales.

"I'm *joking*, jeez. Obviously, none of the ones we planted were poisonous." Garrett rolls his eyes. "Four points for you."

> Next, Adin. Not bad at all. You did pretty good in all the skills but couldn't get a fire going. You did earn a point for having the start of one, though. Yeah, I know, we're generous like that—eight points.
>
> Siddharth: It was *very* funny watching you spend two hours whittling a little man out of wood instead of making a weapon like we hoped. However, because you whittled a little Garrett Moxley—and demonstrated strong craftsman skills or whatever—we gave you points for that anyway. You earned nine total.

CONFESSION TAPE—Siddharth Patel, Contestant

[He holds up a wooden figurine vaguely resembling Garrett.]

I knew he'd eat this shit up.

> Carter: No surprises here, you nailed almost every task and were the first one to get a fire going. Only reason

you didn't earn more points is because you hardly foraged anything—nineteen points.

Now, for our first alliance, Vendredi and Beck. Very impressive, you two. The shelter you set up was one of the sturdiest, and you completed nearly all the tasks, besides making a fire. Twenty-one points combined, plus, three bonus ones for being in an alliance, for a grand total of twenty-four.

Our other team, Seyoon and Dean. They say two heads are better than one. Last night, you put that to the test and . . . it's true! Combined, you earned more points than anyone. You foraged practically half the forest, accomplished all the skills, got a shelter up, *and* were the only other players to make a fire.

. . . However, unfortunately, your shelter didn't last through the night, so we couldn't give you full points for that. Twenty-five points, and with the bonus, twenty-eight.

I glare at her. She chuckles nervously.

"Hey, that's still way more points than anyone else," she says.

Ah, ah, I'm not done. Because you teamed up, you'll have to split those points. Meaning, fourteen points for each of you. Likewise, twelve for Vendredi and Beck. Luke, bring out the updated leaderboard, will ya?

All of us stand to get a better look as Luke drags out the giant board. Before he can reveal it to us, Garrett holds his hand out, calling for him to wait. He looks at us and mouths "for dramatic effect" with a shit-eating grin.

CONFESSION TAPE—Vendredi Tengku, Contestant

The worst part of these eliminations is the waiting and wondering. You're stuck with your thoughts. *Did I do good enough to stay in the game? What if somebody beats me by just a point or two?*

Of course, that bastard knows it and likes to drag it out. Make it painful for us. He *lives* to be the most annoying person in the room.

CONFESSION TAPE—Carter Moxley, Contestant

Am I worried I'm going home? No. Next question.

CONFESSION TAPE—Beck McLaughlin, Contestant

I really hope I'm not eliminated. I haven't gotten a chance to investigate the area for Bigfoot yet. Did you know that Washington has the highest reports of Bigfoot sightings in the U.S.? Nine out of a hundred residents have seen him. This is the cryptozoological hot spot of the nation, and it'd be a shame if I couldn't . . .

Huh? What do you mean confession tapes have to be kept under thirty sec—

Finally, after several long, painful moments, Garrett nods sagely, and Luke turns the board around to display the final scores. My breath catches.

1ST	CARTER MOXLEY	29 PTS
2ND	DEAN PARKER	23 PTS
3RD	VENDREDI TENGKU	20 PTS
4TH	SEYOON SHIN	17 PTS

4TH	BECK MCLAUGHLIN	17 PTS
5TH	SIDDHARTH PATEL	16 PTS
7TH	ADIN ZAVARY	14 PTS
8TH	AENEAS HUDSON	8 PTS

I can't believe it. I'm still holding on to second place. Seyoon perks up to see that her name isn't on the bottom of the list anymore. However relieved everyone is, nobody celebrates out loud. We all turn to Aeneas, whose face has fallen.

> I'm sorry champ, but Aeneas, it looks like your time on *Forest Feud* ends here. An assistant will gather your things and meet you at the Loser Limo to take you home.

Aeneas pulls themself together pretty quickly. They stand up, a bittersweet smile on their face, and nod shyly at the rest of us campers around the circle. An assistant comes out with their suitcase a moment later, and off to the trailhead they go.

CONFESSION TAPE—Aeneas Hudson, Contestant

> I'll be alright. My therapist and family will be proud I stepped out of my comfort zone.
>
> Besides, I'm kind of glad I won't be followed by cameras anymore. I kept accidentally looking directly at them. Sorry if that ruined any of your footage.

That concludes the scene. Garrett says a few more remarks to the camera about staying tuned for next week's challenge, and then we're released for breakfast. I wasn't close with Aeneas by any means, but it's still jarring to see a fellow competitor leave so abruptly. That could have been me or Seyoon if last night's challenge hadn't gone as well as it did. Using a points system for elimination instead of by vote like the old show did is way more stressful. You never know how secure your standing is, meaning more tension and drama for Garrett's show.

I realize now that all those fucked-up experiments psychologists were performing in the sixties to push people to their breaking point may have gotten outlawed, but they didn't go away. They just film them and call it reality television now.

As everyone gets up to head to the cafeteria, Garrett steps in front of me and Seyoon, blocking our escape path.

"Hey, you two, could I interest you in a homecooked breakfast?" he says. "I'm quite the chef."

I'm shaking my head before he can finish his sentence. "No, thank you."

"But I made muffins?"

Seyoon blinks. "Are you trying to poison us? That's creepy. You're creepy."

Garrett's smile flatlines, annoyed. "Your mom was much more pleasant than you are."

"Yeah, I'd agree."

"Can you two brats just follow me so we can have a conversation away from the cameras?"

That piques my interest, and I can tell Seyoon's thinking the same thing. I don't trust Garrett, but if the man who thrives on attention suddenly doesn't want to be filmed, then I'm curious enough to hear why.

We warily follow Garrett to his private cabin. Surprisingly, it's as nondescript as the other ones. The only indication that it's his is the wooden post in front of the porch that says Host. Once inside, a physical weight lifts from my shoulders. It's a relief to break away from the constant cameras and attentive crew members, even for just a minute.

Garrett tells us to wait in the living room while he excuses himself to the kitchen. I use the opportunity to snoop. I take back what I said earlier—his cabin is anything *but* nondescript. The place is covered wall to wall in *Forest Feud* memorabilia, for one thing. From promotional show bills, stills from different challenges, and contestant posters. No surprise, about 80 percent of them are of a younger, less-gray Garrett. Among the other 20 percent are contestants I recognize from the fifteenth season. I subtly scour them all, pausing at a small frame hanging in the hallway. This one isn't a promo poster; it's a sun-washed Polaroid of Garrett, my dad, and Seyoon's mom. The three of them are laughing at something out of view, with their heads thrown back, big smiles on their youthful faces, and their arms haphazardly reaching out for each other.

The unadulterated joy radiating off Dad takes me aback. I thought their alliance was strictly strategic. But were they actually all friends? From the looks of it, *good* friends.

Suddenly, Seyoon creeps up behind me.

"We should clog his toilet," she whispers.

"*What?*"

"It'd be funny, right? Or we could steal his remote."

"No more ideas from you, please. Let's just see what he wants."

We sit at his tiny dining table, and after a few more minutes, Garrett comes back carrying a muffin tin and wearing a bright blue apron that says Mr. Good-Lookin' Is Cookin'! I'm almost tempted to tell Seyoon to steal the remote after all.

"Hope you brats like blueberries," he chirps, setting the muffins between us. He picks up a box out of the recycling bin and shows it off proudly. There's a picture of him on the front in a chef's hat.

"Moxley Muffins?" I say.

"You've heard!" He sounds delighted.

Unfortunately so. As a lifetime fan of *Forest Feud*, I'm quite aware of all of his corporate sellouts to cash in on his fame. There was Moxley Mountaineering Mittens, his hiking-gear stint. Then Moxley 'Mallows, a line of eccentric flavored marshmallows. And of course, Moxley Markers, Moxley Makeup, Moxley Magnets, etc. Basically, if it started with the letter *M*, he already had a trademark patent on it.

He watches us expectantly, his hands neatly folded in front of his apron.

"I'm not eating those," Seyoon says.

Garrett looks sad enough that I hesitantly reach for a muffin and take a small bite.

"Oh." I can't hide the surprise in my voice. "This is actually good."

He takes a seat across from us, popping one in his mouth whole. "Aren't they? Wish I could take credit, but all I did was show up to media day and look pretty for the picture on the box."

Seyoon eyes me for a few seconds, and when I don't keel over, she takes one too. Her eyes widen. She's reaching for a second before Garrett speaks again.

"Go ahead and turn your mics off," he says.

"But we were told to keep them on at all times?" Except after film hours or if we're in the bathroom, these clip-on mics are meant to pick up every word, hum, and fart.

"Who told you that? Some crew member?" I nod. Garrett flaps his hand. "Well, the guy who pays *that* guy is telling you otherwise. Go on."

Curious, both of us reach for our collars and flick the little switch on the mic.

"Whardifbouf?"[4] Seyoon attempts to speak through a mouth full of muffin.

Garrett leans back in his chair and fakes nonchalance. He looks so ridiculous in the apron, it's kind of pissing me off. "I feel like it's my responsibility as both the host and your unofficial uncle to see how the two lovebirds are doing."

"Lovebirds?" I squeak—*say*.

"Uncle?" Seyoon nearly chokes.

"Alright, I knew I was pushing it with that one. But with how close me and your parents were, it's within the realm of possibility that I could have been a sort of godparent to you. And in that alternate universe where I am a respected and beloved guardian, it's my duty to check in on some rumors floating around that you two are K-I-S-S—"

"They're *just* rumors," I cut him off before he can keep going. "We're not—it's not like that. We're not dating."

"Really? Huh." Garrett leans forward and snags a muffin, taking a bite before continuing. "Can you pretend to be?"

---

4. What's this about?

What?

"What?" Seyoon voices my thoughts. She shakes her head and stands up, shoving another muffin into her pocket. "Never mind, forget it, I don't want to hear any more. I was right, you're a creep, and we'll be on our way now. Thanks for the muffins."

She's already walking away, but something about the amused look in Garrett's eye makes me wait. He looks like he expected that reaction. Like it was a test. I'm good at tests, and one of the reasons is because I consider all the possibilities before selecting a choice.

"Why?" I ask. Seyoon stops once she realizes I'm not following.

"It's not because I particularly care whether you two are actually experiencing the marvelous horrors of young love, if that's what you're wondering," Garrett drawls, his bubbly, TV-host voice completely gone now. Even the slightly dumb glaze in his eyes has disappeared. He looks smarter and more calculating than I could have expected from him. "It's because this is a great opportunity for you two, and as someone who's been in your shoes, it'd be a shame if I didn't tell you. A worse shame if you didn't at least consider it."

"Go on?"

Garrett, finally getting the undivided attention he craves, preens. "You already understand the benefits of an alliance. Teams are strong, and strength is feared in competition."

A hundred examples come to mind. Jenny and Emma in season three, who worked so well together that everyone stayed out of their way. Then there was Theresa, Mauve, and King in season fourteen. They dominated the game to the point that their strongest rivals bargained with them to target other people. And Hector and Thomas, who, in their semifinal challenge, were pitted against two other contestants who gave up halfway through because they knew they couldn't beat the dynamic duo. A great alliance has gotten more than a few contestants to the finish line.

"However, everyone knows an alliance can be broken by the smallest thing," Garrett continues. "But if the others think you're united not just through sportsmanship but *love*? That'd make for an unbreakable bond. Might be intimidating. Might be beneficial." He takes a huge bite of his muffin, chewing with his mouth open. "God, wow, I can't believe how good these are."

Seyoon slowly approaches us again, standing behind my chair. The wheels are spinning in her head, I can see it on her face. Garrett's making a lot of sense. A sentence I never thought I'd say. "Why would you want to help us out? You're not a nice person."

"I'm wounded!"

"Sure you are."

"Yeah, you're right. Nothing a little twerp could say would keep me up at night after all these years in the limelight."

"Then, just tell us the truth."

"The truth is, romance boosts ratings," Garrett says plainly. "Audiences eat up a good showmance, and yours is the jackpot. The kids of former contestants who were in an ill-fated alliance, now falling in love on the same show? You're star-crossed lovers, doomed by the fact that only one of you can win. Shit, wait, that's a good line, I need to write that down . . ."

I hate to admit it, but he's completely right. It's gold. This is the stuff they throw out in a writing room and have to scratch because it's too good to be true. Damnit.

"Besides," Garrett goes on, still scrambling for a pen and paper. "You'd be doing me and Blakey a favor. We're trying to get funding approved from the network for a nice spinoff show starring yours truly and my precious nephew." He fans his hand dramatically. "*Moxley to the Maximum.* I think if we prove to the powers that be that America still loves *Forest Feud,* they'll give us the moolah."

Seyoon tugs at the back of my collar. "Yeah, I knew it was for selfish reasons. Come on, Dean, let's go. Grab that muffin."

I do, following her lead. We see ourselves out, but before the door closes behind us, Garrett calls out, "Hey, just because I'm selfish doesn't mean I'm wrong!"

Seyoon slams the door hard enough to shake the frame. "God, I hate him."

She makes grabby hands for the muffin I stole, so I pass it to her, distracted. She mutters something else about con men and phony TV, but Garrett's words in my mind drown out her voice.

"Maybe we should at least talk about it," I say.

Her face freezes mid-chew. A crumb falls from her mouth. "Whaf?"

"But not here." I gesture to the crew of camera operators only a dozen yards away. "Somewhere private where we won't be filmed. Although I'm not sure where . . ."

Seyoon chews thoughtfully. "I have an idea."

18

THIS BATHROOM STALL IS MY SAFE PLACE

SEYOON

"This might be a little *too* private."

Dean squirms, but there's not much room to move when he's jammed against the stall door. I throw my hands up from where I'm wedged uncomfortably behind the toilet.

"Oh, I'm sorry, your highness. Is this porcelain throne not good enough for you? Besides, can you think of somewhere else where we won't be overheard or caught on tape?"

He sighs in defeat. Outside of Garrett's cabin, the bathroom is the only place where we're allowed to turn our mics off. Hey, you think I'm happy about this? I'm not. This is an awkward enough conversation to have as it is; the toilet in between us isn't exactly helping. And we can't just stand next to the sinks. There's a tiny window in the door—frosted, for privacy—but it's not worth risking someone walking by and seeing us.

"Let's just hurry up and talk through our options," Dean says.

"By options, you mean pretending to be a couple so that Garrett can market us as his star-crossed lovers or whatever and cut himself a big fat check?"

"Look, I'm not saying I like the idea, but he did make a good point. If the others think we're together like—like *that,* our alliance will be more credible. A united front is a good strategy to have in a game like this. I've seen it done before."

I narrow my eyes and cross my arms. His argument isn't convincing me, and he knows it.

"Listen. Earlier today, when the others found us . . . like *that* and started thinking we're a couple, I overheard a few people talking," Dean tries again. "They're scared of us. They know we pose a real threat together. But on our own? They think we're weak."

The cold from the tile wall against my back runs down my spine. "Weak?" I ask, straightening.

Dean visibly swallows. "They mostly think *I'm* the weak one. But they also pointed out our rankings in the first challenge."

At the mention of the first challenge, sticky humiliation slathers over my skin. Everyone saw me fail. Worse: *Try* and fail. They knew from that very first moment that I wasn't good enough.

But I am. I have to be.

I bite the inside of my cheek until the taste of copper overwhelms my senses, distracting me from the shame sloshing around my gut.

Dean visibly swallows, unnerved by my silence. He shifts his weight onto his other foot. Then he takes a step forward, impossibly close in this already-tight stall.

"Seyoon." Dean says my name like it's a favor. I crane my neck to meet his gaze. "You're stronger than me. We know it. That's the thing; if I wasn't in an alliance with you, everyone would peg me as an easy target. Because I am. But when I'm with you . . ." He pushes his hair out of his pink face, turning away. "When I'm with you, I can do things I can't on my own. Like start a fire. And be thought of as someone strong. I actually believe I have a real shot at winning when I'm with you."

My mouth parts. Dean speaks before I can.

"But I know you need to win, too, and you don't need me for that. Or anyone, really. So . . ." He breaks off into an awkward laugh. Dean steps back, scratching his neck. "I'm not making a great case for why you should do me this favor, am I?"

A huff of amusement falls from my own lips. "Not really," I say, but I trail off.

Dean thinks I don't need him to win? That I don't need *anyone*?

I expected that sentiment to make me feel good about myself. But instead, my stomach drops further. It rings a little too close to what Amelia told me the last time we ever spoke. During our last game being friends *or* teammates. I took it as her being bitter. A sore loser. But . . . but it wasn't *us* who let rivalry get in the way of things. It was me.

I stay mostly still, but it feels like everything inside me is falling into a crack in the earth, leaving only the hollow shell of my body behind. "I . . ."

I know the real reason I've never gone to a slumber party. I know why I was never invited to weekly coffee runs with the gymnastics girls. I know the track team didn't just *forget* to invite me to post-meet hangouts. I know. I already *know*.

I've prided myself more on being a winner than a teammate.

Dean waits patiently at the other end of the stall, holding his breath while mine leaves me in shallow spurts. He watches me as if I'm some spooked animal, like he's trying not to startle me into turning him down.

What kind of teammate am I to give him the impression that I don't need him just as much as he needs me?

I lick my lips and say, "Why do you think I wanted to form an alliance with you?"

Dean blinks. "I assumed for the bonus points. And to stick it to Carter and Garrett."

"It's because I wanted to work *with you*." I punctuate my point by stepping forward and tapping his sternum. "The asshole who placed second in Mountain Marathon because he's smart, and the nerd who's seen every season of *Forest Feud*. You're strong in the ways I'm not." Suddenly too exposed under Dean's wide-eyed stare, I cross my arms and shrug. "You're the expert when it comes to strategy stuff. If you think pretending to be in a relationship will get us ahead of the game, then . . . I trust you. Let's play the part, lover boy."

He huffs in disbelief. "Really?"

"Yeah. Unless this was just an excuse for you to flirt with me?"

He sputters, his face beet red now, and I crack, bursting into laughter.

Dean glares at me. "Do you ever get tired of being such a jackass?"

"No, it comes very easily to me. Much like everything else."

"Yeah, it does." He rolls his eyes, but then after a small, quiet moment, he shoots me a smile. "Thank you."

"Don't thank me. This is for me, too. Teammates, right?"

I hold my fist out to him. He bumps it with his own.

With that settled, Dean turns the lock on the door and lets himself out. I follow after, stretching my cramped arms above my head.

"If we're doing this, we probably need to sell it to the others, right?" I ask his turned back. "Should we consummate the relationship or something?"

Dean whips around with a petrified look on his face. "*What?*" he squeaks.

19

IF THE PADDLEBOARD'S A-ROCKIN' . . .

SEYOON

Okay. Apparently, *consummate* doesn't mean what I thought it did.

"I thought that's what it's called when you announce a relationship," I hiss so none of the others around us can hear. "Excuse the hell out of *me* for not knowing what every single word in the English language means. Damn."

Dean pinches the bridge of his nose. "Can we please stop talking about it?" he whispers.

It's B-roll day today: a full eight hours of shooting candid footage so viewers can see how we interact outside of challenges. Except, I don't know how candid it actually is when every scene is carefully scripted. Our first location of the day is the lake, which is where we're all headed to now, clad in swimsuits and padding barefoot down the grassy knoll. The clip-on mics aren't waterproof, so we don't have to wear them, thankfully, but there's still countless boom mics following us around.

At least until we get in the water.

Dean crosses his arms over his bare chest and steps closer. "Your plan better work, whatever it is."

"It will. I'm confident."

"Always are," he mutters under his breath.

After we decided to commit to the showmance, we both knew we'd have to make sure everyone really believes we're together. There can't be any room for speculation. Since then, I've been brainstorming all the ways we can convince the others we're more than bunkmates and reluctant allies. As someone who's never been in a relationship—a *real* one, anyway, Emmanuel doesn't really count—I had a tough time figuring it out. But then when I found out we were going to be corralled together all day for filming, the perfect idea plopped itself into my head.

We finish our short trek from the cabin to the lake, where a million pool toys have spawned overnight. I grimace at all the cameras stationed nearby. It's not just the other campers who will witness this stunt we're about to pull—it's also everyone who'll watch this back at home. Umma. Appa. Amelia. My skin tries to break out in shivers, but I rub them away. Now is not the time to be getting cold feet.

"Fuck, it's cold," Dean says as he dips his toes into the water.

Blake starts directing us to do different activities, grouping people in one area, then changing her mind and switching the pairs around. I raise my hand and ask if me and Dean can go paddleboarding.

"Great idea. Carter, tag along with them," she says. "We need more interactions between the three of you."

"No," I interrupt. "Um . . . me and Dean want to have some privacy, actually."

It's mortifying, but it works; everyone pays attention. Adin snickers. Vendredi leans behind Blake and shoots me two thumbs-up, mouthing *Nice.* Garrett, who's been more preoccupied with lathering himself up with sunscreen than helping Blake stage the scene, does a double-take.

"Well, alright then," Blake says nonchalantly, but I see her perk up, interested.

We cling to a paddleboard and begin swimming out—but not too far. We have to make sure the others have a perfect view of us. I climb up on the paddleboard first, straddling it with both my legs hanging off the sides. Dean clambers up to join me. His expression scrunches in a way I'm starting to recognize as his embarrassed face. He carefully scoots closer to meet me in the middle of the board. Water drips from his curls and down the plane of his bare chest. Finally, he sits close enough that his knee bumps mine. The waves rock us gently from side to side. The surface of the water glistens like sparks of a campfire.

"Alright," he says. "We're out here. What's your brilliant plan? It's got to convince the others *and* the viewers at home because, I don't know about you, but I don't want to be known as the douche who *pretended* to be in love just to get ahead in a game."

I scrunch my nose in distaste. I know that's exactly what we're doing but . . . no one else needs to know that. "Neither do I. But don't worry, I have the perfect idea."

As Dean stares at me expectantly, a foreign feeling implants in my belly. Kind of like the nerves I get at the starting line of a race, but worse. I flatten my palms against the textured rubber of the paddleboard to ground myself, then paste a smile on my face to hide any hesitation that might crack through my expression.

"We pretend to kiss," I say.

He blinks. The sunshine against his eyelashes casts long shadows on his cheeks.

"Hmm," he hums.

"What?"

"I'm just perplexed by what goes on inside that brain of yours."

"Is it or is it not convincing?" I reply. "We mash the sides of our face together, and from this far, it looks like we're making out. Foolproof."

"You seemed awfully confident about this idea, and the whole plan is to pretend to kiss?"

"Well if *you* have more experience in the romance department that you're keeping a secret, I'm open to ideas."

His lips flatten into a thin line. "Seyoon, I'm president of my school's literature club. No, I don't have more experience in that department."

"Really?"

"Rude."

"I'm not being sarcastic. I'm surprised."

He squints suspiciously. "Why?"

My gaze roams over him. In the privacy of my own mind, I can admit that Dean isn't ugly. Fine, he's *okay*-looking.

Alright, he's really hot. There, happy? Jesus Christ.

There's something undeniably charming about Dean's bright eyes and mousy features, and it's pretty cute when he grins all shy, dimples peeking out. And when he's really getting into the heat of the competition, and his smile turns into something wicked, it's downright—

Alright. That's enough. I shift uncomfortably on the paddleboard.

Dean's suspicion morphs into plain confusion at my drawn-out silence, so I swallow the sudden thickness in my throat and blurt, "Well, you said you're president of the book club, right? People love a man in politics."

To my total surprise, Dean laughs. It bubbles out of him, and he looks just as caught off guard by it as I am. I snort and, luckily, that clears some of the air between us.

"Fine, let's give it a try then," he says. He jerks his chin at me, and a curl bounces on his forehead. "Come here."

My pulse thuds hard in my ears.

"No, you come here."

"Are you seriously doing this right now?" he asks.

"It's my idea, *I* should take the lead."

"I'm not letting that happen."

"Afraid you'll like it?"

"You are the worst—"

I interrupt him by snaking my hand around his neck and pulling him toward me. Dean's eyes widen, but I stop tugging when he's centimeters away, his nose bumping against mine. I put my other hand on the side of his face so it looks like I'm cupping his cheek, but it's really to conceal the fact that our lips aren't actually touching. They're close, though.

So close I can feel it on my mouth when he lets out a single, stuttered exhale.

There's a wolf whistle and a few excited hoots from where the others are, and I grin.

"Listen, it's working," I whisper, even though there's no need. They can't hear us from over here. But something about being so close to Dean right now makes me want to lower my voice. Or maybe it's because I don't have enough breath to speak any louder. His skin is soft and hot under my touch. My face burns where his nose brushes. "Let's make it more convincing."

"Um," Dean croaks, his voice husky and low. "Uh."

His raspy syllables are the only thing separating our mouths. Then I feel a touch—his—tentatively grab my bare hip, right below the fabric of my swimsuit bottom.

On reflex, my fingers curl in the hairs at the nape of his neck, lightly scratching the skin there and tugging on a blond ringlet. Dean's eyes pop open. His gaze flickers down to my lips, then back up. My own eyes trail down to his mouth, then lower—

Then he pushes me away, and the paddleboard capsizes, sending us both flailing into the lake.

The water is an icy shock to my system. I float back up and gasp for air, more breathless than I should be. Dean pops up a moment later, his face still fiery red.

"What the hell was that for?" I ask. My lips tingle from where they almost touched his.

Dean grabs onto the paddleboard and begins swimming back to shore in a hurry.

"Nothing!" he squeaks, panic lacing his voice. "I'm just going for a swim. Over there. Okay, see you, buddy," he gets out all in one breath.

I tread water, staring after him with a mixture of disbelief and shock. Dean paddles faster than he's ever gone before. Whatever his deal is, it doesn't matter. Because my plan worked.

Everyone thinks we're together now.

Huh.

CONFESSION TAPE—Carter Moxley, Contestant

They both have awful taste in companions.

CONFESSION TAPE—Siddharth Patel, Contestant

I guess that alliance *is* solid.

20
THE CONVERSATION PIT OF HELL

DEAN

I thought the time I barfed my guts out at Applebee's would be the most humiliating moment of my life. This afternoon, however, is proving that new and worse levels of public shame are always within my reach.

Siddharth and Adin make obnoxious smooching noises whenever I walk past. Beck and Vendredi coo if me and Seyoon so much as *look* at each other. I'm sure my face is going to stay red like a beet forever. But our plan worked. It's *working*.

Blake orders all of us to film at a few more locations around camp. The cafeteria, around the campfire with fake marshmallows to roast (so they don't burn during all the reshoots), and through the woods on one of the nature trails for a totally leisurely, not at all scripted walk. The long day of filming, cameras in our faces, and producer puppeteering is starting to wear on everyone's patience. Mine included.

We're finally at our last set of the day: the rec room in the Communal Cabin. It's a large common area with windows that stretch from the oak floors to the vaulted ceiling, showcasing the trees swaying in the evening breeze outside. Branches occasionally sweep by and graze the glass, like long fingers reaching out for us. There's a foosball and pool table in one corner, a kitchen in the other, and in the middle, comfy sofas form a conversation pit. Noticeably, there's no television in the room. They're strict about not giving us access to the outside world. Even now, out of habit, I find my fingers twitching for the phone that isn't in my back pocket.

Seyoon plops on the couch, and I sit next to her. I misjudge the distance and accidentally brush our thighs together. Her skin is warm, just like it was when I grabbed her hip on the paddleboard. The sensation of her breath tickling my lips, her fingers at the nape of my neck, and the memory of how her brown eyes looked like molten gold in the sunshine flood my mind all over again. I haven't been able to stop thinking about it all day. She shifts on the sofa, and I jolt.

Seyoon whispers in my ear, "Can you act normal, please?"

I glance around, then subtly cover my mic. "I'm trying. This is awkward. Don't *you* feel awkward?"

Seyoon tucks a strand of her hair behind her ear with a smirk. "Nah. Nothing gets to me. I'm too good at everything I do." She muffles her own mic now. "Even pretending to be in love with President Nerd."

God, she's annoying. I'm about to let her know as much when my attention is drawn to her cheek puckering as she chews on it from the inside. I narrow my eyes at the action. She does that a lot. I used to have that habit, too, until I switched to picking at the skin around my nails when I felt anxious.

Huh.

"You have a bad poker face," I say.

Seyoon frowns and tucks another strand of hair behind her other ear. "No, I don't."

"You totally do. You don't know what you're doing, either. I knew it."

A pretty shade of pink crawls up her throat. She closes her fist over her mic tighter and leans in close. "Okay, *fine*, it's a little weird that everyone thinks we're sucking face, but if it's what will get us closer to that grand prize, nothing else matters." Seyoon sits back, an easy confidence sliding over her features. "No one can throw me off my game. Not what the others think, not a million cameras everywhere, and not even you."

That makes something burn in my gut. Jealousy. I don't have even a fraction of the self-assurance Seyoon has. I wear my doubts as a second skin, my insecurities as an oversized coat.

Well. If she can pretend like none of this affects her, maybe I can too.

Blake and Garrett corral everyone onto the sofas. The cameras start rolling again, each stationed at different corners of the room to capture every angle.

"I know you kids are tired from a long day of filming," Garrett says, "and probably sick of each other's company, which is perfect." Blake kicks him in the heel nonchalantly, and he winces. "I mean, *not* ideal for our purposes at all. But don't worry, all you have to do here is have a conversation. Easy peasy, right? You'll just—"

Carter groans. "We've been doing this for hours already. You don't have enough footage of us talking by now?"

"Shut up, dude," Vendredi snaps. "You complaining only slows us all down."

My eyebrows raise. Her uncharacteristic sharpness pulls some of us out of our heat-stricken, hungry, exhausted dazes. Vendredi leans heavily on the arm of the adjacent sofa, kneading the bridge of her nose. She mentioned a headache earlier, but it wasn't enough to get her out of filming. It must be getting to her. Blood rushes to Carter's puckered face.

Blake clears her throat and shoos Garrett away. She turns to us with a more genuine smile. "Thank you all for hanging in there. I promise, we're almost done. I even have a little incentive to motivate you."

Siddharth perks up. "Money?"

Adin leans over him. "Food?"

"Sleep?" Beck asks pathetically.

TSW Studios would like to assure viewers at home that Forest Feud *provides adequate meals and breaks to its contestants.*

"No. Better," Blake says with a sparkle in her eye. "Whoever gives the most entertaining and convincing performance will receive a hint that will help them in tomorrow's challenge."

Now *that* wakes us up. Seyoon and I exchange a look.

Tense energy thrums in the space between the seven of us as assistants hand us props and adjust our positions. Blake steps back behind the line of cameras.

"Beck. Can you ask Seyoon and Dean how they got together?"

She falls into character like a flip being switched. It's extremely apparent how much being on another reality show and having two former contestants as parents give her an advantage.

"So," Beck starts, voice airy. "You two looked cozy on the lake today. When did"—she wags her finger between us—"*this* start?"

Blake nods, impressed. Before I have time to think of something, Seyoon hops in.

"After the first challenge," she says. She scoots impossibly closer—our thighs fully pressed against each other now—and lays a hand on my knee. I jerk on reflex, and she squeezes, digging her nails into my skin. *Act normal.* "There's so much history here, you know, with our parents being in the same season. We connected instantly."

"Dive deeper into that, Seyoon," Blake prompts. "What drew you to him?"

Her fingers twitch on my knee. "Um, well . . ."

She swallows visibly, gnawing on her bottom lip as she thinks. Some part of me preens. Seyoon can bluff as much as she wants, but she also has no experience in this department.

Maybe I *can* throw her off her game, despite what she'd like to think.

Ignoring the anxiety screaming in the back of my mind, I lean back and snake my arm around Seyoon's waist. She jolts.

"I was first drawn to Seyoon because of her *humility*," I say, managing not to laugh. "I thought the way she handled losing that first challenge after saying she was going to beat me was really admirable. It takes a lot of courage to keep your head up high after that."

Somebody snorts in the corner. I wipe my mouth to keep it from turning up. She must catch the mirth in my expression anyway, and I see the exact moment she figures out what I'm doing. Her nails dig in deeper around my patella. It's worth it. After everything she's put me through, I'll admit it. It feels a little good to get Seyoon as flustered as she always makes me, for once.

Alright. It feels *really* good.

But I shouldn't have underestimated her desire to come out on top.

Seyoon twists toward me and flashes an alluring smile, eyes half-lidded like she's charmed. "That's *so* sweet. But not as sweet as when you wrote me a poem comparing my eyes to the night sky."

Is she out of her mind? Don't answer that. I already know.

"I didn't—"

Seyoon lifts her brow, a silent provocation. *You ready to yield so soon?*

Like hell I'm going to let her win something *I* started. "I didn't have anything better to compare them to," I say. "Your beauty outshines anything in the world. The closest thing would be . . . the heavens."

Whatever tiny shred of dignity I might've had walking into this room just shriveled up and died. Hopefully, I will too.

The camera closest to us walks over, probably to capture the way both our faces are on fire. Seyoon's mouth falls. For the first time, she's speechless. Something about being the one to elicit that kind of reaction from her makes electricity tingle along my spine.

"Wow," she laughs. "You're quite the romantic, huh?"

"I mean," I force myself to say without cracking. I'm suddenly grateful for all those cliché romance books we read in book club. "Nothing comes close to you whittling my face into a tree. It's really *you* who's the sentimental one."

Adin gasps and puts his hands over his heart, then seems to remember where he is and settles back down.

CONFESSION TAPE—Adin Zavary, Contestant

> Alright, I'm secretly a huge romantic at heart. There, I said it, you happy? I love sappy rom-coms and soap operas and all of it. But don't tell anyone, okay? Especially not Sidd.

Blake leans over the back of the adjacent sofa, a nearly maniacal grin on her face. The glint in her eye—hungry, almost—is very familiar. That's not the prim, calm director we were introduced to on the first day on set. *That's* the host from the old days of *Forest Feud*. The one who had a reputation for personally contriving drama between her contestants.

I figured she must have mellowed out in the two decades that have passed since then. But maybe not, given the way she's rapidly tapping her fingers on the sofa back, attention laser-focused on us and us alone. She certainly looks entertained by our performance. Hopefully entertained enough to give us the incentive.

Blake pokes Beck. "Ask Dean when he first realized he was in love."

Beck does so. Everyone looks at me. The sound director gestures urgently at the boom mic operator on the other side of the room, who runs closer. Every camera has swiveled to train on me. My body turns to ice.

"Um—" I say. *Everyone I know will see me be a blubbering, blustering idiot in love.* It's setting in for the first time. "Well, first off, this is still new, you know? 'Love' is a little strong. Maybe?"

Seyoon has a satisfied smirk on her face. *I've won*, it screams.

I want to wipe that smirk off her face *so bad*, it turns me feverish.

"However," I say. I pause to smother the nerves buzzing deliriously in my bones. It takes all my strength to keep my hands and legs from shaking. I lick my lips. Seyoon's eyes dart to my mouth, then back up to my eyes. Whatever shows there makes her smugness falter. Good.

"If I had to trace when I knew I *liked* her down to a single moment . . ." I start again, my voice taking on a gentler, more raw tone, not necessarily by choice. My gaze trails over Seyoon's face.

The best lies need to have some truth to be believable. It's how we'll convince Blake to give us that clue.

Seyoon's hand on my knee twitches, heavy and hot. The sensation brings me back to the first time she touched me. It was during Mountain Marathon. Like the reckless, overeager moron she is, she leaped onto my zip line. We could've fallen. I nearly did—until she reached out and grabbed me, uncaring of how it opened her fresh wounds back up.

"It was probably when she kept me from falling off the zip line in the first challenge," I answer. I'm only looking at Seyoon now. It's easier than at the cameras for some reason. "And it wasn't because she saved my life. It was because she did it without thinking. Like . . . like helping someone was a reflex for her. Even in the heat of competition, she helped a rival out. That's what made me start to like her."

Silence punctuates my words. Seyoon is stiff, like she's not breathing. At some point, I leaned in. I watch her watch me, uncaring for once of the others and the cameras circling around us for several long moments.

Adin hiccups—and it rips me from the trance I had tripped into.

"Holy crap," he says. "That is *so* romantic."

Garrett erupts into cheers from where he'd sprawled across the pool table. I expect Blake to yell at him for ruining her scene, but she's too busy fist-pumping the air behind the couch.

"*Beautiful,* you two!" she shouts. Loose silver hairs fall carelessly across her bright face, her usually perfect bun now falling apart on her shoulders. "Yes, *yes*! Okay, let's keep this energy, everyone. Siddharth, I have a question for you to ask the group now . . ."

Blake expertly directs the rest of the scene, her enthusiasm bleeding into the following conversations about family, each of our hopes, what we stand to lose if we're cut from the game. Questions—and their heavy answers—that would usually have me on the edge of my seat. Having this information about my fellow competitors is crucial, so I try tirelessly to tune in. But it's impossible with Seyoon's incinerating, weighty stare on me.

I'm snapped back to reality when it's Vendredi's turn to answer a question. She looks miserable, still nursing a headache and leaning heavily on the arm of the couch.

"No, I actually don't care what my mom thinks about me being here," she sighs. "I'm not interested in fulfilling a family legacy or anything like that. I'm doing this because it's my dream to be an actress."

On the opposite couch, Carter scoffs. "What a shallow answer."

Vendredi stills. "Excuse me?"

"Your mom is the whole reason you're here, and you're not going to give her any credit?"

Vendredi leans forward, gripping the sofa arm. "You don't know shit about the situation between me and my mother."

Blake creeps up on Carter's side. "Ask her to explain," she says like the devil over his shoulder.

Carter crosses one leg over his knee. "Then, explain it to us."

Vendredi is clearly restraining herself. I glance between her and Carter, then the cameras. Which are, thankfully, finally off us.

Her voice is steady when she speaks, but heavy, like the calm before a storm. "You think you know who Mariah Dillworth is because you watched her on television. Well, I don't care how good of a player she was. I know how terrible of a mom she *is*. And that's none of your business."

Carter gives her a once-over, his long nose scrunching with distaste. "No one here cares if she was a good or bad mom. What we care about is how entitled you are to not acknowledge that you're only here because of her."

She shoots up to stand, face twisted with fury.

"What are you going to do? Hit me?" Carter drawls. A small smirk ghosts his mouth. "That wouldn't be a good look for you."

Everybody stays still, even the crew members.

Vendredi clenches her fists. Unclenches them.

"I'm leaving," she spits.

Blake tries to stop her, but Vendredi steps to the side and exits the rec room, slamming the door behind her.

Siddharth is the one sitting closest to Carter. He turns to him and shakes his head. "Dude. What's your problem?"

CONFESSION TAPE—Carter Moxley, Contestant

Blake said the most entertaining performance wins a clue for tomorrow's challenge. Was that or was that not *entertaining*?

I'm not going to apologize for playing the game, even if it hurts people's feelings. Come on. Some of us have a million dollars to win.

The air is heavy. The cameras keep rolling, but none of us says anything. Carter ignores Siddharth entirely, continuing to pick at the threads on his pants. Eventually, Garrett hops off the pool table and joins us.

"I can't take it anymore. That must be enough footage, right?" he asks. Blake sighs.

"Yeah, it was. Alright. You're all free to go. Except you—" She points at Carter. "I want you in the confession booth now while everything is still fresh."

Seyoon's up first, on her feet and out of the room quickly. As others move to leave, I follow her, past the cafeteria and onto the porch. Night has fallen fully by now. There's just enough light emanating from the cabins to make out Vendredi sitting by the empty bonfire pit. Seyoon jogs toward her. More hesitantly, I join.

Vendredi's leaning over her knees with her head buried in her arms. She turns when she hears our shoes crunching in the grass and quickly wipes her face. She's been crying.

"Oh. Hi," she says.

I don't know how to comfort somebody in need. I never have. What's the right thing to say in a moment like this?

Seyoon crouches next to Vendredi. Curious, I watch, wondering if she'll try validating her feelings or maybe start by telling her everything will be okay. Seyoon waits until Vendredi sits up enough to meet her gaze. Then she smiles and says just one thing.

"Want to pull a prank on Carter with me?"

A beat of quiet. Then, a laugh barks out of Vendredi. She sits up fully, and even in the dim light, I can make out the genuine smile carving a spot on her face for the first time tonight.

"Hell yeah, I do," she says.

I huff in amusement, my eyes glued to Seyoon.

Yeah. Helping others really is like a reflex for her, huh?

21

I MAY NOT BE GOOD AT TITLING REVENGE PLANS, BUT MAN, AM I OKAY AT ENACTING THEM

SEYOON

Vendredi, Dean, and I form our plan by the bonfire pit, one I've named Operation Give That Little Shit Something to Complain About For Once. However, O.G.T.L.S.S.C.A.F.O. isn't very catchy, so we're just calling it the revenge prank for now.

We're still scheming when Blake finds us. "There you are!" she says. She's in a great mood—this was her best day of filming, after all.

Vendredi stands up, already sighing. "Look, I'm not going to apologize to—"

"Apologize? To Carter?" Blake laughs. "Save it, I'm here to thank you. That, and pull you out for an interview." Blake nudges her toward the confession booth. "I always support my contestants airing out their grievances. But only on camera. Off you go. I'll be there to join you in a minute."

Vendredi, relieved, heads off. "See you tonight!" she calls out to us. I shoot her a thumbs-up.

Blake chuckles. "You two. Oh, you kids keep me young." She stands over me and Dean, a huge smile across her face. "That back there? That was great. Forget the legacy trio alliance I wanted—a showmance is *much* better." She starts walking backward toward the confession booth. "In case I need to say it out loud, you won the clue for tomorrow's challenge."

"Seriously?" I ask.

"Yep. And if you keep this adorable romance up, there might be more incentives headed your way."

Then she leaves, and it's just me and Dean.

I shove him in the shoulder. Hard.

"Ow!" he cries out. "What was that for?"

"For saying I carved your face in a tree like some obsessed stalker!"

"That's what you get for saying I wrote a poem about your eyes."

"Well, you're the one who started waxing *actual* poetry about them." I cup my chin in my hands and turn my face up to the sky. "Like the heavens," I repeat dreamily.

"Shut up, *please*."

Dean turns away from me, but I spot the sliver of a grin creeping over his face. I laugh, holding on to the log for balance.

Giving him shit is fun—*really* fun, he's easy to fluster—but this? Sitting in the afterglow together? This is fun too.

"Despite how . . ." Dean waves his hand in the air. "Truly awful, and painful, and degrading as a human being that was, I think we did pretty good."

"They're all definitely convinced we're in love, that's for sure." I try not to stumble over the word. Now's not the time to get shuttered by embarrassment. I'm Seyoon Shin, I don't *get* embarrassed. Don't quote me on that, though. "You were right," I say, bumping his shoulder with mine. "Playing the couple act was a good idea. Thanks."

"What for?"

I bite the tattered inside of my cheek to stall. “For being a good teammate, I guess. You’re helping both of us get ahead.”

He’s quiet for a few moments. “Well,” Dean says, “it’s not *entirely* horrible teaming up with you, either.”

“You *are* in love with me!”

Dean does his huffy-laughter thing again and stands. “Whatever helps you sleep at night. I’m hitting the showers. Good luck with your prank.”

“What do you mean? Aren’t you joining?”

He pauses. “You want me there?”

“Of course.”

Dean blinks. Had he really thought I wouldn’t? He perks up and says, “Okay. Cool.”

I grin. He’s trying to hide it, I can tell, but it’s clear he’s happy about the invitation. Probably also at the chance to screw with Carter, but I have a feeling there’s more to it than that.

I think maybe we’re on our way to being friends.

Here are three things I know about Carter:

1. He’s the most annoying person I’ve ever met in my life.
2. His uncle is the second-most annoying person I’ve met.
3. He’s a *heavy* sleeper. And a very routine one, at that. Carter falls asleep promptly at lights out, and nothing can get him up besides the 7 a.m. alarm that blares through camp every morning. He snores, too. That sleep apnea is no joke.

When telltale honks echo through the sleepy cabin, it's our cue for O.G.T.L.S.S.C.A.F.O to commence. The name has started to grow on me.

I throw off my blankets and hear Vendredi do the same in the next bunk. The mattress above squeaks as Dean climbs down the ladder. I reach out blindly in his direction, grazing his arm in the dark. He holds on to my wrist, and we pad gently over to Vendredi, careful not to trip or step on a squeaky floorboard and wake everyone up.

But then, of course, I run my toe into the corner of Vendredi's nightstand.

"*Fu—*"

Dean covers my mouth with his hand. We stay very still and listen. There's no interruption to the rhythm of Carter's snores or any of the even breaths in the cabin.

A thought to lick his palm invades my mind. No reason not to, I guess. He shudders and lets go. I can't see him move, but I jump when his lips brush the shell of my ear.

"You're the worst," he hisses.

"No, trust me, I can get worse."

Another hand reaches out for us. I blink. My vision finally adjusts to make out the silhouette of Vendredi in the dark.

"Ready?" she says, barely above a whisper. I nod and look at Dean.

He hesitates. "You sure you guys want me here for this?"

"Of course. We're partners," I answer. "That includes in crime."

That's good enough for Dean. The three of us tiptoe over to Carter's bunk bed. He's flat on his back, tucked in tight under his blankets, hands folded over his stomach. Vendredi leans over and snaps her fingers twice in front of his face. Nothing.

"The fuck's wrong with this guy?" she whispers. "He looks like a corpse."

Carter lets out another long snore then, reassuring us that nope, he's alive. Yippee.

"Come on," I say. "Like we planned. I'll take the right side, you two grab the left."

We scramble to get in position. I wriggle my fingers under the mattress near Carter's head while Vendredi and Dean get a grip on the opposite two corners. In unison, they pull the mattress, and I push. It slides off the frame an inch. Everyone freezes. Carter's face is just a few inches from my hand. I hold my breath.

"*Hurr-acgh.*" He lets out. *Phew.*

"Let's go. Slow and steady," I hush.

I dig my nails into the plush underside of the mattress as we carefully slide Carter and his bed off, pausing every time there's a break in his snores. I have to carefully clamber across the metal frame once we get the mattress free.

Dean wheezes as we walk backward toward the door. "He's heavy."

"We're almost there," Vendredi says. "Shit. The door. Who's going to—"

"What are you guys doing?"

The three of us freeze. Carter lets out another helpful snore. I whip my head back to see Beck sitting up in bed, blearily wiping sleep from her eyes. *Fuck fuck fuck.*

"Um . . ." I say, loud enough for her to hear across the room, but not to wake Carter, or Adin and Siddharth in the corner. "Putting Carter outside . . . Would you get the door?"

Silence. Then, "Sure."

Beck pads over and lets us out. A gust of cold night air rushes into the cabin.

"Thank you, Becky," Vendredi says, grinning at her. Beck nods, half asleep, before returning to bed.

We rotate ourselves to get the mattress to fit outside the door. Carter sleeps through it all, even when we hoist him above our heads and carry him down the tricky porch stairs. It's hard navigating in the dark, but we make do by moonlight and memory. My arms are on fire once we finally get down to the lake. Luckily, it's past filming hours, so we don't have to wear our mics or worry about getting caught by any pesky camera operators.

"Let's push him in," Vendredi says.

"Yeah!"

"No," Dean replies.

We boo him but oblige, instead leaving Carter high enough on the rocky shore so he won't be washed away. Should a stray wave come up and drench his blankets, that's Mother Nature's prerogative.

We run back to camp and collapse on the grass before finally bursting into laughter. I roll around, mushing my face into the dewy ground, reveling in the sweet, earthy smell in my nose and the warm, fuzzy feeling wrapping around me. The moon gives off enough of a glow to make out Vendredi's and Dean's faces near mine, equally flushed from laughter.

"Can't believe he didn't wake up," Dean says. His hair is splayed in the grass like a halo.

"I had faith in Seyoon's plan," Vendredi says, readjusting her bonnet. Seeing how upset she was earlier was heartbreaking; I'm glad the light is back in her eyes. "Where'd you get that idea, anyway?"

My smile falters. "Saw it in a movie or something."

Dean hums. "I don't want to inflate your ego any more than it already is, Seyoon, but I have to admit, it was a good prank."

I give in to my urge to ruffle his hair. It's softer than I expected. "You're so in love with me, it makes you look stupid."

"Watch yourself."

Vendredi laughs. There's a glimmer of amusement in her eyes as she looks between us. "You guys remind me of me and my girlfriend when we first started dating," she teases. "I know we're on a reality show and all, and it's probably not the most ideal place to form a lasting relationship, but I have a good feeling about you two. You complement each other."

My ears warm. Dean sits up. I make the mistake of locking eyes with him.

"Um," he says. "I'm—I'm probably going to get some shut-eye now." Dean stands. There's a loose twig caught in his curl, but I don't bring it up. He pulls his hoodie over his head and shoots us each a hesitant but earnest smile. "This was fun, though."

Vendredi and I watch him hurry back to the cabin. He looks back once, right before he closes the door.

"Sorry," Vendredi says, sheepish. "Didn't mean to embarrass you guys."

"It's okay. It's just . . . new, you know?" I say, an inkling of guilt biting my side. It's different when the cameras are off. When they're on, Dean and I are performing. Now, though? Now I'm just lying to her face.

"Well, if you want advice, you know where I sleep. Juliet and I have been together for almost three years. I'm *very* well versed in this sort of thing."

Vendredi wags her eyebrows at me, and I snort. A question that's been nagging at the back of my head all night creeps to the forefront of my mind now.

"Actually," I start. "There was something I wanted to ask you. Not about relationships. But something you said earlier."

"Hit me."

"You mentioned not caring about family legacies or what your mom thinks of you." She stiffens. I feel bad but press on lightly. "I know you didn't want to talk about it in front of everyone, but do you want to tell me about it?

It's uncomfortable to admit. Vendredi looks sympathetically at me. Maybe it's what gets her talking.

"It's complicated with my mom. She was never around, and even when she was, she wasn't *really* there, you know?"

I swallow. I do.

"Luckily, I have an amazing dad. He's all I need. And he totally supports my goal of going into acting." Vendredi shrugs. "That's the only reason I'm here. To get my face out there, not to follow in my mom's footsteps or anything. I don't even care about winning the prize after seeing how that kind of money changed her."

My mind whirs, trying to wrap itself around the idea of *not caring*. It's impossible. I sit up on my knees. "You don't want to win so you can rub it in your mom's face?" I ask. "Not even a little bit?"

Vendredi laughs—the last thing I expect her to do. "No. I don't think of my mom that much. I certainly don't think of her here. Wherever she is right now, I know for a fact she's not thinking about me either."

My lung collapses, air oozing out of me like a deflated balloon. "Oh."

She stands and offers me her hand. I take it, grateful, because my knees don't feel as steady now. I probably overexerted my muscles hauling Carter and his mattress. Yeah, that's it.

"Why'd you ask?" Vendredi says as we head toward the cabin. I match her slow, leisurely pace, watching the way the grass flexes under our feet. Suddenly, I'm embarrassed to explain how much it means to me that Appa sees me win. How badly I need to prove him wrong. The only thing it proves is that I haven't stopped caring about what he thinks, even though he doesn't give a damn. Admitting that, even just in the privacy of my head, makes me feel small.

Vendredi hears something in my silence I didn't mean for her to. "You don't have to tell me. It's none of my business."

She didn't have to tell *me* either, though. I clear my throat.

"I had this best friend," I blurt. Vendredi stops walking. I realize it's because I stopped first. My feet plant in the ground, toes digging into the cold soil, as if to bury myself under it. Oh God. Why did I say that? Since when does the Agonizing Amelia Incident of Junior Year have anything to do with why I'm here?

"Yeah?" Vendredi encourages.

It was Amelia, by the way. She's who I got the mattress prank from. One time, I fell asleep first at one of our sleepovers, and she carried me and my sleeping bag into the backyard. It became one of our longest running jokes, taking turns dragging the other person farther away from the house each time, then dying of laughter when the other would bolt awake in confusion. I don't know why I didn't just tell Vendredi that when she asked.

"Yeah," I say. Something blocks my throat, and I have to swallow a few times before I can get any words past it. "She was a grade ahead of me. We became friends because she was the captain of my volleyball team. We were really close, we did everything together, including all the same sports. But, um . . . when I moved this year, we played against each other for the first time. My team beat hers. I'm really competitive, and I let it get to my head. I was a dick, basically. We haven't talked since that game."

Vendredi's brows furrow. "That's what broke your friendship?"

"There was . . . more."

Not that Amelia would know. Because I didn't tell her why I had to move. Or about Appa leaving us. I never told her how the last thing he ever said to me was that I disappointed him, not that he loved me. It wasn't like she didn't try to be there for me—but I didn't let her. She called about a million times, but I wouldn't answer.

Why? Good question. I wish I had a good answer. But the reason is pathetic: I don't like being the kind of person who needs a shoulder to cry on. That's all. I hate being weak, someone one who needs help. A *loser*. It's easier being the shoulder. The helper. A winner.

I don't know why I'm like this. But it's why I've always struggled to cross the boundary of friendly to *friends* with anyone besides Amelia. Maybe it's why I'm only giving Vendredi a half truth now.

Vendredi steps forward and wraps her arms around me in a hug. I freeze.

"I get it," she says. "I let my competitiveness get the best of me, too, sometimes." Vendredi steps back. "It doesn't matter what you're trying to prove by being here, or to who. All that matters is you're here now, right?"

The thing blocking my throat rises, coating my tongue in acid. Guilt. I wish I wasn't like this. Because I want to cross the boundary of *friendly* with her too. I learned the hard way with Amelia that the only way to do that, though, is to give more than half truths. I think of Umma. What would she want me to do? I know she's probably worrying about me here, just like I worry about her at home. She wanted me to make friends.

"Right. Thank you, Vendredi," I say. "You're . . . you're a good friend."

She beams, and it's so bright, it washes away some of the bitterness. "I didn't come here to make any, but you know what? You're a good friend too."

I want to be. I hope I can.

22

SUNSHINE, FUNKO POPS, AND RAINBOWS

DEAN

I set my hand of cards down on the mattress with a grunt. "You're cheating. I know you are. You're too quiet."

Seyoon's face contorts into the most incriminating expression I've ever seen. "How *dare* you besmirch my name. I would never cheat."

"Maybe not in a challenge, sure. But when it comes to gin rummy?" I lean forward and make to grab her cards. She yelps and leans away, scooching to the safety of the other end of her bed. I point my finger at her. "See, an innocent person wouldn't react that way."

I knew I shouldn't have trusted her when she approached me this morning with the battered deck of cards she found beneath her bunk bed. But we had some time to kill before everyone finished getting ready for the day. Seyoon's hard to say no to, anyway. Not like I wanted to. She doesn't need to know that I've come to genuinely enjoy her company. Her ego's big enough as it is, thanks.

Seyoon shows off her toothy grin and fans herself with her cards. "It's not cheating. It's, uh . . . Portland rules. Yeah, this is always how we play. You should get familiar if you want to move to my city."

I'm about to tell her where she can shove her Portland rules when the cabin door bursts open. Everyone in the room jumps. Carter stands in the doorway, dripping lake water.

"Okay," he says, an eerie calmness to his voice despite his facial muscles twitching with rage. "Who wants to die?"

He is met, predictably, with silence.

"That's . . . rhetorical, right?" Adin asks.

Carter storms over to his bunk and shoves Adin's shoulder. Adin's too big for it to make much of an impact, but he does pout and rub his arm. Siddharth reaches down from his top bunk and shields him, frowning.

"Was it you, huh?" Carter says. "Did you and your boyfriend move my mattress out in the middle of the night?"

Vendredi snickers from her bunk. Carter whips his head around. He walks over and stands in front of her with his arms crossed. "What's so funny?"

"You're tracking lake water in, dude," Seyoon complains.

He turns to glare daggers at Seyoon. "You know something about this?"

"And if I did? What are you going to do about it . . . hit me?" She stands, crossing her arms and giving him an amused up-and-down. "That wouldn't be a very good look for you."

It's what he said to Vendredi yesterday. I snort, unable to stop myself. Carter directs the full force of his hatred on me now.

"I can't wait until you two tear yourselves apart," he spits. Then he turns and stomps out of the cabin. It'd be more intimidating if it weren't for the moist *THWOP THWOP THWOP* sounds his wet socks make on the floorboards.

Siddharth climbs down from his bunk. "You guys pranked Carter? That's *so* sick."

"Thank—"

I cover Seyoon's face with my hand, muffling her. "We can neither confirm nor deny," I say, laughing nervously. Pranking Carter in the secrecy of night with no cameras around is one thing. Admitting it to a cabin full of competitors we're not sure we can trust? Entirely—

"Ugh!" I yank my hand back. Seyoon's saliva coats my palm. Why do I keep doing that? She's going to lick every time, I know this.

We get ready, have a quick breakfast while ignoring Carter fuming in the corner of the cafeteria, and get on the bus to the filming location for today's challenge.

Once we're in the forest, they set us up near the starting point for Mountain Marathon and get to work powdering our noses, adjusting our mic packs, and preparing us for the challenge. The cameras film from every side. I'm losing hope that I'll ever get used to it.

"Hey, lovebirds," Blake says, approaching us with a crew in tow. "Can we grab a quick shot of you two? Don't shy away from PDA. How about a little hand-holding? A romantic gaze into each other's eyes?"

I turn to Seyoon, managing to mostly avoid an uncomfortable grimace. She blinks, then holds her hand out to me. I slide my palm against hers—rough and calloused, like a gymnast's—and entwine our fingers together. The camera pans down to our hands.

"Adorable, darlings, love it." Blake checks something off her clipboard before heading down the line to harass another contestant.

I glance down at where my hand connects stiffly with Seyoon's. How long am I supposed to hold on? Probably for a while. Couples like to hold hands, and we want people to think we're dating. Yeah, I'll keep holding on then. It's not like it's unpleasant. Our fingers slot together surprisingly well. I'm vividly aware of the way her knuckles feel against the pads of my fingertips. Soft, in case you were wondering. My heart is racing. I've never held anyone's hand.

Seyoon squeezes mine and hums. "You're really clammy."

Okay. Moment's over.

Not long after, Garrett gives us the spiel for today's challenge. Or at least, the first take of the spiel.

> Who's ready for the third challenge of the season? Edit in some applause there, Blake.
>
> Last time, you put your survival skills to the test. Today, we'll be sending you back out into the woods, so let's hope you remember a thing or two to help you out there. The name of today's game? Trailside Treasure Hunt.
>
> Hidden somewhere in these woods are the most precious valuables money can buy: limited-edition Garrett Moxley Funko Pops. That's right. These treasures are hidden in locations that are significant to your respective relatives' seasons of *Forest Feud*. Your job is to brave the forest, find your Funko Pop, and bring it back before time runs out.

Adin raises his hand. "What if more than one person has a relative in the same season? My uncle and Sidd's sister played together."

> And here I thought you were all brawn, no brains. Great question. There is one Funko Pop per relative to find, each for ten points. They're grouped by seasons. So, say there are three players with parents from the same season . . .

The camera slowly pans to me, Seyoon, and Carter, in case there are any viewers at home who don't quite make the connection. Overkill.

> . . . Those three Funko Pops will all be hidden in the same location. Got it?

Carter doesn't even bother raising his hand. "Do we get extra points for bringing back more than one doll?"

> They're not *dolls*. Ugh. Yes, you can earn extra points, but only for collecting Funko Pops from *different* seasons. No bonus points for snagging all the treasures from one location. We're trying to make this fun for the audience, which means difficult for you, the contestants.
>
> I see some confused faces. "But, Garrett, this challenge sounds so easy." You might not think that when you find out there will be a *double* elimination this round. That means two of you will be waving bye-bye to that sweet, sweet cash prize.
>
> Is everyone rightfully nervous now? Perfect! You have ninety minutes on the clock. Starting . . . now!

"A double elimination?" Seyoon says. She glances around and frowns. "I'd hate to see anyone here go home. Except Carter, who can go to hell."

"I can hear you, Fourth Place," Carter quips.

Before they cut us loose, an assistant hands each of us a map of the forest. There's a red line marking the perimeter we can explore, about a mile in radius, with several landmarks on the map: the Nisqually River, a campsite, a hiking trail, and more. Garrett sidles up to me and Seyoon as we pore over the paper.

"I have something for you two that I think you'll like," he says.

"Is it time away from you?" Seyoon chirps.

"Rude. Just for that, I'm giving this to Dean."

He pulls a folded note from his pocket and plops it in my hand. "The incentive you two won yesterday for giving Blake the best performance." Garrett pats each of our heads. "Don't get lost out there."

Everyone splits off into the woods, trailed by the usual team of camera and sound operators. I catch Blake whispering to some of the techs, and when Seyoon and I head out, there are double the usual number of cameras following us. A restless buzz thrums under my skin as the techs circle us on every side, constantly in my periphery. There are already cameras installed in the trees—is this really necessary?

Once we're away from the other contestants, we unfold the clue. The scrawl is messy and haphazard.

Vince, Garrett, and Jungeun, sitting in a . . .

Seyoon squints. "Is this cursive?"

"I think Garrett just has bad handwriting," I say, then read it aloud. "The answer has to be *tree*. Problem is, which one?"

"What a shit clue. They want us to look for a needle in a haystack. No, a needle in a pile of other needles. See? Even the metaphor sucks."

I purse my lips and gaze out across the woods, thinking back on the fifteenth season and any particularly memorable locations this could be hinting toward. The scenes flash through my brain like a highlight reel. I gasp when I realize.

"The treehouse!" I scour the map, searching, and *yes*, there it is. I point it out for Seyoon. "In the final challenge, the obstacle race led to a treehouse at the finish line. Do you remember?"

"Oh—you're right!" She beams at me. "Nice work, partner."

I try not to preen too visibly at the praise.

According to the map, there's no paved road or hiking trail to get to where the treehouse is located, which is clear on the other side of the perimeter, so Seyoon and I get to work trekking through the woods. The others must be scrambling high and low in search of their own Funko Pops, but wherever they are, it's not nearby. It's just me, Seyoon, and the tiny militia of underpaid film workers behind us.

Seyoon grunts, stepping over a fallen tree. "Good thing we got that clue, huh?"

"That's all thanks to your sweet little spiel yesterday." With the cameras in earshot, I can't call it what it actually was: a damn convincing performance.

Seyoon shoots me what's supposed to be an obnoxious grin, but it's kind of accidentally charming. "That was all from the heart, lover."

"Lover?"

"Yeah, I'm testing out some pet names. We're dating, it makes sense. You don't like it?"

I don't understand how she can say things like *we're dating* so flippantly without combusting. Damnit. She really is better at everything than me. "Feels one-note," I say to shed off the embarrassment.

"What about 'babe'?"

"Please don't."

"Pretty boy?"

"Now you're just teasing me."

She loops her arm on a nearby trunk and swings around it, twirling in front of my path. "Yeah, maybe. But you make it so easy . . . *sunshine.*"

That one makes my stomach flip. Ignoring it, I press the back of my hand to her forehead.

"What are you doing?" she asks.

"Checking for a fever. You must have contracted a flesh-eating virus from swimming in the lake every day, and it's gnawing away at your brain."

She doesn't bat my hand away. Well, now it's going to stay here. Okay, too long, I'm removing it.

"What, you don't like 'sunshine'?" Seyoon asks.

She's pouting. *Jesus.* No, even he wouldn't have the patience for this.

"It doesn't suit me."

Seyoon steps away from the tree and plods forward, knowing I'll follow. "Yes, it does," she throws over her shoulder. "When you actually smile instead of frowning like you're constipated, it lights up your whole face. You turn warm. Plus, you know, you're the one thing here I can be sure of besides myself. Same way I can count on the sun to rise, I can count on you to have my back, right?"

I stop walking. My shoes plant themselves among the layers of moss and fallen pine needles.

"Is that . . . ?"

I stop myself from asking: *Is that what you really think of me? Or is that for the cameras?*

It shouldn't matter, because we're both playing pretend. And yet, my pulse skyrockets all the same.

Seyoon's not paying attention though, instead looking off into the distance. "Wait a minute. I think I see it. Yeah, that's it. Come on!"

She takes off running, and I follow her, getting whipped in the face by the branches she pushes out of her way. I crane my neck up, spotting a small, rundown hut high above the rest of the trees. We stop at the base. If I weren't positive this was the right place, the several cameras attached to the nearby trunks would pretty much confirm it. A strange blend of nostalgia and grief washes over me when I remember that twenty years ago, Dad was here, right where I'm standing. I feel closer to him now—thousands of miles away—than I ever did while under the same roof.

The thought hurts. And it doesn't help, so I push it away.

There are wooden planks, makeshift ladder rungs, nailed directly into the tree. Seyoon starts climbing them without hesitation.

"Hey, you don't know how sturdy those are!" I call up. She ignores me, obviously. With a sigh, I dig my nails onto the shallow edge of the first plank, testing the strength of it, then pull myself up.

"So, what do you think?" Seyoon asks as she climbs a few rungs above me.

"About what?"

"Sunshine. It's cute, right?"

My arms are shaking by the time I'm all the way at the top, about thirty feet up in the air. Seyoon reaches the platform first. Her head ducks out over the side. We're so close to the roof of the forest here that when the breeze shifts the foliage around, the sun filters through in blinding streams. I have to squint to look at Seyoon.

The golden rays backlight her gentle, smiling face, forming a near-perfect crown.

She extends her hand down. I take it, grateful, as she helps pull me up over the edge.

"It suits you better," I tell her. Then I glance back the way I came.

"Don't look down if you're scared of heights," she says. Too late. Fuck.

"Okay, let's—" I scramble away from the edge. How are we going to get back down? Later problem, Dean. "Let's go inside. Maybe there's something there."

The platform is about as wide as a car, and the tiny tree house sitting on it is even smaller. The exterior is simple, with only a door and a dusty window next to it. There's not even a handle, so Seyoon simply pushes it open.

"Are you kidding me?" she says as soon as the door swings open.

At first I think she's talking about the half-assed construction job. Literally—only the front half of the tree house is built, leaving a gaping hole in place of where the final wall should be, revealing the miles of forest on the other side.

But no. Worse than the OSHA violation staring us in the face is Carter, with three Garrett Moxley Funko Pops stuffed under his arm, still in their collector cases.

"How the hell did you beat us?" Seyoon asks. "We had the clue."

"Because I'm not an idiot. Obviously, the significant location for the fifteenth season would be where the betrayal took place. Duh." Carter adjusts the boxes in his grip and turns his nose up. "Now, if you'll excuse me, I need to figure out a way to carry all of these down."

Seyoon holds up her arm when he tries to leave. "What are you taking all three for? Those are ours. You don't even get extra points unless you take ones from different locations, remember?"

"Oh, I know that. This isn't so I can get extra points." He hip-checks her out of the way, and she stumbles into the adjacent wall, the planks of wood there rain-warped from decades of water damage. Carter smiles, but his eyes are flat. "This is so *you* can't get any."

Seyoon's jaw falls. "You're an asshole."

"Me? I'm the asshole? *You're* the one who dragged me and my mattress into the lake!"

"Because you were a dick to my friend!"

I step forward, my hands raised defensively. "It was supposed to be a harmless prank."

"Aha!" Carter shouts and jumps, his pointed face turning redder by the word. "So, it *was* you two!"

He accidentally kicks over the only object in the tiny, three-sided treehouse: a rusted bucket. A spider crawls out and flees for its life. Carter heaves for breath, then clears his throat and composes himself again.

"Tell you what. I'll give you the dolls if you apologize." He smirks. "On your hands and knees."

Seyoon barks out a laugh. "We are not *bowing* down to you. Or apologizing—unless you say sorry to Vendredi first. You really hurt her feelings."

"Have it your way." He turns on his heel and heads for the doorway.

"Wait," I blurt. "We're sorry. Give us the Funko Pops."

"Dean!" Seyoon shouts. I wince.

Carter pauses. "She has to apologize too. And mean it." He twists his face around. There's a sharp, sly smirk inching across his mouth. "Or you could always split up. I'd give you a doll then."

"That's not happening."

"Neither is me groveling on my fucking knees." Seyoon crosses her arms defiantly, her nose scrunched with distaste. "How about you start by apologizing for shit-talking my mom on the first day? Or cutting our zip line?"

"You run your mouth *this* much and still can't say 'I'm sorry'?" Carter scoffs. "It's only two words."

"Here's two words for you," Seyoon bites. "Fuck you."

He pushes the door open with his foot. "Good luck finding other Funko Pops. There's only twenty-five minutes left on the clock."

Shit, there is? Carter's right. The forest is too big. There might not be enough time to search the perimeter. No, there definitely isn't. I think back to the scoreboard. Seyoon was in fourth place. Could we take the zero-point hit? I could, probably. But not her. Especially not with the double elimination Garrett promised. The seconds that pass as Carter nears the edge of the platform are agonizing as I deliberate. But there's no doubt about it.

We need those stupid Funko Pops. Or else she's going home.

"Just apologize," I hiss to Seyoon. Her eyes pop open.

"What? No. He treated Vendredi like shit. He treated me *and* you like shit. I'm not going to let him walk over me anymore, and neither should you." She grabs my hand and forces me to meet her gaze. "We can find other dolls, Dean. You've seen every season of this show, you'd know where to look. And I can get there fast enough. I believe in us. Don't you?"

Carter gets down on his knees to begin descending the rungs. He's taking the artifacts. If he leaves with those, if we don't find anything else, Seyoon could get eliminated.

I don't want her to go home.

"Seyoon, please! Your arrogance isn't worth losing the points, just apologize to him!" I shout, the panic rising in me bleeding into my voice.

She jerks back like I hit her. Fuck. *Fuck.*

Desperate, I run out the door and kneel down, grabbing the back of Carter's shirt collar to stop him before he's out of reach. "We're sorry. We're *both* very sorry, okay? I promise she is."

He turns his head up to look at me, and I startle. Carter doesn't look surprised that I came running back.

"Since you got on your knees to apologize, I'll accept it." He tosses two of the artifacts up on the platform. Chuckling, he starts back down. "Better stay on your knees so you can beg for forgiveness now, lover boy."

Nausea floats up my stomach as I watch him go, the sheer drop-off and height only making my vertigo worse.

I sit back and warily glance at Seyoon. She's standing in the doorway with an expression I've never seen her wear before. Disgust. No, *disappointment.* She's disappointed in me.

My stomach plummets as though I've tumbled off the platform.

23

DO I GET ANY CREDIT FOR NOT RESORTING TO VIOLENCE? BECAUSE I SHOULD

SEYOON

Dean and I are the last ones back to the meet-up spot in front of the buses. Actually, Dean is the last one, because I'm storming twenty feet ahead of him, pretending like I don't hear him calling my name. Garrett, Blake, the rest of the film crew, and the remaining contestants are waiting there for us.

"There are our slowpokes," Garrett says. "But hey, you made it with almost two minutes to spare—and each with a Funko Pop! Woah, what's with those faces? You feeling sick? Try to vomit *after* the point tallying, please. We're on a tight schedule here."

It's easy to ignore him with the ringing in my ears. Vendredi's concerned face is the first one that sticks out from the crowd. I beeline for her, a safe haven, when Dean jogs over and circles around, blocking my way.

"Not. *Now*," I bite out, harsher and louder than I intended. Everybody within earshot turns and stares. All the cameras are pointed at us. Usually, they don't bother me. But right now, I want to smack them away from my face.

"Seyoon, please. Don't be mad," Dean says quietly. I'm not sure if that's a request for the cameras or if he's just trying to tell me what to do. And how to feel. *Again.*

That's it.

"I can't believe you," I snap. The words burn up my throat. "How could you not back me up? *Again!*"

His shoulders straighten. "We needed those points, Seyoon. No—*you* needed them. I was trying to help you."

Vendredi hesitantly approaches. "Hey, guys, what's the matter?"

In the bleeding edge of my awareness, I notice Blake pull Vendredi away and whisper something about not obstructing the shot. Whatever she's saying isn't nearly as important as the fury pulsating through me.

"I'm mad," I spit, getting in his face, "because you wanted me to get on my knees and apologize to the guy who's been nothing short of a raging asshole. I'm mad you asked—*expected* me to disrespect myself like that. You called me arrogant for having *principles.* But you know what's most upsetting? That you still refuse to speak up for what's right."

Dean stiffens. I've prodded a sore spot. I see it. The shift. His eyes, soft and shining just hours earlier, narrow and darken with resentment.

"If it wasn't for me, if I didn't get us *this*—" He snatches the Funko Pop from my hands and shakes it. Figurine Garrett rattles around the plastic, his bobble head shaking in protest. "You would be going home. But your ego is too big to acknowledge that you needed my help, that you're not the winner you think you are. How do you expect me to back you up if you won't even trust that I'm looking out for you? What kind of partner does that make you?"

I flinch back and immediately regret losing my ground. Dean's tone and his cold, cutting glare slice through me. Peeled open now, I become aware of the hundreds of eyes watching us. Dozens of cameras trained on my furious expression. My breath stalls. How is this the same boy I was just joking around with? The one who eagerly helped me prank the resident bully last night? The one whose soft edges were drawing me in, closer and closer to calling him a real friend?

But I should've known better. All of that before was *because* of the cameras. This? This is in spite of. I'm an idiot for thinking I could trust an alliance built on a lie. Dean's an actor, a competitor—not my friend.

My lip curls back with a sneer. I shake my head. "Then, maybe we're not good partners after all."

I shoulder-check him on my way past, but with the height difference, I kind of just plow into his ribcage and stumble away. *Ow. Walk it off, Seyoon. Savor your mic-drop moment.*

Carter hums smugly and says, "Guess the power couple's run is up."

Somebody hurries after me, clambering onto the bus. It's Vendredi, thankfully. I throw myself into a seat in the back and glare out the window. She sits beside me.

"Are you okay, Seyoon?" Her big, round eyes dart over my face, concern written in the pinch of her brow. Guilt twists my gut.

"Yeah, I'm fine," I manage to say, although not convincingly.

Vendredi lingers, looking uncertain about what to say. I cringe inside—the last thing I want to do right now is talk about my *feelings.* In the end, she just puts her hand on top of mine. "Can I keep you company?"

Affection surges through me. "Yes, please."

The others start boarding the bus hesitantly, like they're scared to be trapped in a contained space with me. I slink down so I'm out of view and away from their invasive stares, and so I don't have to look at the back of Dean's head. Vendredi taps my hand, drawing my attention back to her.

"Hey, if you and Dean are actually breaking up," she starts, keeping her voice down. "You're more than welcome to join my and Beck's alliance. Granted, we didn't find our Funko Pops, so it might not make sense from a strategic standpoint but . . ." Vendredi raises one eyebrow hopefully, smiling. "The offer's on the table. If you want it."

That makes everything sink in. Me and Dean are broken up. It's hard to imagine doing any of this without him. My leg bounces. I dig my nails into my thighs.

Luckily, Vendredi accepts my small smile and silently mouthed *Thank you* as a good-enough response for now. She scoots in closer and loops her arm through mine, and it makes the bumpy, terrible ride back to camp a little better.

24

THE MOST DIABOLICAL THERAPIST THE FIELD OF PSYCHOLOGY HAS SEEN SINCE FREUD

DEAN

CONFESSION TAPE—Dean Parker, Contestant

[rehearsed, stilted]

Getting us enough points to stay in the game doesn't mean I don't have a backbone. It means I'm a smart player. I'm *not* the bad guy here, okay?

[He shifts awkwardly, then starts again.]

Sure. I didn't have to call Seyoon arrogant for not wanting to bow down and beg forgiveness from the guy who started it. I get where she's coming from. But Carter's obviously never going to take the high road and apologize. So, somebody has to, right?

. . . Maybe to Seyoon, though, the high road was standing up to him.

I shut up. I don't think I'm helping my case as much as I hoped.

I lean back against the wooden wall of the confession booth with a heavy sigh. The studio ring light around the camera burns my retinas. I drag my palms over my face, feeling more drained than I did after Mountain Marathon.

I just need to get my side of the story on tape so that the editors can't spin the narrative too far from reality. And so my intestines will stop twisting and tying themselves into knots when people cast me long side-eyes around camp. That's all. I'm not trying to convince myself I was in the right. I *am* right. Well, I'm not wrong. But . . . neither is Seyoon.

There's a knock at the door. I lean forward and push it open.

"I was just wrapping up," I say, only to see it's Garrett, leaning on the side of the shed.

"By all means, don't let me interrupt," he says. "We hardly ever get you in the confession booth. We have a severe lack of your vulnerable side on tape, Mr. Brick Wall."

I give him a tight-lipped, straight frown but say nothing, and he points at me and goes, "Yeah, see?"

Dealing with Garrett's antics, especially without Seyoon here to help, is the very last thing I want to do right now. Oh, the thought of Seyoon makes my stomach hurt worse. Maybe I should see if the medic has Tums. The elimination scene got pushed to tonight, so I can hide in the infirmary until then. "Well, I was done. The confession booth is all yours."

"*I'm* not here to confess my sins."

"That's not what I was doing."

Garrett half smiles. It's not as condescending as usual. He opens his mouth, and I brace myself for something idiotic or exhausting, but he surprises me by asking, "How you holding up, kid?"

I blink. He almost sounds earnest. Maybe he is. "Fine."

"You're more like your dad than I thought you'd be." That makes me feel good about myself for the first time today, until Garrett continues. "You're just as hardheaded."

"My dad's not—"

The instinct to defend Dad dies on my tongue. Even I can't deny that.

Garrett steps into the tiny shed. "Scoot over."

There's barely enough room for one person on the makeshift bench, let alone me and a grown man. I stifle a sigh and press myself against the wall as Garrett plops himself down. He reaches over and fiddles with the camera, turning it off. I raise my brow. I figured Blake sent him over, but she'd want this on camera. He should too. Garrett sits back, crossing his leg and holding his knee like he's a therapist. The thought of Garrett as a therapist, even as a hypothetical, is so horrifying, I can't suppress a shiver.

"So," Garrett says. "How are you *really* doing?"

"I said 'fine.'"

"Well, you did kind of get dumped in front of everyone."

"Fake dumped. You know we're not actually together. It was *your* idea. Why wouldn't I be fine?"

"Because you've been prattling excuses in here for the last half hour like you're trying to prove to yourself that you are."

The ring light is still on, and it lets me get a good look at Garrett's face. It's jarring, how he can be such an overeager idiot for the cameras one second, then so eerily intelligent the next. I swallow, shifting under his intense, curious gaze. I cross my arms over my chest and lean farther away.

"You don't need to pretend like you care, one way or another," I say. I nod to the camera on the other wall. "You turned that thing off already."

"Do you really think that little of me?"

"Yes?"

Garrett doesn't laugh it off like I'd expected him to. "With my history with your dad, I guess I can't blame you. We *were* good friends, though. Up until the end."

"Then, why'd you betray his trust?"

"Like you did with Seyoon today?"

The blood drains from my face.

Some of that sharp brightness in Garrett's eyes softens. "Hey, I get it. If anyone understands what you're feeling right now, it'd be me. That's why I asked how you're doing. 'Cause I know it's a pretty shitty feeling to play the game, and to play it as well as you did."

Viewing Garrett and myself in the same light makes me uncomfortable, but now that he's drawn the comparison, I can't help but see it. I'm not the strong, macho player Dad was in his day. Seyoon's mom was athletically inclined, too, and clever. Garrett was the odd one out in their trio, the runt. I didn't expect him to make it to the final three, but once he did, I thought the other two would sweep him. But then he tricked them into going down the wrong path in the final obstacle rope course, and I realize that's exactly why he won. Because everyone underestimated how smart he was. No one expected much from him. The same way I still don't, now. The same way people never expect much from me, either.

Seyoon, though? Seyoon expected more from me.

I stuff my hands into my hoodie pocket, twisting my fingers. "Do you . . . regret being that kind of player?"

He hums, sucking his teeth, thinking. "No. But I do wish I had made things right after."

It just confuses me more. Why would Garrett want me to make things right with Seyoon? How does he benefit from that?

Garrett chuckles and stands. "Those wheels are turning so hard in your head, I can practically hear them. You know, you *can* just take some things at face value instead of overthinking every single thing anyone says to you."

I have never done that before in my life and have no intention of starting now.

Garrett pats the wall of the shed as he exits. The guilt sloshes against my insides, painting them slick, threatening to drown my lungs in oil. I try to ignore it the whole trek to the infirmary, thinking it'll wash away any second now.

I'm an idiot. The whole world will see how I let my emotions, my fears, get the best of me. Dad and Meredith will see that I didn't take Seyoon's side, that I didn't speak up for what was right. Because even though I know I was right, she was too. Thinking about the fool I've made of myself in front of everyone at camp—and, once this airs—the *nation*, makes my stomach sink like I swallowed a stone.

But what sticks with me through it all, heavier, worse than the embarrassment, is the shame. I disappointed Seyoon.

I finally admit what I've been repressing all day: that I'm more upset with myself for letting her down than anything else. Why? What she thinks of me shouldn't matter. We're competitors at the end of the day. I shouldn't care about her.

But I do. I really do.

25

THIS EDITOR'S SUITE IS NOT VERY SWEET

SEYOON

I'm glad elimination got pushed. For the general safety of the public, that is; I'm in no shape to be around others. But at the same time, having nothing to do is only making the agitating, restless anger in me worse.

I'm on my way to hang out in the Communal Cabin so I don't run into Dean (and fold him like a pretzel in a fit of anger), when Luke, Garrett's assistant, intercepts me.

"Miss Shin—"

"You can just call me Seyoon. I'm, like, twenty years younger than you."

"Twenty is . . ." Luke sighs so hard, I think I've aged him another five years. "Never mind. Blake wants to speak with you. Follow me."

I trail after him as he leads me to the Crew's Cabin. It feels illegal to enter, like sneaking into the teacher's lounge at school (which isn't actually a very interesting place and wasn't worth getting detention for). It's similar to the Communal Cabin, with several large foyer rooms and high, vaulted ceilings. There are folding tables everywhere; makeshift workstations for the crew members to fiddle with their equipment on and review the hundreds of papers scattered across every flat surface. At the far end of the first floor are several doors. Luke opens the one with the sign EDITOR'S SUITE and ushers me inside.

The room is almost entirely dark, with the only light coming from the dozens of monitor screens spanning an entire wall. Different videos flicker across them all. There's one of Carter running through the woods. Another of Beck foraging berries. B-roll footage of camp. At least five screens feature Garrett's shit-eating grin.

A corkboard on the wall nearest me displays several sticky notes and documents. One of them reads *Show Proposal—"Moxley to the Maximum,"* and I remember the spinoff show Garrett mentioned he and Blake were planning, starring him and Carter. Barf. The only maximum I'd like to see them receive is a maximum sentence.

Blake is alone in the room, fixed in front of the monitors. She twists around at our entrance.

"Seyoon, there you are. Thank you, Luke," she says.

Luke nods and exits, shutting the door behind him. Blake gestures for me to join her in front of the screens.

"Neat, isn't it?" she asks. "Welcome to the editor's room. Where the magic quite literally happens. We sift through hundreds, if not a thousand hours of footage here."

Blake reaches for the keyboard and types something in, pulling up a brand-new clip. She doesn't even need to press play for me to recognize it as the scene from this afternoon, in the treehouse.

The Seyoon on the monitor's face contorts from stunned hurt to rage in a second, twisted with lines I didn't even know existed. I self-consciously rub my cheek. Dean looks unfairly composed compared to me. Even when he's pissed, the only sign is a tick in his jaw and a wrinkle between his brows. He doesn't wear his heart on his sleeve like me. I'm the one with a terrible poker face, as he and everyone have pointed out.

Blake turns the screen off with another tap of the keyboard. "I was trying to figure out what caused your lover's quarrel."

"It wasn't a—" I can't even get myself to say it. My lips flatten. "Me and Dean aren't actually dating. Garrett told us we should pretend to be in a showmance because it'd help our alliance. But it's just pretend."

She hums. "Yes, I know. I told him to suggest it to you guys. I'm glad you were receptive."

I blink dumbly. "You knew we were just acting this whole time?"

"I did, but the other campers don't, so no need to worry. That's what you were hoping for, right? You want to present a unified front. Intimidate the competition." Blake makes a fist in front of her face to emphasize her point. With her other hand, she presses the keyboard, and my angry, pixelated face pops back on the screen. "This, unfortunately, doesn't quite present a unified front."

"You can thank Dean for that," I grumble. "He's the one who didn't want to side with me."

Blake pulls up another chair and motions for me to sit. I do but squirm. This feels like all those times I've been asked to stay after class so the teacher could tell me to "stop disrupting the learning environment." A.k.a., shut the hell up. She never told any of my equally rowdy male classmates anything, mind you.

Blake sighs. "Have you seen the first season of *Forest Feud*? No? I don't blame you. Pilot seasons are always rocky, plus we were one of the first reality game shows to really hit mainstream. We had so much to figure out and learn. Hell, I must have been more nervous than my contestants." She laughs. "I remember wondering how things would pan out then, throwing twelve teens in the woods for a few weeks."

"What happened?" I ask.

"Pretty much the same thing that's happened this season. Alliances form. Enemies form faster. Somebody has a mental breakdown by week three. These patterns feel predictable now, but back when we were starting, we didn't know what to expect. I do now, though." The woman leans forward, her hands crossed tightly and a serious look in her eyes. "There was a showmance in the first season, too. Then the guy started fooling around with another contestant. The girl was understandably upset. They had a big, dramatic falling out in front of everyone. Oh, it was beautiful. Highest-rated episode of that season."

"And then what?"

"And then they all turned on her. Damnedest thing. The boys sided with the guy, of course, but some of the girls did too. In the original run, we had elimination by votes. She was out that same week. Oh, and don't get me started on how the viewers tore her up at home."

I stiffen. "But it was the guy's fault! He cheated on her!"

Blake throws her hands up. "I know. But he made himself sympathetic. He stayed calm while she screamed and sobbed and cussed him out in front of every camera." She sits back and lets out a sigh. "Men are allowed to react, but women can only ever *overreact*. It's a flawed belief that we see echoed in the audience of every single season. The show, your competitors, the viewers at home—they don't care about who's right or wrong. They just want to punish the weak."

I swallow. My angry pulse throbs in the back of my head. "I'm not weak."

"I know that. But I also know what happens to girls like you in these situations." Blake gets up and walks to the other table, grabbing her clipboard. She flips through a few pages, and I spot a film schedule dated for tomorrow. "That's why I want you and Dean to make amends. We'll make sure the others are there to see it, too, so they know you're still together. Still strong."

The rolling wheels of my chair squeak against the linoleum from how fast I stand up. "What? I'm not apologizing to him. That's not fair."

She sets down her clipboard. With a sympathetic smile, like she's a parent coddling an upset toddler, Blake approaches and pats my shoulder, soothing me. Damnit. It is kind of grounding. *Am* I acting like a toddler?

I can't help it. I think it's part of me. This *thing*. This intrinsic *something* about me that makes me unlovable, unlikable, unable to really connect with anyone. Maybe it's what got *me* here, pulled into the backroom and asked to behave, and not Dean.

When I finally look up, Blake's eyes are soft. "I know Dean wants to make things right too," she says.

That catches my attention. "You spoke to him?"

She nods, expression perfectly neutral. "He was only trying to look out for you and make sure you both made it to the next challenge. He cares about you, Seyoon. I can't force you to reconcile with him, but there were benefits to teaming up with him, weren't there? Those haven't gone away. Both of you know this. Think about why you're here. What you want. You came here to win, right? For your mom?"

The mention of Umma goes straight to my chest. I wonder what she's doing right now. Probably breaking her back at one of her two jobs, or at home, all alone. Remorse stings me. I can't forget why I'm here. For her. Everything I do here is to make sure that she has a better life when I come back.

I'll do anything to make that happen.

I nod slowly.

"Then, win. And do whatever it takes to get there."

I tilt my head up at Blake and offer a meek smile. "I will. Thank you."

26

DOES THE DUDE-BRO HANDSHAKE REALLY NEED A SPECIAL VARIANT?

DEAN

The nurse kicks me out of the infirmary for elimination, dashing my hopes of hiding out there with the excuse of a stomachache. I crunch on chalky Tums, dragging my feet to the bonfire circle where everyone else is already sitting. The only available seat is on the side opposite Seyoon. I'm too cowardly to glance in her direction, afraid I'll be met with that look of scorn that's still burned on my retinas.

The stand-up stage lights they've erected around the crackling fire are so bright, they almost make me forget it's nighttime. Garrett stands with his back to them, his silhouette lit like some dramatic hero. He catches me looking his way. Any of the candid sincerity he lent me back in the confession booth—if it was real at all—is tucked neatly behind his flashy TV smile now.

Welcome to our third elimination of the season—and our first double elimination. Campers, before we dive in, let's debrief. Unfortunately, not everybody was able to find their doll—*treasure*. Vendredi, along with Beck and Adin, you struggled to snag a

> Special-Edition Limited-Run Garrett Moxley Funko Pop. What happened?

Vendredi purses her lips, not happy about being called out. "There was a lot of ground to cover and not enough time. Looking back on it, Beck and I should have divided and conquered, but we stuck together for our search." She rubs her arm. "Plus, I haven't seen my mom's season in forever. I wasn't sure what location might be significant."

There's a pregnant pause. I wonder why Garrett doesn't continue, until I notice it's because multiple cameras are angled toward Carter, waiting for another snarky soundbite. For once, he exhibits good self-preservation instincts and keeps his mouth shut.

> There you have it. For those of you who did retrieve a figurine, you've earned ten points. As long as they were from *different* locations. Meaning, Seyoon and Dean, even though you each collected a Funko Pop, it's only ten points between you. But don't forget—our two alliances get their bonus points, too.

"But they broke up," Siddharth points out. "We all heard it. Should they still get the alliance bonus?"

My blood runs cold. Garrett glances backward at Blake. She gestures him over, whispers something in his ear, and he nods.

> Because they completed the challenge together and only ended their alliance *afterward,* they'll still earn the bonus this time. However, moving forward, they won't. Satisfied? Then, let's reveal the new standings.

No more bonus points moving forward. Because we're not together anymore. Right.

I turn my attention to the leaderboard while ignoring the dull pang in my chest.

1ST	CARTER MOXLEY	39 PTS
2ND	DEAN PARKER	29.5 PTS
3RD	SIDDHARTH PATEL	26 PTS
4TH	SEYOON SHIN	23.5 PTS
5TH	VENDREDI TENGKU	20 PTS
6TH	BECK MCLAUGHLIN	17 PTS
7TH	ADIN ZAVARY	14 PTS

I've somehow managed to hold on to second place for the third challenge in a row. Pride sparks momentarily in me when I think of how happy Dad will be to see. But more importantly, Seyoon's still safe too, despite us each only earning six and a half points. Even after everything, the knot of tension in me releases to see that she's okay. She made the cut.

And then I hear sniffling.

Beck is wrapped in Vendredi's arms while Seyoon holds them both in a group hug. Siddharth isn't celebrating his new spot in third place either, not with Adin now in the bottom two. I wince. I was so absorbed in the fact that Seyoon and I made it, I forgot two others would be going home.

Adin grabs a shamefaced Siddharth by his shoulders and jostles him hard enough that his perfectly styled hair falls over his face.

"Sidd, listen to me. Are you listening?" Adin asks, dead serious. "Don't feel bad, because you're going to win. Hey—" He turns to one of the nearby cameras now, beckoning them over. The camera operator looks around, then awkwardly creeps forward, practically mushing the front of the camera against their faces. Adin turns his face to a three-fourth angle and thumps his fist to his chest. "You're going to win," he repeats dramatically.

Siddharth blinks, now more confused than upset. His shirt collar is stretching thin under Adin's grasp. "You know what?" he eventually says. "Hell yeah."

"Hell yeah!"

"For you, Adin!"

"For me!"

They go in for what I assume is going to be one of those dude-bro handshakes, but they instead opt for the popular variant: the dude-bro-handshake-turned-back-thumping-hug. A classic among its specimens, one I have not personally mastered myself. The hug lingers for a while though—okay, a *long* while. I'm going to avert my eyes and give them some privacy.

Beck and Adin say their goodbyes, are handed their bags, and head off for their exit interviews. Just like that, two more gone. The cabin will be so quiet without Adin's rambunctious laughter or Beck's quick, excited murmurs to Vendredi. Or without Seyoon's nonstop chatter from the bunk below. I have a feeling I won't hear it tonight. I miss it already.

I muster enough courage to glance in her direction. Her eyes are red, splotchy from saying goodbye to Beck and comforting a much more upset Vendredi. The dull edge of regret nudges its way inside me, slipping under my rib.

CONFESSION TAPE—Adin Zavary, Contestant

How does it feel to be booted off the show? It sucks, thanks for asking.

Ha, nah, it's okay, I'll be alright. I still get, like, partial bragging rights for seventh place. I'm sure it'll be enough to get me elected as student body prez next year. Wrestling captain though? No, I'd probably have to get at least sixth for that.

I'm rooting for Siddharth, now! You better win!

CONFESSION TAPE—Beck McLaughlin, Contestant

I'm disappointed I wasn't able to redeem my loss on *Phantom Pursuers* through this show, but it's okay. I ended up having a lot of fun and making some great friends. More importantly, though, while we were out in the woods for the last challenge, I found *this*.

[The camera zooms in on the tuft of matted brown fur in her hands.]

Based on the texture and color, I'm almost positive this is a sample of Bigfoot's hair. I didn't want to say anything to the others about it at the time because I know Siddharth has cryptozoophobia. Although this distracted me from the challenge, it was worth it.

Blake finds me definitely-not-wallowing on the porch the next morning. Today's another B-roll film session, unfortunately. Now more than ever, I wish I were anywhere but here. I'd even take bailing Meredith out from another bad date over this.

"Morning, Dean," Blake says, as sunny as ever. "Cheer up, champ, your day's about to get a lot better."

"Why?"

She climbs up the steps and leans against the railing. "Because your girlfriend wants to apologize. Isn't that sweet? Excuse my reach, sweetie," she says, manicured fingers reaching for the clip-on mic attached to the back of my shirt collar. I hear a click that I think means she turned it off.

"Am I in trouble?" I blurt.

She chuckles. "Trouble? You're darling. Viewers will eat you up. Listen, Dean. You and Seyoon have some damage control to do after your fight yesterday. This romance of yours only benefits you if your competition thinks you two are solid, right? But now everyone knows you're on the rocks. A public break-up requires a public reconciliation. That is—" One of her thin, plucked brows arches high. "If you still want to work with her. Because she wants to work with *you*."

"She does?" My heart thuds heavily. "I mean, yeah, so do I."

"Of course you do. Come on, then, let's go."

I scramble to my feet and hurry to follow her down the porch and through the clearing. Vendredi, Siddharth, and Carter are being directed around by a modest film crew. I wonder where all the other cameras are, then immediately get my answer when Blake guides me to the space between the Crew's Cabin and Garrett's cabin.

It's a cozy alcove and might even be a private place for a conversation like this, if it weren't for all the crew members, Garrett, and the other campers still within eyeshot. Five cameras surround Seyoon, who looks stiff and uncomfortable against the wall.

Blake fixes my hair and straightens out my shirt. "I've already debriefed Seyoon," she says under her breath for only me to hear.

"She's ready to play her part. I trust you will too." Finally, she switches my mic back on and flashes me a dazzling smile. "Don't feel awkward. Pretend like we aren't here."

Wow. Why haven't I thought of doing that earlier?

I take a deep breath and turn around. Seyoon's watching me. There's a layer of ice over her face that nips at my skin when I drag my feet over and lean on the wall next to her. It takes all my concentration not to let my eyes flicker to one of the many stage lights and cameras mere feet away.

"Hey," I say.

"Hey."

There's a stilted exhaustion to her tone that I don't think I would have picked up on when I first met her. But I know her too well by now to miss it.

"I . . . I'm glad we both survived elimination yesterday," I begin, figuring it's as good of a place to start as any. "I was worried about you."

The side of Seyoon's cheek puckers as she chews on it. It catches my attention, as it always does, and she stops as soon as she notices. Her words are deliberate and precise. "I know you were. I know that's why you sided with Carter in the challenge. You were . . . only trying to look out for me and make sure we both made it to the next challenge."

I blink, surprised. "Yeah. Yeah, exactly."

Seyoon folds her arms over her stomach. Her gaze is fixed just below my eyes. She inhales deeply through her nose. "I'm sorry I blew up on you."

"I'm sorry too. I said some things in the heat of the moment that I regret. I . . ."

The lights are so bright. All three of the other contestants have ditched whatever they were doing to not-so-subtly eavesdrop. Seyoon's standing close enough that I could touch her if I wanted—which I do—and yet she feels completely out of reach.

This isn't right. This isn't how it was supposed to go. There's so much I want to say to her, to make up for, but I can't find the words to, not when every eye in this clearing is trained on me. Every gaze except the one I so desperately need to feel again. The fibers of my muscles strain under the tension of *how badly* I need Seyoon to look at me the way she used to. I'd give anything to hear her spout off another dozen horrible, cheesy pet names just to get under my skin. Or her laugh, the one with the snorts and wheezes. I can't stand her strained formality. I can't stand her being disappointed with me. She's more than a teammate to me—and isn't this just the worst time to admit that? I should have said this to her sooner. She's someone I admire, I respect. She's my friend.

I want my friend back.

But right now, with the world watching, all I can choke out is another flimsy, inadequate, "I'm sorry, Seyoon," and I hate myself for it.

My brain whirs like a computer running too hot, so without thinking, I reach out tentatively for her hand. She lets me hold it. The pads of my fingers draw lines across the scabs still healing on her palms.

Seyoon smiles at me, but it's insincere. There's no sun. "Me too. I know I said I wanted to end things but . . . will you . . ."

I spare her from having to finish. "Yes." I squeeze her hand. "Partners."

Pressure mounts in the cavity of my chest underneath all the words I swallowed down. It festers. Burning, aching. *Spit it out, Dean. Speak.*

Somebody clears their throat. Both of our heads whip around. It's Blake.

"A kiss would seal the deal," she suggests quietly.

Seyoon's face reddens like a tomato. My heart trips over itself.

"Um," she says, tone rising. "That's—"

"Maybe not . . . now. Or here," I answer.

Blake holds her hands up in surrender and slinks back to the line of cameras and assistants. Garrett's among them, an unusually contemplative expression on his features. Our talk from yesterday trickles back into my memory. One thing in particular that he said sticks to me like a burr digging into my skin.

I wish I had made things right after.

Maybe it's not too late for me to.

27

A KIDNAPPING? WORSE: A HEART-TO-HEART

SEYOON

As soon as I've managed to fall asleep, somebody shakes me awake.

I groan in complaint, swiping at the touch and burrowing farther into my pillow. But there's no light to hide from, and as consciousness begins to probe at my sleepy mind, I realize it's still dead quiet inside the room. It can't be morning yet.

Curious, I roll over. My eyes adjust to the dim light until I can faintly make out the shadowy silhouette standing next to my bed. Panic seizes my breath, and I scramble up.

"Fu—*mmrf!*"

A palm covers my mouth. I'm about to bite it when the familiar clean scent of citrus and something woodsy hits me. I settle down. Warily, the person removes their hand.

". . . Dean?" I whisper.

"Yeah."

I punch blindly, my fist connecting partially with something soft. He groans and doubles over.

"What the hell are you doing standing over my bed like a serial killer?" I hiss, careful not to wake up anyone else in the cabin. It's still too dark to make out anything, but rhythmic breathing and snores continue to sound through the room.

"Sorry," he whispers back, breathier than normal. I might've hit a respiratory organ. "Can you follow me?"

I wait, but Dean doesn't elaborate, nor does he go away. If I ask any more questions, we might wake somebody up, so with a sigh, I shove my blanket off and leave the warm, cozy comfort of my bed. Dean waits while I fumble around in the dark for a hoodie, then we head outside.

"You're lucky I don't *need* my beauty rest, but it's still rude to drag me out into the cold at . . . what, two in the morning?" It's definitely past filming hours, at least. The cameras are absent. "What's this about?"

"It'll be worth it, I promise," Dean says. There's a little more light out here from the moon. My eyes strain to trace the hesitant smile on his face.

I don't know what I'm expecting, but it certainly isn't for him to lead us away from camp and down one of the trails in the woods, guiding us by flashlight like he knows exactly where he's going. I follow slightly behind, still upset, but too curious to turn back. We walk for a good ten minutes before he veers off the path and into the forest.

It's a small clearing. A pile of blankets lay across the grass in the middle, with a warm, flickering lantern in the middle.

"Join me," Dean says, already sitting down. I can't get my feet to follow.

"Why?"

"Don't you like stargazing?"

"I love it," I answer warily. "How do you know that, though?"

"You told me. Back during the survival skills challenge."

Did I? I think back to that night, lying stiff as a board next to Dean in our cramped tent, nervously babbling about any- and everything. I *did.*

"You remembered." My voice is so small, one of the breezes filtering through the trees could have carried my words away, but Dean hears. He nods. I rub my throat, suddenly tight. "You were half asleep by that point."

"It was hard to fall asleep when you kept talking my ear off." There's a hint of humor lacing his voice, though. He was listening to me. Not everyone does. "Sit. Please?"

I do, toeing my shoes off and joining him on the blankets. The grass pokes through the fabric and tickles my feet. Dean sits with his legs crossed, facing me, his hands fluttering in his lap, twisting each finger and rubbing over the knuckles. His anxiety seeps through the short distance between us and makes my stomach flip. For the first time, I'm the one having trouble meeting his eyes.

"What is this?" I ask.

"Isn't it obvious?"

The absolute opposite. I shake my head.

Dean pushes his curls out of his face as an excuse to do something with his hands besides fidget with them. When did I start recognizing that for what it is?

"It's supposed to be an apology."

"Those aren't usually this intimate."

"Well, yes, but I figured a romantic gesture is necessary when you're asking a girl to take you back."

My cheeks explode with warmth.

"Even if it's just for a pretend relationship," Dean adds hastily.

I bury my face into my hands. "We already hashed this out earlier. We're back together. You didn't have to do all this."

"That was for the cameras. This is for you."

My head whips up.

"I should have had your back. I should have stood up for you." The lamp plays across the nervous, guilty expression on Dean's face. "I was a terrible ally, and a terrible friend. I said some things I regret. I'm sorry, Seyoon."

I didn't expect this. The earnest apology takes me so off guard that it's a few moments before I'm able to react. Shaking my head, I pull at the blades of grass that poke up through the threads of the blanket, my fingers quivering. "I'm sorry, too," I mutter. "We needed those points, and I know you were looking out for us. For me. I guess I . . . I was upset that you didn't think we could do it. Find enough artifacts on our own. It hurt because I believed in us, but you—" Oh Christ. This is humiliating. "But you didn't believe in *me*."

What he said after the challenge replays in my mind now. As much as I tried to ignore it, or pretend like it didn't hurt, or that my confidence is bulletproof, it isn't. And it *did* hurt.

I try to salvage the mood with a laugh, but it just sounds pathetic and bitter. "Maybe that was egotistical thinking, though. Arrogance. You were right about that. And about a lot of things. It's true, I'm not the winner I think I am. I'm not a lot of things. I'm not smart enough, good enough—somehow though, I'm still *too* much."

Shut up, Seyoon. Shut up. But I can't. And it's not just my hands that are shaking; it's my vision, jumping and blurring like letters on a page. Hot shame douses over me like it did when I tried to read that riddle in the first challenge. The same way it does each time Appa sighs in exasperation upon seeing my report card. Guilt churns my gut in a manner I haven't felt since the last time I saw Amelia, when I didn't have the courage to tell her everything that was wrong with me, so I lied and said that I was okay, that there was no reason I had ignored her dozens of calls since moving.

Why am I like this?

I want to carve it out—the thing inside me, the thing that made Appa leave, the thing that pushed Amelia away—before it consumes me whole. Before Dean sees it and leaves me, too.

Something wet and weak gathers at my lash line. But then gentle fingers graze the thin skin below my eyes and wipe my tears before they can fall.

I look up.

28

CAN TUMS HELP THE BUTTERFLIES IN MY STOMACH? WHAT ABOUT PEPTO-BISMOL?

DEAN

I reach out and swipe Seyoon's tears away almost involuntarily. Something draws me to her; something always has. I turn to her the same way a lost camper looks to the North Star to orient themselves.

She blinks, coming back to me, her eyebrows pinched and her lashes wet. My throat is tight. Does she really think of herself that way? Worse, she thinks *I* think that of her?

"That's not true," I say softly. The pressure that's been mounting in my chest all day starts to deflate with each word. I pull my hand back so I can scoot closer, close enough that our knees touch. "You're not too much. You're better than good enough."

Her lips quirk up without humor, a self-deprecating smile I didn't know she was capable of. "That's nice of you to say."

"No, it's not. It's honest. You're stronger, smarter, and better than you're giving yourself credit for."

"Smart? I can barely read," she argues.

"That doesn't mean you're not smart. Besides, you can read people," I respond. "You understand how they work in a way I never have. You're effortlessly charming. Personable."

Seyoon purses her lips. "I'm impulsive."

"You're brave. You're sure of yourself and your decisions."

"Stubborn."

"Determined."

"Loud," she tests, an eyebrow raised.

"Bold," I say easily. "And energetic in a way that's unfortunately infectious."

"Cocky."

"Sure," I add, smiling a little. "But not for no reason. And even though you're competitive, you never put down other people or cheat to get to the top. You never stray from what you know is right. You lift people up, people like me."

Seyoon looks even more puzzled than before, her eyes scanning my face while she parses something together. "Why are you saying all this?"

"Because it's true."

"You mean that?"

"*Yes,*" I urge. It surprises me how *much* I mean it. This emotion, whatever it is, swallows me whole, consumes me. It scares me. Since when do I care?

No. I deserve honesty, too. I've always cared. I care about everything, all the time, too much. Just because I don't often voice my feelings doesn't mean I don't have them.

This time, I ignore the fear that prickles at the base of my neck and reach out again, showing her my hand, asking for her touch.

The possibility of putting myself out there, of changing this thing between us irrevocably, is terrifying.

Seyoon meets me halfway—like she always does—and slips her hand into mine. Her fingertips skim over the creases of my palm, lighting tiny fires in the pockets of space between our skin.

"This is the truth," I start, locking eyes with her so she can see my honesty as much as she can hear it. "I like who you are, and I like when we're on the same side. I promise, from now on, if you still want to be in an alliance with me, we'll make decisions together." I slide my hand around until our palms are aligned, giving her an opportunity to move away if this isn't what she wants too. "What do you say?"

Crickets chirping in the grass puncture the heavy silence. I usually hate eye contact, but I can't pull myself out of the deep pools of her irises now. When she stares back, perceiving everything I try so hard to keep hidden, I find that it's actually sort of nice to feel seen. At least when it's by her.

Seyoon slots her fingers between mine. Warmth plants itself into the crevice of my chest.

"I like when we're on the same side too," she says, smiling with confidence this time. "Okay. Let's win this thing. As teammates."

Teammates.

Just teammates.

The reassurance should settle me, but all it does is knock something else loose, something left unsatisfied. What more could I want from her?

We settle down on the blanket to stare at the indigo sky. Seyoon begins prattling off the constellations for me, and as I listen to her voice, feel the heat of her body next to mine—the warmth in my chest explodes. Fire scorches in the notches between my ribs, burning in the blood pumping through my heart. It's the most pleasant burn I've ever experienced. I can see why Icarus would fly toward the sun.

The realization creeps up on me, closing in until I can't escape it.

I want to be more than teammates.

I want *her*.

29

WHAT'S A LITTLE MAKE-OUT SESSION BETWEEN FRIENDS?

DEAN

I am, understandably, distraught.

You would be, too, if you were teammates-slash-friends-slash-fake lovers with a beautiful girl who has a penchant for ignoring personal space and wants to spend every minute of the day together.

Alright. Listed out like that, it sounds like a dream scenario. The unfortunate reality is that this is just pretend. At least, for her it is. She said it herself—we're teammates. That's all; we're only working together because of a common goal. We may as well be coworkers. Coworkers who need to pretend to be madly in love so they don't get fired. This would be an HR nightmare.

I didn't get much rest last night, both because of my distressing revelation and because of the rock under my back. We fell asleep stargazing and barely woke up in time to hurry back to camp, piles of blankets in our arms, before anybody realized we were gone.

Good thing today's only a media day—my brain is too fried for a challenge. The professional photographers roll into camp, lugging big camera bags and equipment to shoot promo photos for the show.

The hour in hair and makeup is painful, but not as painful as spending the whole morning getting my picture taken.

"The *final five*," Garrett says with bravado as the photographer poses us in the middle of camp. "Once the show starts airing, we'll be pushing major promo around you kids. Isn't that exciting?"

"This could help my chances of being scouted by a talent agent," Vendredi mumbles through her smile.

"This could help *my* chances of looking really, really cool," Siddharth says, posing for the camera.

My eyes keep drifting to Seyoon the whole time. I'm fucked. Why *her*, of all people? I mean, she's my type to a T. And also way out of my league. Under different circumstances, I could stretch the limits of my imagination to conjure up a reality where Seyoon could maybe, potentially, *possibly* return my feelings. But that's not this reality. Because in *this* one, she wants one thing and one thing only: to win.

It's the most important thing to her. I know that.

I tear my gaze away before my chest starts panging again. My cheeks hurt from fake-smiling each time a flash goes off. This is exhausting. Being on TV is draining. I miss the library at school. I miss reading with my book-club friends. And reality-TV nights with Dad. And hanging out in Meredith's room. Oh, I *miss* Meredith. She's the only person I could talk to about—

Somebody elbows me. Seyoon. "Earth to Dean? They're doing solo shots for Carter now."

Everyone but me has exited the shot. Carter glares impatiently.

I scurry out of the way. Seyoon steers us away from the crowd of photographers and crew members to a quiet corner of the glade. The stylist did her hair nicely today. Loose waves cascade down her back, and her bangs frame her face perfectly. Either the heat or makeup paints a rosy glow on her cheeks.

She glances around and, satisfied that no one's paying us attention, turns off her clip-on mic and gestures for me to do the same.

"Did you hear what Siddharth and Vendredi were talking about earlier? Before the group photos?"

I shake my head. My attention was otherwise preoccupied.

"They were talking about *us*," she whispers. "Sidd thought it was weird we wouldn't kiss yesterday when we made up on camera. Vendredi said we *might* still be together, though, because I didn't take her up on her offer, but this isn't good. They think our alliance is on the rocks."

"Wait," I stop her. "What offer?"

She stiffens. "Oh. After we . . . broke up last challenge, Vendredi asked me to join her and Beck's alliance."

My heart sinks. The noise of the crowd mutes to a dull hum.

"I didn't take her up on it, obviously," Seyoon hurries to say. "She was just being nice. She thought things were over between us."

I must still be making a face, because Seyoon grabs my hand and squeezes it. "Dean. *We're* partners."

I know what she means, but my body tingles to hear her call us partners. It's nice to imagine she means more.

Okay. Jesus. Less pathetic next time, please.

"Right. Yeah," I say. "Well, it's not good that our public apology wasn't enough"

"You think? Come on, President Nerd, you're the strategist here. How do we prove we're not just back together but stronger than before?"

I look out on the horizon, thinking. The lake shimmers under the sun, blinding me.

"Last time we tried convincing people we were together, we faked that kiss on the paddleboard," I say. "So, we'll probably need to top that."

She snaps her fingers. "Genius. Come with me."

I'm not given much choice. We sneak farther away, behind our cabin, just into the treeline of the surrounding woods. It's cooler here in the shadows, but Seyoon's face only blazes redder. My heart works overtime at the proximity. *Why* did I have to develop a big, fat, annoying crush on her? This is what I get for fraternizing with the enemy.

"What are we doing here, Seyoon?"

"You said we needed to top our plan from last time. What's better than a fake kiss? A *real* one."

We both blink dumbly at each other.

"Huh?" I say.

"'Huh'? Didn't you hear me?"

"Yeah, I did, that's why I said 'Huh?'"

Seyoon frowns, maybe to distract from her blush, which is starting to spread everywhere, even across her throat and under the collar of her—focus.

"This worked last time, didn't it?" she says.

"Yeah, but," I sputter, "that was just pretend. And for the cameras. No one can see us back here."

"We don't need the cameras to see *this part*. And pretend's not going to cut it—I don't want to risk the others *or* the viewers figuring out we've been faking it the whole time. Everyone will hate us for tricking them."

Seyoon drops her gaze, and from the way her voice lowers, I can tell this is her real motive. "I . . . I hate that I wasn't able to do this. Kiss you. I froze when Blake asked us to during our make-up scene, and that bothers me. After I stalled in the first challenge, I promised myself I'd never freeze again. I want to prove that I can do this." She drags her eyes back up, gazing at me through long, straight lashes. "So . . . do you want to? You know. Kiss me?"

Of course I want to. My eyes haven't stopped tracing the curve of her lips the whole time she's been talking. They're a deep orange-red from the lipstick the makeup department put on her. But this wouldn't feel right. Not now, not when I want to for a very different reason than she does.

It takes all the willpower I have to step away. "We shouldn't."

She takes a step forward and plants her palm over my racing heart. Those soft, pouty lips utter, "Please?" and my brain short-circuits.

Well, I used all the willpower I had to step back earlier. I'm out now.

Hesitantly, I hold her hips, just like I did when we faked this on the paddleboard. I drag my fingertips up, grazing her waist through the fabric of her shirt. Seyoon's eyes are wide and curious, flickering across my face, lingering on my mouth. She lifts her right hand up and snakes it around the back of my neck.

"Are you sure?" I ask.

She nods. "You?"

"Yeah. But . . . I don't . . ."

"That's why we're practicing, right? Besides, this isn't the real thing. It doesn't have to be perfect."

I can't pretend that doesn't sting. But it's true. This isn't real. It doesn't mean anything to her. It doesn't have to mean anything to me, either.

She pulls. I don't have it in me to push anymore.

Our lips meet. My first thought is how pleasantly surprised I am that they're softer than I imagined. And warm. Her mouth is pliant beneath mine as our lips slot to fit each other. The blood rushes to my head so fast, I hear it in my ears. The kiss is chaste—over in a second. Both of us pull back.

That was my first kiss.

Seyoon huffs, smiling. "See?" she says, her other hand looping around my neck. "It isn't hard."

Not exactly.

I lick my lips. Her eyes dart to the motion. "One more?" My fingers splay over the small of her back. "For good measure."

Her throat bobs. Seyoon nods. "Sure, okay. Practice makes perfect."

She stands on her tiptoes to help with the height difference and kisses me with less hesitation this time. I hum, humiliatingly, but Seyoon seems to like it. She pulls back just long enough to take a breath before I chase after her to steal it.

"Oh, *now* you're a quick learner," Seyoon teases against my mouth. "Not even this will shut you up, huh?"

She giggles into the kiss—and it hits me all at once. I'm kissing Seyoon. I've never kissed anyone before, and now I know what her lips taste like and have felt the shape of her laugh. It's so intense of a thought that my head swims. If it weren't for the tree I've pressed her up against, I might fall over. When did I push her up against the tree?

And then, from camp, we hear our names being called.

"Where are Seyoon and Dean?" Blake says. "We need solo shots of them."

We jump away from each other, although we're still well out of sight from the others. My lungs burn like I've run a marathon. Her eyes flicker to my mouth area, then she grins, satisfied. There's no time to question that look before we hurry out into the clearing, acting normal.

"We're here!" Seyoon chirps. Her voice cracks, and part of me preens.

Blake turns around. She looks between the both of us. Then she sighs.

"Get to hair and makeup first, then come back here. And please, no more fooling around—we're on a tight schedule," she says.

Confused, I reach up and touch my mouth. My fingers come away red with Seyoon's lipstick. I realize why she said we didn't need the cameras back there.

Blake calls for Siddharth to take his turn, and he skips up. On his way past, he wolf-whistles at us. When I look, Vendredi's staring, too, her eyebrows arched up. Half a dozen cameras are turned our way.

I turn on my heel and head for the makeup tent, head bowed. Seyoon hurries to catch up.

"No one will be doubting us anymore," she says around a grin. "That was a hell of a convincing performance, if I say so myself."

My steps falter slightly. I watch her features closely, looking for any sign that her terrible poker face will slip. None. She smiles plainly at me. As if nothing happened. As if she's totally unaffected.

I want to kick myself. She said it herself. This isn't real. I know that. What *is* real is the finish line we both want to get to: the whole reason we're even together. Winning is the most important thing to Seyoon. She's not the type who'd let herself get distracted. Not like me.

This doesn't mean anything to her, I remind myself. It doesn't have to mean anything to me either.

I won't forget why I'm here again.

30

SURELY MY OWN POOR DECISIONS CAN'T BACKFIRE ON ME. NOT IF MY INTENTIONS ARE PURE

SEYOON

On the morning of the fourth challenge, Vendredi walks into the bathroom as I'm blotting the water from my hair after a shower.

"Morning. Where's your better half?"

I grin, sticking my tongue against the gap in my front teeth. "She just got here."

"What a flirt. You kiss Dean with that mouth?"

My face turns pink in the mirror. She stabs her finger at my reflection. "Aha!" She wheels around to point at the real me. "So, you guys *were* making out. What is going on with you two?"

"Nothing! We're teammates. And lovers. Teammates who love each other."

"I thought you guys were for sure broken up after your huge fight."

"We made up. You saw."

"Yeah, I did. Felt a little forced."

I flip my head over and scrub the towel over my scalp again so she can't see what my face betrays. "Uh, well . . . imagine you and your girlfriend, Juliet, had a fight, and you had to make up on camera. Of course it's going to look awkward. Dating on reality TV sucks."

Guilt churns my stomach. I don't want to lie to her, not after how close we've gotten, not after how honest she's been with *me* about her mom—but I can't reveal that me and Dean aren't even together. It'd be a crack in our front. Something we can't afford so close to the finals.

Still. It makes me feel like shit not to be honest with her. Lying to my friends is what caused the Agonizing Amelia Incident of Junior Year, after all.

Vendredi turns the faucet on. When I hear her start brushing her teeth, I deem it safe to stand back up and lean against the sink.

"I guess you're right," Vendredi says around her toothbrush. "So, are you guys solid now, or what?"

"Yeah, we're solid." A small smile worms its way onto my face. "That night, Dean took me out to stargaze, and we talked it out properly. Away from the cameras."

"Well then, I'm glad. Really. I'm happy for you, but . . ."

My eyebrows furrow. "But what?"

She spits and rinses the toothpaste from her mouth. "But what are you guys going to do if you both make it to the finals?"

My heart pounds harder. It's a good question. One I've been nudging out of my periphery for a while, but as we get closer to the end, I can't ignore it much longer. Dean and I formed this alliance on the basis of helping each other get to the final challenge, but we haven't explicitly talked about what comes *after* that.

I push my wet bangs out of my face and gaze at my reflection, stalling at the sight. With my face bare and my hair down like this, I look so much like Umma. Homesickness strikes me in my solar plexus and leaves me a little breathless.

"Dean and I both came here to win," I answer Vendredi. "When we get to the finals, it's game on. Winning comes first. Everything else second."

"Hm," she says, interestingly. "In that case, I feel a little better asking you this."

Curious, I face her. Vendredi leans back against the counter, trying to look nonchalant, but I recognize the sharp look in her eyes for what it is. The look of a rival.

"You're my biggest competitor. It's tough, because I want to be your friend, but I also want to beat you." She laughs. "I think you're the only person who can understand I mean that as a compliment."

The exciting rush of adrenaline I get before crossing a finish line licks at my heels now. I grin. "Yeah, I know what you mean. So what?"

"So," Vendredi says slowly. "How about *we* team up?"

My grin falters.

She goes on. "Beck's gone, so I don't have a teammate anymore. With the finals right around the corner, things are going to get tough. Let's pool our strengths, at least until the finale."

"But what about Dean?" I ask.

"We can be a trio. Just like we would be if you had taken me up on the offer to join me and Beck."

The reminder that she already offered me something she's asking for now makes me wince. I'd be a shitty friend to say no, wouldn't I?

Vendredi's confidence wavers here. She laughs awkwardly. "And, to be honest, being in last place doesn't feel great. My main goal in coming on the show wasn't to win, initially; it was to get some exposure, hopefully land an acting agent, but since I've made it this far,

I want to see how much further I can go. I . . . I could use some help from a friend. We could help each other."

The conversation feels slippery. I lose hold on my thoughts even as words start spewing from my mouth. "I know we could. But . . . but Dean and I are partners. Maybe I could talk to him and see . . ."

My words sound half-hearted, even to me. It's true that Vendredi would be a great ally, and more than that, she's my friend. I don't want to disappoint her. But does inviting a third person into our alliance actually help? It's so late in the game. It would defeat the unbreakable-couple front we've spent this whole time building. Plus, that's another person to split points with. That's one more friend I'd have to put to the side when faced with the finish line.

Winning comes first. It *has* to. For Umma.

Softly, I say, "I'm sorry."

Vendredi's expression falls. "No, I understand. That's the nature of the game. I wouldn't expect you to put our friendship above a competition. You're too good of a player to do that." Her gaze drops to the tile, and she smiles awkwardly. The easy, comfortable air between us is disturbed.

She pushes off the counter and makes to leave. My heart seizes with every step she takes. Fuck. Vendredi offered to let me join her and Beck's alliance when she thought I needed it. And I can't return the favor when she needs it now? *Fuck.*

I get along with most people, but it's rare that I can make a real connection with someone the way I have with her. My intensity usually gets in the way of things. It did with Amelia. But not Vendredi. She's the first person who's matched my competitive streak and challenged it instead of being scared by it. I never thought that was possible.

I'm a good player, sure—but am I a good friend?

I want to be.

"Vendredi, wait!"

She turns around at the door. I know if she leaves and I don't say anything, what we have will forever change. Just like it did with Amelia. I can't let that happen again.

I can't lose another friend.

"What about this?" I say. I wear my teeth into my bottom lip. "If . . . If Dean, by *some* chance, happens to go home before either you or I do, we team up then. How's that?"

Vendredi thinks about it. She shuffles over slowly, giving me nothing to work with. Eventually, when she's in front of me, she holds up her pinky. Her mouth turns halfway up.

"I'll take what I can get," she says. "Deal."

I lock my pinky with hers, relieved.

It's fine. I'm not betraying Dean or his trust. Because I won't let it get to a point where either of us goes home before the finale.

31

ARE YOU SERIOUSLY HITTING ON MY MOM RIGHT NOW?

SEYOON

Garrett greets the five of us gathered around the bonfire pit later that morning. He's dressed in a particularly ugly blazer this time. Is that—is that zebra-print? I can't take this any longer. He needs to be jailed.

There's a bounce to his steps as he prepares to launch into the spiel for today's challenge. I can't tell if he's excited or nervous. Either way, not a good sign.

> Can you believe we're already over halfway through the season? We started with twelve, and now, only five of you remain. Oh, my heart could break thinking about it. It hasn't been easy getting here. You know, I think we could all benefit from a mid-season morale booster. So, before I get to today's challenge, I have a surprise for you all. Don't say I never did anything for you.

A trumpet blares through camp. Not a real one; it's just Garrett pressing a button on his sound remote. Who gave him that? All of us tense, waiting for whatever awful surprise he has in store for us to jump out . . . but nothing.

And then, from the camp's entrance, somebody whistles.

A woman with brown skin and bright red lips stretched in a sly smile climbs up the hill and walks toward us, waving. She looks maybe in her early thirties, and given her nice sweater and slacks, she decidedly doesn't seem like a producer or tech for the show, but who knows what—

"*Didi!*"

I startle at Siddharth's voice. He jumps up and sprints full speed at the woman. She beams and opens her arms. Siddharth launches himself at her, choking her in a hug.

A few others crest the hill now. A big, burly man with a thick goatee practically runs into camp. Dean stiffens. "Oh my God," he says. "Dad?"

No way. *No way.* Hope balloons in my chest. I'm already walking toward the hill. Two more people pass under the entrance arch, blocking my view—but then there she is.

It's Umma.

I've sprinted over to her before I make the decision to run. Her arms encircle me. Wetness gathers at my lash line, and I can't push back an overwhelming surge of emotions when I feel her gentle hands rub my back. I hug her tight and blink back tears on her shoulder.

I mean to say a million things, from shouting in excitement to yelling in confusion, but what comes out of my mouth is a meek, "보고싶었어."[5]

"I missed you, too." Umma kisses the top of my head, then pulls back and beams at me. All of my worries from this morning melt away.

---

5. I missed you.

Garrett makes a big speech off to the side about how kind he is to have orchestrated this, but it's easy to tune him out. All around us, happy families reunite, laughing and catching up. Umma asks me to tell her everything. I hold her soft hands in mine and fill her in, from the challenges, to the terrible food, to the very real friends I've made.

"What about you?" I ask, pulling back and scanning her face to see if she's succumbed to starvation or an illness or some other terrible thing that could have happened in the time I wasn't with her. "How have you been?"

Something flits across Umma's face that makes me anxious. "Actually, Seyoon—"

"Jungeun!"

We both turn to see Dean's dad barreling toward us. It's clear where Dean got his height from when his dad stops in front of us, hulking over Umma with a big, toothy smile peeking through his beard. He looks pretty similar to how he did on TV, but nothing like his son. Where did Dean get his sad, orphan-mouse features from?

Without hesitation, his dad pulls Umma into a side hug. She laughs, a bit surprised, but hugs him back.

"Vince. I can't believe it's you."

"I know it. Look at us, back here twenty years later, our kids following in our footsteps. Speaking of." He turns to me and sticks his hand out, eyes crinkling with warmth. "You must be Seyoon. It's good to meet a friend of Dean's."

Dean finally catches up, a hesitant smile flitting on his face as he watches us interact. "Yep. Seyoon's become a good friend." There's a funny pitch to his voice.

That makes Umma perk up. She reaches for Dean and shakes his hand, too, smiling so warmly that he squints as if blinded. "Dean, then. It's wonderful to meet you."

Our mini family reunion catches Garrett's attention, if him trying to slink away unnoticed is anything to go by. Vince steps over and plucks Garrett by the collar of his shirt.

"Don't think you can run away without saying hello," Vince says, patting him on the back hard enough that he stumbles forward.

Umma smiles pleasantly, but there's a glint of something more in her eyes. "You weren't trying to avoid us, were you?"

I prepare for a tense reunion. Dean does the same, watching closely. Umma can't hold an ounce of resentment in her bones, obviously, but Garrett's petty and dramatic to his core. Just look at his blazer.

Garrett feigns surprise, a noticeable sheen of sweat starting to cover his face. "What? No! I didn't even see you guys there. Didn't even notice you, that is. Notice that it *was* you," he babbles, a hint of red on his cheekbones. "Vince, you're looking good. Jungeun, you're more beautiful than ever. Not that you weren't beautiful back then, 'cause believe me, you were. I mean—how are you?"

My jaw falls. Garrett Sleazeball Moxley is melting into a flustered puddle of goo. Because of my *mother.*

"Are you seriously flirting with my mom?" I say, not hiding the disgust in my voice.

Garrett gives me a look like he would strangle me if Umma weren't right there.

Vince leans back and laughs, holding his belly. "You haven't changed at all, Garrett, even after all this time. Hey, what happened to keeping in touch? I sent you a few messages over the years. Too busy to make time for your old camp friends?"

Dean's eyebrows raise, as if surprised by this information.

"Or," Umma interrupts, "did the guilt of betraying us keep you from picking up the phone?"

Garrett shrinks into his blazer as if it could protect him from withering under her scrutiny. "Jungeun . . . Vince, I—"

Umma waves her hand. "It's alright. That was years ago. I'm not angry."

"Yeah. Water under the bridge," Vince says. There's a wrinkle between his eyebrows, but then he looks at Dean, and it smooths out. "Besides, you're giving our kids the opportunity to finish what we started. That's what counts. Thanks for making sure Dean hasn't fallen into a creek or frozen to death in the woods. He's not really the outdoorsy type. I was a little worried he'd—"

"Okay, yes, thanks, Dad," Dean mutters, embarrassed.

A sharp look flits across Umma's expression. She reaches out and holds one of Garrett's hands. He looks down at her, his eyes wide. With her other arm, she wraps it around my shoulders and pulls me into her side.

"That's right," she says. "Thank you for giving our kids a fair chance."

I'd pick up on what she means even if she weren't squeezing Garrett's hand so hard that his knuckles turn white. He didn't give Umma or Dean's dad a fair chance when he told them to go the wrong way in the final challenge.

Garrett looks briefly at me and Dean, his face creasing with remorse I didn't think he was capable of feeling. He drops his head and squeezes Umma's hand back.

Then Garrett steps away and awkwardly clears his throat. "I better wrangle everyone up before Blake yells at me for slowing down the production schedule again. We'll be heading down to set soon." Garrett turns to leave, thinks about something, then turns back around. The tiniest smile ticks up on his face. It's more genuine without his veneers spilling out. "It really is good to see both of you again."

Vince's smile takes up his whole face. Umma, to my horror, *blushes*. "You too."

He walks away then, stealing a megaphone from one of the crew members and yelling into it. "Wrap up the sentiments, campers—it's time for the fourth challenge! Don't worry, you don't have to say goodbye to your families yet; they're coming with us. Chop, chop!"

We all head down the path to the parking lot. It's not until we're settled in the back of the bus together that I bring up our conversation from earlier. "You were going to tell me something."

Umma shifts in her seat. "First, don't panic."

"Well, now I might."

Her lips flatten into a line. "I was let go from the grocery store last week," Umma says. "I only have the hotel position now, and they've been giving me less and less hours these days."

"What? Why would they let you go?"

"They were upset that I was taking time away from work for—" She cuts herself off.

"For what?"

"We don't have to talk about it now. It's not important."

"*Umma*."

Her pursed lips tremble. Eventually Umma gives in. "For all the meetings with the divorce attorneys and the court hearings.

A . . . a date has been set to review custody over you, and I've been told it's unlikely I'll get full custody, not with my finances where they are."

It feels like my entire core has been hollowed out. My lips mouth something, but there's not enough air in my lungs to make the sound.

Umma pulls me back in for another hug, rubbing her hand over my shoulder blades relentlessly, almost as if soothing herself instead of me. "It's okay. As long as I find another well-paying job before the hearing, it should be fine. It *will* be fine, 알았어?"[6]

No. It's not fine. It's *not.*

They're going to take me from Umma. They're going to stick me with a man who's never wanted me. They're going to leave Umma all on her own.

"When's the court hearing?" I pull back and ask.

"September twenty-fifth."

That's well after the season finale. If I win that cash prize, Umma will have everything she needs to prove to the judge that we're financially stable on our own. But if I don't . . .

She kisses my forehead and makes me look into her eyes, saying everything without uttering a single word. Umma always has hope. It shines in her pupils. It usually reflects back in mine, but right now, there's a black hole in me sucking all the light away. And the air. My breaths come shallow and quick.

As the bus starts rolling down the road, I can't stop thinking about the possibility that in a few months, life for us may never be the same. There might not be an *us*. If I don't win the cash prize, the

6. Understand?

courts will order that I stay with Appa. Umma will have to eat dinner alone most nights without anyone there to scoop an extra paddle of rice into her bowl because she doesn't eat enough if I don't make her. She'll watch her Korean variety shows all by herself because even though I don't enjoy them, I always sit on the couch with her when she watches. Who will keep the seat next to her warm? And who will sing songs in the car to help ease her road anxiety?

My arms tingle in a way they never have before. It's like the blood in my veins is acid, popping and bubbling. What if I *lose*? The thought makes me sick. It's a possibility I've always managed to fight off as doubt wriggling in the back of my head. But I can't pretend it's not there. I let myself, for one moment, consider losing. Picture myself boarding the bus and going home today. Or next week. Or at the finals.

No. No, I can't let that happen. My leg shakes. The muddy river running next to the asphalt road outside the window is blurry through the panicked tears welling in my eyes.

I always wanted to win. But now I *can't* lose. Or else I could lose Umma. Which means losing everything.

I won't lose. I won't lose. I won't. I won't.

I can't.

32

MAN, FAMILY REUNIONS SUCK

DEAN

The long, bumpy drive to set is never exactly fun, but it's made so much worse when I'm being interrogated the whole time.

"Come on," Dad says with a lilt to his voice I already don't like. "Tell me more about your guys' alliance."

I glance around the crowded bus pointedly and tap my mic. They've strapped our parents up with their own before we boarded, too. "Can't right now. It's not a good idea to talk strategy so openly."

Dad's whole face lights up. "Smart. Attaboy." He leans in and whispers, although it's unlikely anyone can hear us over the rumble of the road and all the overlapping conversations. "But give me *something*. Come on, I'm dying here."

Knowing Dad, he's not going to quit prying until I give him what he wants. But I'd rather jump out of the emergency exit right now than tell Dad about our little showmance. Actually, I don't know which would be more mortifying: that, or letting him think we're really together. Oh Christ, he'd definitely do something embarrassing if he thought that, like ask Seyoon what she sees in me. Or worse, give us *both* The Talk. It's not below him. I know he would.

Maybe I should tell him the truth. But how, without anyone else figuring out what we're talking about? I consider the safest way to convey at least a nugget of the truth. Enough to get him off my back.

"Do you remember Joanne and Vinnie from season one of *Forest Feud*?" I ask. They were two contestants who formed an alliance and ended up dating midway through the season. Dad nods; of course he'd know that. "This is less like that, and more like Yolanda and Matt." The iconic pair from season fourteen, who pretended to be in love so they'd be voted fan favorite. It was a shitstorm online when it came out that they were just faking it the whole time—another reason Seyoon and I have to keep the cameras fooled just as much as our competitors.

It seems to click for Dad. "Wait, does that—"

"Dad, *enough*."

I don't know who's more surprised, me or him. I've never been the type to put my foot down with him before. Dad's jaw pops open, and I crumble. "Just . . . not here. The game's still on."

Dad blinks, then shuts his fallen jaw. "Alright," he concedes. "I'll leave you alone. For now."

He ruffles my hair. Whatever—it's the stylist's problem, not mine.

After what feels like forever, we arrive at the private lot, then turn onto a different road until we reach a large, flat clearing. Entirely out of place among the nature reserve is the giant, wooden stage with a tall, metal backdrop adorned with velvet curtains. Stage lights encompass the roof, grazing the branches of the evergreens towering over. Four lecterns line the stage, each with a microphone, and to the side of the stage, there are five chairs. In front of the curtain is a huge screen with FOREST FACTS FRENZY! flashing in obnoxious letters.

My heart leaps. "That's—"

"The challenge from the tenth season!" Dad finishes. We look at each other and grin.

We all load off. Our guardians are guided to the spectator seats, and we're directed behind the lecterns, each with a red button and a tablet. Seyoon and I share one, of course. There's an odd glaze to her expression she doesn't shake off even as Garrett hops onto the stage and the cameras start rolling.

> Welcome, contestants and families, to Forest Facts Frenzy!
>
> For those not familiar, this is a fan-favorite trivia challenge from the show's original run. You'll be tested on your knowledge of the old seasons and iconic contestants who came before you, including yours truly. It's fitting given we're a reboot, right?
>
> The format is straightforward. On each of your lecterns is a big red button. I'll ask you a question, and the answer options will appear on the screen. The first person to buzz in gets to answer, but if you're wrong, the rest of you get the chance to steal.
>
> And now for my next demonstration of kindness: Each of you gets ten points to start. Blake, load 'em up.

Rewatching every season of *Forest Feud* my whole life is finally about to pay off. This challenge was made for me. I seek out Dad, who looks as thrilled as I feel. He shoots me two thumbs-up from the sideline and mouths, *You got this*. It feels good to make him proud.

Blake, behind the setup of cameras, signals at one of the tech assistants. The sound of coins clanging against each other plays from the speakers above as the screens in front of our lecterns reflect ten points each.

There's a short interlude for the videographers and camera techs to adjust their equipment from filming Garrett's intro to the next section of the scene. Seyoon's still pale, and it hits me why. I nudge her leg with my knee under the lectern.

"Hey," I whisper. "You don't need to be nervous. I know you haven't seen the other seasons, but I got us. You can count on me."

She scans my face. She chuckles half-heartedly. "I know you're trying to comfort me, but your woeful gerbil eyes aren't exactly reassuring."

"Are you flirting with me?"

Seyoon barks out a surprised cackle, and I warm up a bit to have been the one to make her laugh.

She relaxes into a small smile. "Thanks, Dean."

The production crew is ready. Blake, sitting in a director's chair off the stage on the ground behind Garrett, signals for filming to resume.

"Campers, I'll go easy on you for the first question," Garrett says. He shuffles the notecards in his hands. "Ready? Who was the first person to win *Forest Feud*?"

The answer options pop up on the big screen behind us as well as the tablet on our lecterns. My eyes quickly scan over each option in just a second or two. Easy—

BZZRT!

Carter slams his buzzer before my hand's off the table. "A. Ryan Alley."

The sound of coins jingling rings out as five points are added to Carter's screen. He looks smug.

"How the fuck did he read that so quickly?" Seyoon hisses, panic lacing her words.

There's no time to answer her, because Garrett's already moved on to question number two. "How many years was *Forest Feud*'s original run on air?"

Seyoon's quick reflexes get her to the buzzer first. "Fifteen."

Garrett makes an incorrect buzzer sound with his mouth.

Adrenaline flushes through me as I slam the buzzer again. "Seventeen," I correct. "There was a season that got delayed."

"Hmm, one of you was wrong, and one of you was right. Do they get points for that, Blake?"

The woman purses her lips, thinking. After a minute, she nods. "For that round, yes. But since you two are on a team, please make sure you are giving a unified answer."

Seyoon's white-knuckling the side of the lectern. "Relax," I whisper. "Let's take it easy, okay?"

She nods hastily, but there's still something wrong. "Easy. Yeah. Relaxed."

Then Garrett's back to it, leaving us hardly any room to think. There's a scramble to the buzzer every time—a race I keep losing. Fuck. I can read the answer options quick enough, and I know which one is correct, but my reflexes can't compete with Carter's, Siddharth's, or Vendredi's. Seyoon could, but she's too busy carefully reading over the options on the tablet much longer than everyone, looking startled when someone else answers before she's finished.

"How many times has a contestant thrown up on screen?"

"Oh!" Siddharth screams, practically jumping on his lectern to slam the buzzer first. "C. One hundred times."

"Wha—one *hundred* times? You really think we shot, edited, and aired a hundred contestants hurling? Wrong."

"Aw, man."

"Which toe did season-four contestant Robbie Evans lose in the first challenge?"

Bzzrt. "D. His big toe?" Five points to Vendredi.

The sound of coins jingling over the speakers grates on my nerves, a reminder of all the points we're *not* getting. I glance over at the parent section and regret it. Dad's standing up, biting his fist like it's taking every ounce of his strength not to jump on stage and interject himself. Seyoon's not looking much better. Her foot bounces restlessly on the stage.

Garrett flips his card. "What number—"

Seyoon slams the buzzer so hard the plastic cracks. "C."

What the hell is she doing?

"Hey!" Carter yells, pointing at us like an angry debate candidate. "The answer options haven't popped up, she didn't read them. That's cheating."

Garrett huffs. "Maybe not cheating, but it's certainly annoying. From now on, anyone who buzzes in before reading all the answer options will face a ten-point deduction. Got that?" He directs the question to Blake and the woman running the computers depositing points onto our screen. Blake nods.

Seyoon drums her fingers nervously next to the buzzer. "What happened to taking it easy?" I hiss.

"Sorry." She winces. "I . . . I can't read the options fast enough. A one-in-four chance of getting it right didn't sound bad."

"That's a three-in-four chance of getting it *wrong*. Let me do the answering, alright? You're going to get us a penalty."

"But everyone's beating us to the buzzer! We're going to lose," Seyoon snaps. "We *can't* lose."

My head jerks back. I examine her splotchy face, her chest heaving with breaths, the way her pupils jump around. "I know we can't. I won't let us, okay?"

She blinks, nodding, but she doesn't seem as reassured as I'd hoped she'd be.

The game goes on, with more questions being tossed left and right, some no-brainers, some that we all struggle with. I manage to sneak a few more points in, but none of it seems to settle Seyoon, who looks out of it every time she glances at her mom on the sidelines.

Garrett shuffles his cards. "Alright, this question is worth double points. You hear that?" Seyoon leans forward. "When did *Forest Feud* switch from a voting-based elimination to a point-based system?"

Not even a single millisecond after all four options appear on screen, a buzzer goes off. *Who the hell can read* that *fast?*

In shock, I realize it was Seyoon.

Fuck me.

"Well?" Garrett asks.

"Um," Seyoon says. She turns to me expectantly, desperately. I quickly look back at our table to review the answer options.

Siddharth yells and points at us. "Hey, hey! That's cheating! They didn't finish reading the options before buzzing in! They're buzzer-happy!"

Garrett throws his hands up. "Seriously?"

Her mouth opens and shuts like a fish. She looks between her mom, then me, then Garrett. "I'm sorry," she says, voice thin and nervous in a way it never is. "I panicked. Sorry, it won't happen again."

But a noise like the Pac-Man death sound effect plays over the speakers anyway, and we both watch in dread as ten points drain from our counter.

Vendredi leans across the aisle to hit Seyoon in the shoulder. "Dude! Get it together. What's gotten into you?"

"I'm . . ."

Her hands are shaking. There's motion just past her, at the side of the stage. Her mom is standing up now, expression folded with worry. Seyoon notices, and the tremors start to wrack her arms. Dad's still standing too. He's shaking his head with a frown, looking right at me. My stomach knots.

Despite everyone's eyes on us, I grab her hand. Seyoon looks up, her face a bright, cherry red.

"You promised yourself you'd never freeze again. That's what you said the other day." I try to smile for her. "Come on, sunshine. We can't lose, right?"

Something about my words has the opposite effect than I intended. Her face pales like she's going to faint or be sick or some other non-Seyoon-ish reaction. She shuts her eyes. "I'm sorry."

Then she clambers off the stage.

"Seyoon!" I call, but she ignores all of us and hurries away from the set, embarking down the road we came on. Her mom doesn't hesitate before chasing after her. I move to follow, but Vendredi holds her arm up to block me.

"If you don't play, *neither* of you will earn any more points," she says sternly.

I swallow. I look after Seyoon's rapidly disappearing form; at Garrett, Blake, and the cameras; and at Dad. I can comfort her later, but only if we're both still here.

I continue to play. It's the best thing I can do for her.

Somehow, I'm able to push Seyoon's terrified expression out of my mind and focus on the trivia. I crack my knuckles. Wipe the sweat from my palms. I focus. I will the muscles in my hand to jump to the buzzer faster. Inevitably, the questions get harder and include more obscure references that only someone who has watched reruns of the show every week for their whole life would know.

Just my luck.

"Final question, folks, this one for bonus points as well," Garrett says. "In season five, the runner-up blamed one thing for his loss. What was it?"

Everyone else stares puzzled at the options on screen. Everyone but me. I hit the buzzer. "D. The runner-up was Tate Pillipchuck. He blamed his competitor's annoying breathing for distracting him, not knowing they had chronic obstructive pulmonary disease. He later went on an apology run on all the major morning talk shows."

I get the points, and an eyeroll from Carter. Finally, I feel confident about a challenge.

After the game ends, Garrett goes to the tech setup and reaches over the woman working it to stab his finger on her keyboard. All our point boards fade to black.

"No spoilers," he says, doing a pretty good job at forcing cheer and playfulness into his voice. If I hadn't just spent the last month listening to him blabber, I'd think it was real. "We'll reveal the final point standings at elimination."

Filming wraps. They load up the equipment first, giving us a few minutes to catch our breath before heading back to camp. I plop down on the edge of the stage as everyone starts clearing the area and walking toward the bus. I see Dad catch up to Garrett and talk to him for a few minutes, then he comes to join me. Our legs hang off the edge.

"Damn," he says. "I didn't see the final score, but there's no way you're not in the lead. You *killed* that, Dean. You made your old man real proud."

I chuckle, the adrenaline finally wearing off and leaving me drained. "Thank God for weekly TV nights."

Dad's grin fades. "That, uh, was unfortunate about that partner of yours, though. Is she . . . always like that?"

The urge to defend Seyoon rises like bile. I swallow it down on reflex, until I remember the way her voice cracked when she apologized before running off stage, and the words spill out. "Seyoon's the strongest person I've met, in these games or out."

Dad sighs. He's not listening to me, not really. He scoots closer and lowers his voice. "Hey. I checked with Garrett on the rules. If you end your alliance before elimination, they'll divide your points by which questions you answered. You'd keep the majority, obviously.

That means you won't pay for the deduction she got, and you won't split what you earned."

His words ping-pong around my brain. I don't know which train of thought to hold on to first. "Why would you ask Garrett that? I'm not going to—"

"Did you or did you not come here to win?" Dad cuts me off.

Because of course he's not listening to me. Of course he doesn't understand me. He gives me a sympathetic look, but it just makes me feel like a child.

"Buddy, I know this is tough. I've been there. That's why I'm trying to help you. Learn from my mistakes. Your alliance has to end sometime."

It has to end sometime.

I've known that from the very second Seyoon suggested we team up. Only one of us can win. The numbers run automatically in my head. Did I answer enough questions? Who earned the most points? It was such chaos, there's no way I could have kept track of what was going on, but I know it must be tight. Splitting the points will make things tighter.

And yet, that's the last thing I care about right now.

I stand up. My vision swarms, but I hold my ground and my voice steady. "Seyoon's not just my teammate. She's my friend. I'm not going to betray her, and I don't care if you disagree."

Dad rises to his feet too. His face pulls down. "What has gotten into you? This isn't like you."

It occurs to me that I can still turn back. I don't have to shatter the safe, comfortable dynamic we have. The *only* thing we have. The idea of venturing forward is terrifying.

But if Seyoon were here, she'd speak up. And knowing her, even for the small amount of time I have, has turned me into the kind of person who doesn't want to be paralyzed by fear anymore.

"This *is* me, Dad. And this is my decision to make, not yours." My voice raises with every word, steadier than I actually feel. "I know you think I need you looking out for me, but I don't. I need you to trust me. *We* need you to trust *us*—me and Meredith."

"Meredith?" he asks, stunned. "What does this have to do with Meredith?"

"*Everything*." I take a deep breath and try again, calmer. "I know we're your kids, but you can't treat us like children anymore. You may not understand our choices, but you have to respect them. Can you do that for us, please? Both of us."

I've never seen this look on Dad's face before. The wide eyes, the screwed brows, the parted mouth. This is it. New territory. Even though it scares me, the knowledge that Meredith would be proud of me makes it easier. I'm finally standing up for myself. For her. For Seyoon.

Dad's silence is dreadful. But, eventually, he sighs, and it sounds like conceding.

"You really are like your mom," he says gently. "You're right; I don't understand. But I guess I don't have to. I love you, Dean, and I don't want to push you away. I'll respect whatever decisions you make, here and back home." He rubs the side of his neck. "Meredith's too. I trust the both of you to do what's right for yourselves."

I take a careful deep breath. "Really?"

Dad smiles. "Yeah. Of course. I know you won't let me down."

A smile spreads across my own face, mirroring his for the first time. "I won't."

33

OKAY, STUART LITTLE'S NOT SO BAD, ACTUALLY

SEYOON

Umma, the kind, merciful soul that she is, pretends to believe me when I tell her I'm just feeling sick. Maybe it's because I do look pale and weak, or because both of us know that telling the truth wouldn't change anything. On the solemn ride back to Mount Rainier, she lets me rest my head on her shoulder and rubs my abdomen, quietly humming the Korean song she would sing to me when I was a child with a stomachache.

We film a goodbye scene in the parking lot. I tune out whatever Garrett says. When it's Umma's turn to board the bus, I hug her, ignoring all the eyes and cameras trained on us. I let myself be swallowed in the feeling of being small again, of searching for comfort in my parent instead of feeling like I need to be the pillar. Umma's always been strong. I know this. I just want to be strong for her so that she doesn't have to be all the time.

"미안해,"[7] I mumble.

"무슨 소리야?"[8] she chastises. "I told you already. Winning isn't everything."

---

7. Sorry.

8. What are you saying?

"But I didn't come here to embarrass your name and legacy, and if I don't win, I'm—"

"There is no legacy to uphold here. These games aren't all we are." She pulls back and pats my cheek, smiling. "The only name you should worry about making is your own. You don't need to be a winner to be Seyoon."

For the first time, the two separate in my mind, and I consider who I am outside of how well I do.

The truth is that I don't know.

Once all the parents leave, we head back to camp and hardly get a chance to collect ourselves before it's time for elimination. I think I'm going to be sick for real this time. If I throw up on the campfire, does that make me more sympathetic, or pathetic? I don't have it in me to lean over and ask Dean how the rest of the challenge went. I'm too ashamed to face him.

The cameras roll, and Garrett launches into his spiel. The slow, ragged beating of my heart drowns out anything he says. I clench my eyes shut and dig my nails into my knees. It's happening. There's nothing I can do to stop it.

It's only when gasps surf the semicircle of contestants that I dare look up. Luke has turned the leaderboard around.

The new scores are revealed.

1ST	CARTER MOXLEY	79 PTS
2ND	DEAN PARKER	71 PTS
3RD	SEYOON SHIN	65 PTS
4TH	VENDREDI TENGKU	52 PTS
5TH	SIDDHARTH PATEL	46 PTS

Even without attempting to do the mental math, it's obvious from the jump in rank I got that Dean earned us an *unthinkable* number of points. All on his own. And he still split them with me. Finally, I turn to him, my jaw nearly on the grass. He's already looking at me.

The corner of his mouth turns up, his dimples appearing, as if to say, *We made it.*

Would you look at those rankings! Everyone played a mean game, but no one could compete with Dean's *Forest Feud* knowledge. I think you know more about the series than I do, quite frankly.

Siddharth, I am truly sorry to see you go. Really—you're our personality hire. Do you have any final . . . what are you doing? Why are you coming up here? Are you—oh, aw, a hug. Now, isn't that sweet? Thanks, kid. If it was up to me, you'd be staying.

CONFESSION TAPE—Siddharth Patel, Contestant

Man. It's my own fault. My sister talks a lot about her time on the show, but I have a habit of tuning out what she says. Boy, did I regret that when it came to all those trivia questions. It's alright, though. I had a hell of a time here, and I made some great friends. Hey, at least now I can hang out with Adin again.

The main reason I wanted to come on the show wasn't to win, anyway. I just wanted to impress my nieces and nephews. Get some cool points with them. But they're a tough crowd. I think even if I *did* win, they'd still make fun of me.

Siddharth wraps each of us in a bone-crushing hug, including every single crew member in the area, which takes some time and ruins some of the footage when he tackles the camera operators. Once we say goodbye, we're dismissed to enjoy an evening off for once.

Dean approaches me. I brace for anger, or at least a snarky comment about my ego failing me now, but he doesn't seem upset.

"Hey," he says gently. "What happened earlier?"

"I . . . got sick."

Dean steps a little closer, pressing the back of his hand to my forehead. I scan every inch of his face, checking for signs of resentment. Judgment. But nothing.

"You *are* hot," he says, pulling away. "Your temperature, I mean. Obviously, you know what I mean." He shuts his eyes. "Can we talk?"

That's the last thing I want to do right now, because I know Dean's going to pry the truth out of me, with his pouty lips and his big, brown eyes. Damn him and his Stuart Little–like aura and compassion. I don't have it in me. "Uh," I say, looking around for an excuse. "Actually, I was going to go for a swim."

"Can I join?"

Which is how we end up sitting on the dock together, shivering in swimsuits, our legs dipped in the cold water.

The entire lake is painted lilac, a glimmering reflection of the cotton-candy sky above. The few icecaps still left on Mount Rainier's peak are pink in the dying light. Only the crickets humming in the grass and the easy sloshing of the waves rolling up on the rocks underscore the quiet. It helps slow my rapidly thumping heart. Dean's presence helps, too.

He bumps his knee against mine and points at my water bottle. "Do you mind?"

I hand it over, and he thanks me before taking a long swig. His Adam's apple bobs as he drinks. I follow the motion with my eyes, up his throat and along the curve of his jawline. His eyes are shut. Long, blond eyelashes graze the delicate skin of his cheek.

When we first met, Dean wouldn't have ever dared think about asking to drink from my bottle, and if he did . . . well, I'd still let him, but I would think it was weird. Something's changed. I don't know when it happened on his end—because I have been perfectly terrific company the whole time—but for me? Maybe it was when he took me stargazing. Or when he helped me prank Carter. Or when he jumped in the lake with me, doggy-paddling while apologizing for acting like a jerk. No, actually, it was that first night, when he wrapped my hands up in gauze. I knew then that I wanted to be his friend.

And we are now. Dean and I are friends.

I tug the inside of my cheek between my teeth so my lip doesn't wobble. I let down my friend today. I let down Dean. It's not easy for me to make a real friend, someone I trust enough to be vulnerable around—

"Hey, you fucker, I said you could have a sip, not the whole thing!"

Dean only grins, passing me back my empty bottle. "I saved a drop in there for you."

I huff, taking the final swig. I don't think about the fact that our lips touched the same rim, because why would that matter? We've *kissed.* Which also doesn't matter, because it was for show. Our friendship? That's what's real. That's why this hurts.

Quiet swells between us. Eventually, Dean prods. "So," he asks. "Why can't you lose?"

I think it's one of the dumbest questions I've ever heard, until I realize he's specifically referring to what I said during the challenge before my epic, caught-in-4K-quality freakout. I sigh and look over at him. The last rays of daylight wrap Dean's features in a warm, tangerine hue. He meets my eyes these days with so much more confidence than when we first met.

He's pretty.

The thought springs in my mind like a flower perking up in the rain. I would tell him that, but I don't know how to explain I mean "pretty" in the same way the sunset is coloring the sky right now. The kind of beauty that you need to take a step back from to fully appreciate every detail.

Even though I've never needed a shoulder to cry on, I find myself, for once, actually wanting one. Dean's shoulders look pretty sturdy.

"If I don't win the cash prize, my mom and I could lose our home," I say, muttering to the water below. I don't see any cameras around, and since we're in our swimsuits, we didn't have to put our mics on. In this quiet, empty moment alone with Dean, I feel safe enough to be vulnerable. Honest.

"My parents are going through a divorce right now," I continue. "My dad's a bum, but he's the one with a stable job, not her. If I don't win the money, the courts could force me to live with him. My mom had just let me know the situation's getting worse. That's why I was out of it during the challenge. So . . ." I kick my foot under the water and watch the ripples bubble to the surface. "I can't lose. Because I can't lose her."

"Oh," Dean says. "I'm . . . I'm so sorry, Seyoon." He frowns at our distorted reflections in the lake. "I'm realizing I never asked why you were here."

"I guess it didn't come up. I assumed it was the typical stuff for you, redeeming a family legacy, etcetera, etcetera."

He snorts. "Well, I am doing it to make my dad happy, partially. But I'm mostly here for my sister. She wants—*needs* to leave our tiny town. Winning is how I can help make that happen."

"You're a good brother."

"You're a good daughter."

My chest warms. I know there's not really incentive to, but I reach over and lay my hand atop his. He flips it over so we're palm to palm. It doesn't mean anything. It's just a touch. Friends hold hands too.

"I'm sorry about earlier. I didn't help us earn a single point. I even cost us some," I say quietly. "Thank you for sharing yours with me. You saved my ass. I don't know how you got all those answers right—you're incredible."

He scratches his head. "It's nothing."

"Just take the compliment, dude."

Dean laughs. "Really, though. It's nothing. Remember how much I needed you in the survival skills challenge? We balance each other out. That's why we're partners." He smirks. "Besides, we'll win so many points back, it won't matter that we have to split them, right?"

"I said that to you."

"I know."

"You still want to work with me? Despite everything?"

"Of course I do. Because of everything."

It's startlingly honest. Dean seems to realize this and rubs the side of his neck, looking down at our interlocked hands instead of at me. No one's ever wanted me *because* of everything. Dean has seen me at my lowest, my meanest, my weakest. He's seen me when I don't win. And he's still here.

Heat blossoms from my ears to my chest. I haven't proven I'm worth it, yet Dean is *still* here.

His face turns pink, but it could be the lighting from the sunset, so I don't linger on it. Dean swallows. "Seyoon?" he says quietly, like he wants to tell me something devastatingly important. It makes my ears ring.

"Yeah?"

Then Dean inches closer. My breath stalls. He cups my cheek with his palm and presses a gentle kiss on my lips. A graze that lights my senses on fire. My mouth tingles when he pulls away, and I realize I was leaning in, chasing his touch.

"What—" My voice cracks. "What was that for?"

There's something in Dean's expression that makes my stomach tie up into knots. His eyes flit over every part of my face, as if looking for something. An answer. I'm not sure what his question is, so I keep my features neutral. Dean meets my gaze, then he shuts his eyes briefly.

"I think I saw somebody up there. Maybe one of the other campers," he says. "Figured we should show everyone we're still on good terms after the challenge."

For some reason, my stomach dips. "Right. That's smart." He is smart. That's why we're allies.

I glance over my shoulder to check, though, and don't see anyone.

Silence falls over us as we watch the sun dip all the way down. It's not until several minutes later, when I'm thinking of breaking the quiet to suggest we head back, that footsteps sound on the dock behind us.

I turn around and squint to make out who it is in the rapidly dimming twilight. It's Vendredi, clad in a swimsuit.

"Hey, lovebirds, why are you still dry?" She stops just in front of us and points at Dean. "Can you not swim?"

"No, I can, technically. Not well, but—*AH!*"

She pushes him over the ledge, and he falls back into the water with a terrific splash. Dean bobs up a second later, looking like a drowned rat. I burst into laughter. He watches me, and his frown smooths out.

Vendredi opens her arms for me. "Hey, come here."

I stand and warily embrace her. I relax when she rocks us back and forth. "Are you doing better now?" Vendredi says in my ear, her concern palpable.

"Yeah." It's nice to be able to answer honestly. She hums and gives me a big squeeze.

"I'm so glad." Then she pulls us both over the edge.

The frigid water swallowing my body is enough to reset my nervous system. I surface with a gasp, then laugh so hard I nearly inhale lake water. The burn in my lungs is the first ache in my chest today that's felt good. Really good.

34

I'M SO LOVESICK, I MIGHT HURL

DEAN

What Seyoon confided in me yesterday doesn't leave my mind. I tossed and turned all night thinking about it until she kicked my mattress from below. I try to enjoy the day off we have while the crew sets up the next challenge, but even when she dragged me out to play cards with her in the sun and go on a walk with Vendredi, I couldn't stop thinking about it.

God. She's under *so* much pressure. No wonder she's that competitive. If I don't win, life goes on. If Seyoon doesn't? Life as she knows it will be over. She could lose her home, her family. Honestly, I can't believe she's kept it under wraps this long. For a girl who loves the sound of her own voice, she always shies away from talking about the important things. Or, maybe, the things she's scared people will judge her for.

I realize I'm being quieter than usual when, at lunch, it distracts Seyoon and Vendredi away from their spirited debate about which camper would be most likely to survive a zombie apocalypse. Beck would have liked this conversation. I was voted first to perish, by the way.

"What's up with the long face?" Vendredi asks me.

"That's just his face," Seyoon says.

"No, his face is usually like this." She pulls a small frown and pushes down on her forehead to fix her eyebrows in a crabby, unimpressed stare. Seyoon snorts. I scowl, then stop when I realize I'm making that face.

"Nothing's up," I say, looking for an excuse. "I'm just wondering how much more salad Seyoon will cram into her mouth before she chokes."

Seyoon grins around the fork of lettuce in her mouth but swallows before speaking this time. "Aw, you care about me."

"Obviously I—" I shut my mouth so hard, my teeth click. I wet my lips. "I just want you to stop spitting little leaf pieces at me."

Seyoon rolls her eyes but does finish eating before diving back into survival rankings. I watch the way her lips wrap around the fork and rub my eyes until I see spots.

Eventually, I excuse myself to take a shower. The crew are busy milling around as usual. Carter is talking with Garrett and Blake near the center of camp, which gives me pause. Blake notices and waves me over, dismissing Carter before I get there.

"Dean! There you are. I wanted to talk to you," she says, smiling brightly. Garrett, uncharacteristically of him, stays silent and just a step behind her, but still watching.

"Am I in trouble?" It's always my first thought.

"No, not at all. I wanted to ask you how Seyoon's been holding up. I haven't run into her today, but I figured you might be a better person to ask."

That gets my attention. "Why wouldn't Seyoon be okay?"

Blake looks around before holding her clipboard to her chest and stepping forward. Her brows are pinched in worry.

"Well, her breakdown at the trivia challenge was a point of concern, obviously. I know she's under a lot of pressure, and seeing her mother seemed to worsen things."

My eyebrows jump. "Seyoon's told you why she's under a lot of pressure?"

Blake laughs. "No, but I heard her talking to her mother yesterday before the challenge. Caught the lowdown." She taps my clip-on mic. "Come on. You're our resident reality-TV expert; surely you know we're always listening."

The idea of Seyoon's sensitive conversation with her mom being caught on tape *and* broadcast to the world makes my stomach fold. *I'm never going to enjoy reality TV again after this*, I think.

"I just want to make sure the stress isn't getting to her." Apprehension drips from Blake's every word. "With how bad her family's situation is, I know her standing in the game must be weighing heavily on her. Frankly, if she doesn't do well in tomorrow's challenge, she could be going home." The woman lays her hand on my shoulder, squeezing. "As someone who clearly cares about her, I'm sure you're already thinking about this."

The reminder of everything Seyoon—sweet, sunny Seyoon—is going through is an iron grip of guilt around my heart. She has so much on the line, and she never lets it show. An image pops into my mind of her face when we kissed on the dock yesterday. She looked even more beautiful than ever in the soft, private glow of the sunset. I wish I could pocket that moment in time and hold on to it forever.

But we don't have forever. Semifinals are tomorrow. And Seyoon could lose so much more than a million dollars.

"Dean?"

I startle. Both Blake and Garrett are watching me now. Blake seems worried, but I can't get a read on Garrett's expression.

"Sorry," I say. "I hear you. I'll keep an eye on her."

"Good." Blake squeezes my arm once more and steps back. "The number of points you collectively earn—*and* have to split—entirely determines who makes it to the finale." She lowers her voice and smiles. "I hope the both of you make it."

I smile distractedly, then she lets me go. Now it's Blake's words that race in my mind. I want to win, of course. And I also want Seyoon. *Of course.*

For just the tiniest fraction of a second, I let myself entertain the idea that Seyoon kissed me back yesterday for the same reason I wanted to kiss her. That she may want me, too.

It doesn't matter, though, whether it's true or not. Because the reality is that I don't need to guess which one Seyoon needs more: me or the money that will save her family. The only question left unanswered is, which do *I* need more?

When I first realized I had fallen for Seyoon, back under that sky full of constellations she spent all night pointing out to me, I didn't know what I was going to do about my feelings.

But I know now.

35

MY PATIENCE VS. THE AUDACITY. WHO WILL WIN? LET'S FIND OUT!

SEYOON

Either it's just a coincidence or Garrett is an irritating son of a bitch on purpose, but he always takes an extra long time on his intro spiel when it's devastatingly hot outside. He cuts mid-sentence and asks to start over because a bead of sweat rolled down his forehead and "We can't have that on tape. Are you serious? America can't think the sexiest host of all time has body odor. Which he doesn't."

Me, Carter, Vendredi, and Dean shift impatiently in our swimsuits, the rocks of the lake's shore digging into our bare feet. Not the one at camp—we're on another private lot, this one with its own lake. It's about as big as Summit Lake, but it's missing the surrounding forest and mountain scenery. Nothing that can't be added in post.

My attention keeps wandering to Dean standing stiffly next to me in line. I nudge him gently. "What's up with you?"

He startles. "Nothing. I'm just nervous about the challenge." He nods at the lake. "I'm not a good swimmer."

"Is that it? Hey, don't worry, I'll carry us this round." I flip my ponytail and flash him a grin. "I'll earn enough points to get us through to the finale."

Dean smiles back, but it doesn't quite reach his eyes. "Yeah."

He's been off all morning. In fact, ever since yesterday. No, since I vented to him about everything at stake with Umma. A familiar worry creeps up along the back of my skull, whispering into my ear that I've scared him off. I don't remember everything I said that evening, but Dean probably heard, *Hey, remember how I said you should team up with me because I'm really strong? Guess what, I'm actually not!*

No, no, come on. That's not fair; Dean is my friend. He's proven he doesn't think that way of me, even in my lowest moments.

Carter groans, interrupting my doom-spiraling and Garrett's millionth take. "Can you hurry up?" he snaps.

Garrett slumps in defeat. He tries to, at least, but it's difficult with the pink floaty tube around his waist. Did I forget to mention the pink floaty tube? Yeah, that's because I'm trying to pretend it's not there.

Finally, we get rolling.

> Players, congratulations on making it to the semifinals. It's a good thing you packed your swimsuits, because things are about to get—
>
> . . . I'm receiving word from my executive producer that I can't say that things are going to get "wet." But I digress.
>
> Today's challenge is the Aquatic Showdown: a three-part race across the lake. The first part is what I call the Tubes of Terror. Your first task is to hold on to a speedboat as our totally licensed driver takes you very safely to the floating dock in the middle, where the second leg of the triathlon begins: the Leap of

Lake! Like, "leap of faith," get it? There, you'll put your physical skills to the test in this inflatable course, get to the dock on the other side, and swim the remaining half mile to shore for the third leg of the race.

Only three of you will be moving on to the finale after this. However, our friends at the bottom of the scoreboard don't need to worry, because there are *major* points at play here. The first person to reach the shore wins . . . wait for it . . . *wait* . . . forty points. Second place gets thirty. Third gets twenty. And fourth, ten. Meaning, it's still anyone's game. How you perform today could bring you from dead last to the top of the leaderboard, and vice versa.

Everything rides on this challenge. And it's a swimming competition.

I've never gotten so lucky in my life.

Dean raises his hand.

"Yes?" Garrett calls on him.

"I would like to split from my alliance with Seyoon."

Huh?

My brain whirs to a slow, stalling, tripping to make sense of what I think I've heard.

I turn without being aware of it, as if somebody else is steering me by the shoulders. Vendredi's jaw nearly unhinges as she stares at us. Even the crew members look shocked. One of the sound operators drops their mic and hurries to pick it back up. Carter looks ahead, uncaring. Dean doesn't meet my eye.

Garrett's grip on his floaty loosens, and it squeaks down his legs. "Excuse me?"

My senses stumble back into me with the force of a slap on the back. "Dean," I say. A short laugh hiccups out of me. "Stop kidding around."

He turns to me, having the gall to look apologetic. "We both knew this alliance would have to end sometime."

"Well, yeah, but this is not the time! What are you thinking?" I gesture across the vast expanse of water in front of us. "You seriously don't want to split points with me on this challenge? I'm a state-champ swimmer. You can barely doggy-paddle."

"Seyoon—"

"I know I mooched off your points last challenge, but I'm going to make it up." I step forward and reach out for his hand. He pulls away with a wince. Hurt digs spikes along my skin. "What happened to wanting to work together? *Because* of everything?" I throw his words back at him.

Cameras swarm us on every side, nudging Carter and Vendredi out of the way. I feel claustrophobic, stuck between a dozen empty black lens reflections and the cold, empty glaze in Dean's eyes.

The muscle in Dean's clenched jaw jumps. "Seyoon," he grits out, like it pains him. "This is for the best."

For a second, grief overtakes me. *Just like that?* I want to say. *It's over?*

"But," I utter quietly. Pathetically. The sadness burns my throat like a gulp of salt water. "I thought we were friends?"

I hate myself as soon as the words escape my lips and enter the dozens of mic feeds surrounding us. Dean winces and inhales deeply.

"We *were*. But now we're rivals," he says. "I'm . . . I'm sorry, Seyoon."

He's really doing this. I can't believe it. I knew Dean was a good actor, a great strategist. It's me who was the idiot for believing he wasn't acting the *entire* time.

To my horror, heat pricks my eyes. The camera operator behind Dean steps forward to get a close-up shot of me, and I drop my head before anyone can see me crying. The pitying looks from Vendredi and the crew members are like knives dragging across my skin. I turn away from Dean, clenching my jaw so hard that my teeth squeak against each other. He doesn't deserve another word from me.

It's my fault for thinking I could make a real friend in a place like this. It's my fault for letting him see me, all of me, the weak and the ugly bits.

I'm not making that mistake again. And I'm not holding back.

Garrett clears his throat. "Alright then. Dean and Seyoon will not be splitting points this round. Got that, Blake?"

Blake, to the side, nods and scribbles on her clipboard, her expression carefully neutral, as usual. "Noted."

"Okay. Let's *dive* right in, campers."

A few paces down the shore, the speedboat's engine roars to life. Waves lick at the four inflatable tubes bobbing unsteadily in the water, attached by ropes to the stern. Vendredi squeezes my hand before she jogs over. We all wade into the water and each grab an inner tube. Dean and I end up in the middle, with Carter and Vendredi on either side of us. The others wriggle inside, wearing their tubes around their waists. I decide to hold on to mine like a floaty rather than climb inside; it'll make it easier to jump off and onto the dock. I have a feeling the boat won't be slowing down to give us time to climb out.

I hope Dean likes losing is my last thought before Garrett blows a whistle.

The boat takes off, yanking the ropes so abruptly that all of us scream.

Whoever is driving this boat does *not* let their foot off the gas pedal. I grip my tube so tightly, I fear the plastic will pop. The boat hits a current and sends us flying a foot and a half into the air. To my horror, Dean is flung off. His yell fills my ear as he tumbles and lands in the water with a huge splash.

"Dean!" I call out of reflex, only for a wave of icy water to wash over me, flooding my nose and mouth.

Through his megaphone, barely audible above the monstrous roaring of the speedboat and the wind whizzing in my ears, Garrett calls out:

> If you fall off, swim! You're not out of the game until you give up!

I look back as the boat speeds away, spotting the blip in the water that is Dean, swimming desperately to catch up. My stomach knots in worry—until I push the fear away. Not my problem anymore. He wanted this.

The floating dock gets closer and closer, and as I thought, the boat shows no sign of slowing down. In fact, it begins speeding up, if that's even possible. At the very last second, a few feet away from the dock, the boat dips left so hard, I swear it'll tip over and capsize. Our ropes snap around like a whip. Carter and Vendredi struggle to escape their inner tubes—but not me. I let go of my inflatable lifeline and . . .

CONFESSION TAPE—Seyoon Shin, Contestant

> What was going through my head? You mean when I was flying through the air, soaring clear over the dock I had strategically envisioned myself landing on? Yeah, just one thing.

"*Fuck!*" I scream.

My strangled, panicked yell dies when my back slaps the water and the air punches from my lungs. It stings, sure, but not worse than my ego does as I imagine the "*Ooh!*" sound effect the producers will lay over this moment in the final cut.

I bob back up and gasp for air, finding the dock only a few feet away. Okay, not bad, actually.

I swim over and heave myself up on the platform. I'm the first one here; everyone else was flung much farther than I was, having struggled to get out of their tubes in time. Exhilaration floods through my veins, warming me even as the lake water drips from my hair and swimsuit.

From shore half a mile away, Garrett's voice bellows.

> Seyoon is the first one on the dock! Better catch up to her if you want to make it to the finale!

There's no time to strategize the best way to tackle the obstacle course. Between me and the next dock are five giant beach balls and a long, inflatable mat floating on the water. I get a running start and leap onto the first beach ball, so huge my outstretched arms don't even wrap halfway around it. The soaked fabric of my swimsuit helps me grip onto the plastic, and I scooch carefully up to the top, find my balance on wobbly legs, and jump onto the next ball, and then the next. I *knew* this wasn't as hard as they make it look on one of the few game shows I'm actually aware of, *Wipe Away.*

I land on the fifth ball less than gracefully, but without falling off. A leap away is a large, Styrofoam mat floating on top of the water. It doesn't look even a foot thick. How is that supposed to support my weight? Whatever—guess I'll find out.

I hop onto the mat, and water pulls up fast, licking at my ankles. "Shit shit shit," I mutter. There's no good way to get across this before the whole thing sinks, so I put those years of track practice to use and sprint as one side curls up and the water pools up to my shins.

Eight quick strides later and I'm lunging for the other dock. I catch it with just my upper body, my sternum hitting the wood and punching the air from my lungs. I scramble up and check out the scene behind me.

I look just in time to see Carter flailing as he misses the last bouncy ball and falls into the water with a terrific splash. Vendredi quickly takes his spot, agile on the beach balls, not even stopping to catch her balance and instead hopping from each one with ease. Dean is nowhere to be found. I hope he's—

No. Quit that. I need to stop wasting time worrying about him, because Vendredi is catching up.

I turn back around and survey the distance between myself and shore. Half a mile, 800m. I can do this. I went to state champs for this event.

I got second place in this event.

My blood turns cold even before I dive back into the unforgiving water.

It shocks my system every time. The lake is so murky, I can't see or hear through the walls of water on every side of me. I don't know where the others are. Vendredi must've made it to the dock by now, probably Carter, too. Maybe even Dean.

I don't even know if I'm swimming in the right direction—but I can't think like that right now, so I swing my right arm over my head, and then my left, my right, my left again, pushing myself through the water as hard as I can, over and over for what feels like an hour.

And then something grabs my foot and pulls.

I scream. Lake water floods my mouth as I'm dragged under. Whatever it was lets me go, and I quickly bob back up, hacking and coughing, my ears ringing. Scrubbing the water out of my eyes, I whip my head to both sides.

Two feet in front of me and cutting through the water with the ease of a shark is Carter.

No. Fuck. *No.*

I swim faster than I ever have before. Even faster than at state championships when I thought Appa was watching. In no time, my knee hits a rock, and the next time I swing my arm, my hand slams into a pebbled shore. Pain shoots up my wrist, but I ignore it.

I lift my head up, the ground finally shallow enough that I can kneel. Carter collapses on the algae-covered rocks in front of me. The adrenaline from almost drowning ravages through my body. I can't stop shaking. I push myself up on weak, trembling legs and limp over to him.

"You fucking cheater," I hiss between my teeth.

Carter pools his strength enough to crane his neck up and look at me. Between pants, the corner of his mouth twists up in a grin. "What are you going to do about it?"

He jerks his head to the side. I notice then that the film crew, Garrett, and Blake are already here, the Land Cruisers that brought them parked to the side.

Pure, white-hot rage batters against my rib cage. I bite down on my tongue until the pain nearly blinds me.

The sound of somebody gasping and clambering up the shore has me turning around. Vendredi. *Vendredi.*

I look to the water, where Dean is still trying to pull himself to shore.

That's it! That's the conclusion of our semifinal challenge! Carter is our winner, with Seyoon in second place, Vendredi in third, and Dean in fourth.

Still twenty meters out, stranded in the lake, Dean bobs like a lost buoy.

It's some time later when Dean finally drags himself out of the water and onto the rocky shore. I gnaw on my bottom lip, conflicted. I'm pissed at him. I'm devastated he got last. I'm relieved he made it at all.

It doesn't matter that our partnership—our friendship—is over to him. It isn't to me. I still care about him.

I care a lot about Dean.

"Are you alive?" I bite, standing over him where he lies on the ground. With his eyes shut, he nods, just once. My lip trembles. I bite my cheek until it stops. I think about early-morning chats in our bunk beds, floating on the lake together, his lips on mine, and everything in between.

"Why?" I ask, hoping he hears what I mean without having to say it all.

He finally cracks open his eyes. Dean weakly reaches out and wraps his hand around my ankle with a touch gentler than the one that dragged me underwater, running one finger along the back of my Achilles' heel.

"You're bleeding," Dean says, brows pinching.

I look down, surprised to find blood running from a huge gash on the side of my hand, dripping onto the rocks below. I must have cut it when I slammed it onto shore.

"*Why?*" I repeat.

His eyes glimmer with that same *something* that shone in his eyes on the dock last night. It gives me hope for one brief, fleeting moment.

But then he says, "Because only one of us can win."

And just like last night, disappointment sours my stomach.

Even as the crew members pack up their equipment and the others trek back to the bus, I linger, shivering in my wet swimsuit on the rocky shore. The waves of the lake roar at an abrasive volume, grinding down my nerves like water turning rock into sand. I feel myself slipping just the same, the last of my composure crumbling at the seams. Only several minutes and many rapid, heaving breaths later do I realize that it's not the lake roaring in my ears; it's the blood rushing in my head.

It's so loud, I don't hear footsteps behind me until they're right there. Vendredi.

She takes a seat next to me. "So," she says. "What happened?"

I bark out a laugh. "What happened was, I thought Dean and I were real friends. But I was an idiot. He was just playing the game."

He was just playing me.

It was fake. All of it. That's why this hurts so much. Not because our alliance is ending but because I had thought Dean and I were really friends. With the way he threw me to the side so easily, it's obvious now it was all an act—on his part, at least. God, I should have known. He's the reality-show expert, the strategist, the one who pushed us to play pretend in the first place. Of course he'd pretend to be my friend too. But I wasn't pretending.

"I'm sorry, Seyoon," Vendredi says. She pauses. "On the plus side . . . I ran the math. If you and Dean *were* going to split points this challenge? I'd be going home."

My brain clicks and sputters. That means . . . that means *I'm* making it to the finale.

I did it.

I thought I'd feel happier when this moment came.

I turn to Vendredi, who's here with me when she could be back on the bus. I think, maybe, I've wasted too much time thinking about the ones who leave me instead of appreciating those who stay.

It won't happen again.

36

THIS WOULD PROBABLY BE MORE ROMANTIC IF I WERE BETTER AT FIRST AID

DEAN

The guilt eats me up from the inside out. Gnawing on my bones. Leaving me empty.

I wish it didn't have to go down that way. I wish she didn't hate me now. Whenever I close my eyes, I see Seyoon's betrayed expression. My ears still ring with how hurt she sounded. But I know her—she would've refused if I'd tried to reason with her, persuade her to end our alliance amicably so that she didn't have to split her points with me. She would never have agreed, not after I shared the points I earned in the trivia challenge with her. She's too fair. But the second we rolled up to set and I saw that lake, I knew it was the end for me. *You had a good run, Dean, but your doggy-paddling can't carry you across the finish line. Not this time.* I didn't want to drag Seyoon down with me, too, not when I know how much she has at stake. So, I had no choice but to end our alliance early.

In another reality where her family isn't on the line, where we aren't competitors, maybe I could've told her the truth about my feelings. But in this reality, it'd break my heart more to see her lose everything than to find out she doesn't feel the same.

I didn't lie to her, though. What I said was true: Only one of us can win.

And I want it to be her.

There's a suspended tension in the air the rest of the night and the next day leading up to elimination. I spend it walking around camp, running my hand along the logs of the cabin wall, watching the sun dance across the lake's waves, taking it all in for what I know is the last time. I look up at the sky and hope it'll be a clear night so I can see the stars again. I'll miss them back home. I might even miss the woods—something I'd never thought possible.

All day, I keep an eye on Seyoon and wait for her to visit the infirmary and get her hand patched up. She spends her time avoiding me, whispering with Vendredi, and *not* going to the nurse's. Christ. She never changes.

Just before we all have to head to the bonfire pit for elimination, I corner her in the cabin, holding the first-aid kit I packed with me. Seyoon, sitting on her bunk, glares up at me. Her scowl falters when she notices what I'm holding.

"Can I?" I ask gently. The corner of her mouth curls down. "I know it hurts," I prod.

I wait for permission. Eventually, Seyoon grunts and holds out her injured hand. "Whatever. Knock yourself out."

The mattress dips as I sit beside her. Our knees brush, and she moves hers away. I try not to let my heart break. Seyoon presents me with her hand and glares at the underside of my mattress above our heads. It's a bad gash, running down the side of her palm from knuckle to wrist. I pull out alcohol wipes, petroleum jelly, and gauze. I apologize for the sting when I wipe the angry cut, but

Seyoon doesn't react or acknowledge me. I take my time, committing to memory the feeling of her skin on mine and the way she smells. This is probably the last time I'll be this close to her.

My hands tremble as I wrap her palm in gauze. Seyoon notices. "You're still bad at this."

I smother a chuckle. "No. It's nerves this time."

I finish wrapping her up in silence. When I'm done, she pulls her hand back into her lap, inspecting my work. "Why?" she asks. Her voice is like salve on a wound that's been left open to air too long. I know what she means.

"I told you already. Only one of us can win."

"And it's not going to be you. Vendredi did the math. Without my help, you're going home."

"I'm good at math, too, Seyoon."

She finally meets my gaze without a glare. "I don't understand you. I know you want to win as badly as I do. Wanted to."

"I thought so, too. But I want something else more."

"What is it?"

I study her features, wondering if I should tell her after all. My mind helpfully supplies a dozen ways this could go disastrously. Thank you, brain, for defying millions of years of evolution and not developing a self-preservation instinct. It's terrifying, knowing that Seyoon could hurt me—that I'm giving her the power to. But it's because of her that I'm the kind of person who can finally speak up. So I do.

"I wish we hadn't met here. I wish we had more time," I utter. "That's what I want. But I can't have that. So this is the next best thing." I inch forward. She doesn't lean away. "Earlier today, I told you we *were* friends. Because the truth is, you've become more than a friend to me."

Seyoon's eyes widen slowly, as if not sure she believes what she's hearing. "What are you saying, Dean?"

"I'm saying, I lost sight of what was real and what was pretend a while ago." I gaze down at her lips. Mine turn up in a small, sad smile. "I'm not *that* good of an actor."

My pulse flutters watching her figure it out. Turn it around in her head. The next time she looks up, she's the one who has trouble maintaining eye contact for once.

"Dean, I—"

I shake my head to cut her off. I think I'd break if she told me she didn't feel the same. But it would entirely *destroy* me if the answer *was* yes. Because it wouldn't matter—not here, not now.

I lean in for the last time, kissing her forehead. When I pull back, I'm greeted by Seyoon's stunned silence. I leave the first-aid kit with her and stand up.

"You're going to win, Seyoon," I tell her, more confidently than I've ever said anything in my life. I smile. "It's what you do."

The bonfire seems to crackle more aggressively than it has on other elimination nights. It's quiet as the sound technicians adjust their boom mics, the set designer spaces the four of us contestants out on the logs, and the camera operator fiddles with the settings on her video camera. The air feels thinner. The night sky is heavier, a blanket over my head, making it hard to breathe.

Before long, Garrett and Blake join us.

And the very last elimination begins.

> Campers, I'm torn. On the one hand, nothing fills my heart with more pride than to see the strongest four of you here after an entire season of fighting to prove why you deserve the million-dollar cash prize. On the other hand, in just a moment, we'll have to say goodbye to one of you.
>
> Before we go over the final scoreboard, let's review how many points you earned today. Carter, you earned forty. Seyoon, thirty. Vendredi, twenty. And Dean, ten.
>
> Dean, what happened, buddy?

My ears burn from being called out. I hunch in on myself. "Not much of a swimmer."

> Yep, I think we got that. Would've been a good time to be in an alliance, but, alas, it's too late to team up.
>
> Now . . . dramatic pause. This is the moment that will determine it all. Whether you make it into the top three and have a shot at winning the grand prize. I can see what you guys are thinking. *Did I earn enough today to turn things around and shoot to the top of the leaderboard?* Or, *Have I earned enough in the other challenges to hold on to my top rank despite my subpar performance?*
>
> I won't let you stew in your fears any longer. Luke, reveal the scoreboard.

As Luke turns the board around, my pulse hammers so hard that I can feel it in my teeth.

1ST	CARTER MOXLEY	119 PTS
2ND	SEYOON SHIN	90 PTS
3RD	VENDREDI TENGKU	72 PTS
4TH	DEAN PARKER	71 PTS

I knew it. I planned for this. But still, my stomach falls like a cement brick.

A difference of one point. I'm going home because of *one point.*

I'm going home.

37

OH. OH NO. MY ACTIONS . . . HAVE CONSEQUENCES?

SEYOON

Even though I knew it was coming, hearing Garrett say it out loud makes it real.

This is the end.

Dean's leaving.

I try to imagine being here without him. Falling asleep without the easy rhythm of his breathing in the bunk above mine. There'll be no more bickering over something stupid, no more watching how the sun catches the gold in his eyes when he rolls them, making me forget what we were arguing about. There'll be no more stargazing together, or swimming in the lake, or playing card games until one of us accuses the other of cheating. He's leaving, and we'll never get to talk about his confession, the one still tumbling around in my head. No—we'll never talk again, *ever*.

I glance over. He's already watching me. Dean's eyes flicker in the firelight. The possibility of this being the last time he ever looks at me is so awful that the words spew from my lips without a thought.

"Wait."

Heads turn my way. I've stood up without realizing. My heart races faster than my thoughts. I can't feel my legs. I can't hear anything over the rushing in my ears, the blood hammering in my head. I don't know what I'm doing, all I know is I can't—*I can't lose him.*

I can't.

"Can I give some of my points to Dean?" I blurt out, tripping over my tongue to get the words out fast enough. "I know we can't split because we're not in an alliance, but I'm not asking to split. Just—I just want to give him some of my points. Five. How about five? That should—"

Vendredi shoots up, her face twisted. *"What?!"*

And then, all at once, I realize what that means.

"Oh. Oh no," I say, but it comes out as a single exhale, all the wind knocked from my sternum. Before I can do or say anything to fix this, Blake steps forward from behind the camera.

"Let's do it!" she says. She has that same frenzied grin on her face that she did when Dean and I gave her the performance of our lives back in the Communal Cabin. Gone is the smooth-talking, steadfast director keeping things running silently behind the scenes. Back is the host who once offered bonus points to two of the contestants on Umma's season if they aired out their drama with each other in front of everyone.

"There's nothing in the rules against donating points," Blake continues. "Roll from the top—Garett, say you'll allow it, then ask for a recount of the scoreboard."

A few cameras adjust to focus on Garrett's shocked face. He shakes himself out of it like the seasoned professional he is. "Alright. I'll allow it. Let's recount the points to see who our final three will be."

Luke scrambles to move the numbers around on the scoreboard. It doesn't take him more than a minute, but it feels like an eternity until he unveils the updated standings.

1ST	CARTER MOXLEY	119 PTS
2ND	SEYOON SHIN	85 PTS
3RD	DEAN PARKER	76 PTS
4TH	VENDREDI TENGKU	72 PTS

I'm still on my feet, standing like an idiot, when Vendredi steps in front of me. It's as if I'm viewing everything from a distance, suspended high above and watching everything unfold through a glass floor beneath my feet.

There are angry tears in her big, brown eyes, which is when the glass floor shatters.

"I'm sorry," I choke out. I don't know how to articulate it all. "Oh my God, I'm sorry, Vendredi. It's just . . . *Dean*." Like it's an excuse. It's not. But it's my reason.

She raises her voice to make sure everyone hears. "You promised me, Seyoon. You said if Dean lost, you and I would team up."

My stomach falls.

In the outskirts of my vision, I see the blood drain from Dean's face.

Vendredi wipes her eyes. Her voice grows as hard and cold as her expression. She's making the same face Amelia did the last time we ever spoke. "Know this: I don't care about the prize money. I don't care that you won and I didn't. That's the nature of the game." She taps my sternum, her voice momentarily cracking. "I care that someone I thought was my friend stabbed me in the back."

"Vendredi, I—"

"Save it." She looks me up and down and shakes her head. "Joke's on me for forgetting this isn't the place to make friends."

"But I *am* your friend!"

"No, you *were*. Well played as always, Seyoon."

And just like that, she's gone in what feels like the blink of an eye.

CONFESSION TAPE—Vendredi Tengku, Contestant

> Sorry. I wish I had more to say right now, I know you want something eloquent for my outro tape. Something like, "This has been the opportunity of a lifetime, I'm going to cherish these memories." You know. Shit like that. And it's all true, but . . .
>
> But it's hard to feel grateful for any of it right now. I really wish I wasn't leaving like this.
>
> Best of luck to the final three.

Garrett closes out, introducing me, Carter, and Dean as the finalists to the cameras. When he wraps up, Dean gets up and walks briskly away. I trip over my own feet running after him, uncaring of the camera crew that scramble to follow.

"Wait, Dean!"

He turns around and I stop before him, panting for breath. I chafe under his intense, confused gaze.

"Why would you do that?" he asks. "Why would you give me your points?"

"I didn't want you to go home."

"Why not?"

"Because . . ." I don't know how to answer that. I don't know what this twisting, turning, sting inside me means. But it feels tender. Raw. Exposing it to air, to Dean, to the cameras—would burn.

So I just give him a half-truth, something safe, and say, "Because you're my friend."

"Am I? Or am I your backup plan?" he responds, curt. "You teamed up with Vendredi behind my back, Seyoon. I heard what she said back there. You betrayed our alliance. You betrayed *us*."

"It's not that simple! She asked me to, and I agreed, but only if you went home before her. Which I knew wasn't going to happen, because I wasn't going to *let* it happen."

"Oh. Okay. You wouldn't *let* it happen. Thanks for believing in me." I wince at his bite. "Sorry I got in the way of your plans."

Dean turns to leave. As I watch the distance between us grow, reality sinks in with serrated edges and saws a piece of my heart out in the shape of his handprint.

Oh.

This is why I gave him my points. This is why I didn't want to lose him. This is why it hurts so much.

I've fallen for Dean. And it's too late.

Desperate, I chase after him and grab his hand. His fingers twitch in my grasp, and I feel a phantom squeeze around the beating organ in my chest.

"Please," I say.

But then Dean snatches his hand back.

"Don't worry. You're going to win, Seyoon," he spits bitterly. His face crumples now, features aching. "It's what you do."

I realize, finally, that no, not *everyone* leaves me.

Sometimes, it's me who pushes them away.

38

THE MOST CIVILITY CARTER HAS EVER DEMONSTRATED, AND HE WAS STILL PRETTY RUDE

DEAN

The next day is a Friday. I should be watching reruns with Dad or saving Meredith from another bad date. Not here, stuck in this coffin of a confession booth, running through a mile-long list of questions. How the hell did I get here? To the finals, and here, in general, in the middle of the fucking woods. I *hate* the woods.

Blake smiles sympathetically from where she's leaning against the open door of the booth. A P.A. stands nearby and fans her occasionally. "Thanks for being patient, Dean, I know this is a lot, but you're part of the final three. You made it this far—it's important to take the time to reflect. Plus, it's tradition. We always have an interview before the final challenge."

I try to muster up a polite smile, but I think I'm just grimacing. My bones ache with exhaustion. My brain feels like mush from everything that's happened in the last . . . how long has it been? Twelve hours? In the twelve hours since shit hit the fan. "It's fine. I'm ready for the next question."

She flips one of the pages on her clipboard. "Why did you decide to end your relationship with Seyoon when you did?" She leans in with a smile. "Your alliance is obviously going to be one of the big storylines this season. Not just because the romance arc is compelling, but to have you, Seyoon, *and* Carter in the finale is a director's dream come true. The relatives of *the* Final Three competing against each other twenty years later—God, I couldn't have written this any better. So, if you could ham up the heartbreak and conflict of 'falling in love' with a rival, that would be perfect. Thanks, hon. Whenever you're ready."

CONFESSION TAPE—Dean Parker, Contestant

[tensely]

I made the tough decision to end things with Seyoon because we've both been competing for the same spot. And I realized I didn't want to take that from her anymore. That's why I cut things off before the aquatic challenge, so she didn't have to split points with me. I wanted to make sure she made it to the finale. I wanted her to win.

Blake leans forward and lowers her voice, her face somber and curious. "Do you still feel that way after finding out she formed an alliance with somebody else?"

I inhale sharply. A piece of my rib punctures my lung. "It's complicated."

"Tell the camera, not me."

"How many more questions do we have left?"

For the very first time in recorded-human history, I'm relieved to see Garrett approaching.

"Come on, Blake. Can you lay off with the sad questions?" Garrett leans against the other side of the doorway. "Star-crossed lovers are way better for ratings than bitter exes, anyway. How will the bastards at the network approve our spinoff show if the season finale is so depressing that everyone stops watching?"

My nose scrunches as I recall the spinoff Garrett mentioned to me and Seyoon awhile back. "Moxley to the Maximum?"

Garrett lights up. "See? The name sticks."

So do leeches.

Blake stifles a sigh. "Is that why you're interrupting my contestant interview? To critique my direction?"

"No, to ask if I can handle Seyoon's interview later."

"Sure. Anything else?"

"Yeah. I talked to Carter."

Blake stiffens. She recomposes herself and turns to me. "I think we've got enough. Thanks for your time, Dean."

I hop out of the booth, my curiosity piqued, but not enough to stick around longer and risk having to answer any more painful questions. Garrett waves as I leave. Warily, I head to the showers to scrub the day off. When I'm finished, I wrap a towel around my waist and exit the stall. This is probably the only moment of peace I'll have until the finals. I try to savor it—when the bathroom door opens. With my luck, it's another Moxley. One was already *my* maximum.

Carter turns off his clip-on mic and hangs it on the hook where I left mine. I'm intent on ignoring him, but he sidles right up next to me. I clutch my towel tighter.

"Can I . . . help you?"

"Are you and Seyoon really done?" he asks. "Seriously, this time."

I blink at him. "I'm not interested."

"What—*no*!"

"Well, I don't think Seyoon would be, either."

Carter rubs his hands over his face and groans. "That's not why I'm asking, moron. Just answer the question."

I have no idea what his motives are, but I don't trust them. "That's none of your business."

"You look sad. It must be over."

I scowl. But like with his uncle, I know if I try to ignore Carter, he's only going to get more irritating. Begrudgingly, I resign myself to hearing him out instead of hiding in the shower stall until he leaves.

Carter lowers his voice. "Tomorrow, the final challenge is going to be a treetop obstacle race. Similar to the one your dad and my uncle competed in. Just like last time, there's going to be a fork in the road right before the finish line. Take the path on the right. And *don't* tell Seyoon."

All I can do is stare quizzically down at him, waiting for him to elaborate or go away. "What are you talking about?" I eventually manage to string together. "How do you know that?"

"Are you serious? What's my last name? And what's the last name of the host?" Carter rolls his eyes like it's me who's being ridiculous here.

The blood drains from my face. "Garrett is helping you cheat in the finals?"

"You're not stupid, Dean, don't pretend like you are."

My head pulses with an oncoming migraine. Obviously, I assumed that Garrett would be vying for his own nephew to win *Forest Feud*, especially after how he defended him in the first challenge. If I hadn't already come to terms with losing at the semifinals, maybe this confirmation would be more life-shattering. At the moment, it's just another loose thread to try and hold on to in the spinning wheel of my mind. I have enough energy to ask one thing, though. "Let's say I believed you . . . why would you tell *me* this? Now we both have a leg up."

He has the gall to laugh, and I think for a second about kicking him in the shin, but that feels like something Seyoon would do, so I force the thought away.

"We are *not* on equal footing, you and me. I could give you a five-minute head start and still beat you." I rear my foot back to kick, but Carter steps away in time. "It's not ideal to have both you and her with me in the finals, but it doesn't change the fact that I'm going to win. What *can* change is who places second."

Carter steps back and heads toward the door. While clipping his mic back on, he throws over his shoulder, "I'm telling you this because I hate Seyoon more than I *don't* care about you. So, congratulations."

"That's . . ."

"Oh, save it," he snaps. "She'll be fine. Third place isn't bad."

He leaves before I can respond. The spoiled pit rotting in my rib cage pangs for Seyoon. *I should tell her.*

And then I remember how she betrayed me. Us. How she was so convinced I would lose that she formed an alliance with Vendredi behind my back. I trusted her. I was vulnerable with her. I thought she saw me as an equal, a partner. A friend. Friends don't treat each other like stepping stones to the finish line.

She decided then that she didn't need me to win. Why should that change now?

I don't see Seyoon for the rest of the day, and I pretend I'm fine with that.

39

MUFFINS, MOXLEYS, AND MURDEROUS INTENT

SEYOON

Garrett sighs and pockets the list of questions he was reading off to me. "You're exceptionally bad at this."

I cross my arms and glare. Somewhat because of the sun filtering into the confession booth around his silhouette, but mostly because I hate him. "Maybe you're a bad interviewer."

To be fair, my answers to questions like *Why did you promise to team up with Vendredi and then change your mind?* and *What happens if you lose tomorrow?* have been more strangled than spellbinding.

"We're obviously not going to get any good footage out of you right now," Garrett says, "so you might as well help me out with something else."

Anything to get out of answering more questions about how I feel now that Dean's mad at me. I follow Garrett away from the confession booth and to his cabin, which surprises me. He lets us in and then heads straight to the kitchen.

"What do you need my help with?" I ask.

Garrett rummages around his cupboards, pulls out a box of Moxley Muffins mix, and throws on an apron. This time, it's a pale blue one that says in a fancy cursive font: I COOK AS GOOD AS I LOOK. Why did I come here?

"Baking!" Garrett chirps. "I'm hungry."

I balk. "Your assistant couldn't help you with this?"

"It's Luke's day off, and unfortunately, tasty little treats don't qualify him for overtime. Plus, I don't have to pay *you*. Go on, there are extra aprons in that drawer over there."

On principle, I don't want to do anything that would make Garrett's life easier, and I don't get why he can't make these himself, but Moxley Muffins sound pretty good right now. I pilfer through the options, picking a black apron with bold papyrus font that says THIS SHIT IS GONNA BE DELICIOUS! I stand on the other side of the counter opposite Garrett, who hands me a few eggs to crack into a bowl.

"You know what I realized recently?" Garrett starts conversationally. "You're more like your mom than I thought."

"Is this small talk? We don't have to do that. I crack eggs better in stony silence."

"Really. What you did for Dean yesterday, sharing your points with him? It seemed like something Jungeun would do." Hearing Umma's first name said so familiarly makes my ears ring. "Despite what a pain in the ass you are sometimes, you really are a good kid."

My thoughts stall like an old engine. I wait for a punch line to come to soften his words, reduce them to another joke or empty comment. But Garrett doesn't follow up.

"You believe that?" I ask.

"I do."

He means it. His words, with nowhere else to go, sink into me, pressing heavy fingertips into places I didn't know were sore. It's a weird feeling, for Garrett of all people to be telling me this. It's not a bad feeling. Just new. It's the kind of thing I'd always hoped Appa would say to me.

"Well," I say, embarrassed, "Dean shared his points with me before. I was just being a good teammate."

Garrett fetches a carton of blueberries and stirs them in. One rolls out of the bowl, and I play with it in silence.

"I have a question for you," he eventually asks. There's a layer of hesitation to his voice. "Let's say, at the final challenge tomorrow, Dean ends up beating you. Would you regret sharing your points with him then? Would you regret being *that* kind of player?"

I pause and think about it. Tendrils of dread creep through my veins as I really picture it. The view of being behind. Coming home to Umma empty-handed. No longer having a home to share with her. It's the worst possible reality. But the heartbreak in Dean's face last night was a visceral pain, too. So was the look of hurt on Vendredi. The disdain on Amelia's. I shut my eyes.

"No," I eventually decide. "I wouldn't regret it."

"Really?"

I nod. "I've lost before. But . . ." My throat gets tight, and I swallow past it. "But what I regret more is being a bad teammate. That I can't come back from. Not again."

The scraping of the spatula against the sides of the bowl stops. I look up. Garrett is wearing the same creased expression he had when he saw Umma. He purses his lips, considering something. Then he gestures at the collar of his shirt. I get what he means and fumble at my own collar to turn off my mic.

“You remember the final race between your mom, Vince, and me, don’t you? Of course you do. You must also remember how there was a fork in the road, and how I was the only one to go down the correct path.” Garrett exhales through his nose and plants both his hands on the countertop. “I knew which way to go because Blake told me.”

I blink. My neurons are slow to fire, slower to connect. “Blake . . . helped you cheat back then?”

He nods. “And she wants me to help Carter cheat now.”

For a long time, I don’t get it. No, I do, but it doesn’t sink in yet. The anger fills me slowly, like water dripping steadily into a pool.

Then I get it.

I can’t speak. My teeth rattle in my clenched jaw. The blood coursing through my veins is molten. I grip the edge of the counter, trying not to let the rage overtake me. I knew it. I *knew* it should’ve been Umma. If Blake and Garrett hadn’t cheated her over, Umma would’ve won. Her life—no—*our lives* would have been completely different.

Oh God. I feel like I’ve been punched in the gut just thinking about it. We were robbed. My mom, *Umma*—everybody in this life has stolen from her.

Garrett was always a no-good, backstabbing, son of a bitch, but Blake? I trusted Blake. I was wrong to think any of these slimy executives cared about anything other than the weight of their wallets.

"*Why?*" I choke out. It comes out strangled. I don't really mean *why*. I mean *how?* How could you do that to her? How could you do this to me now? How do you live with yourself?

"Because how else are we going to secure a budget for a reality show featuring family winners if one of the titular Moxleys loses?" Garrett dips his finger in the batter and tastes it. "That's Blake's reasoning, anyway. I'm of the opinion that we'll get the funding as long as *Forest Feud*'s a success, but hey. She's my boss. She orders me to do something, and I do it. That's why, for tomorrow's challenge—a race, just like last time—I told Carter to take the path on the right."

His nonchalance only fans my fury.

Garrett has the audacity to look sympathetic. "I'm sorry, kid. You were never supposed to win."

That's it. The pure, unadulterated rage that blows through me is so violent that bile nearly shoots up my throat. I've been angry before, but this is different, worse than any time I've been angry when Appa would raise his voice at Umma or when I caught the other volleyball team at districts cheating. This is like hot oil spitting at my fingertips, so scalding it hurts to hold, tempting me to flick my hand out and burn someone in reach.

"I'm going to tell you something now, and I'm just going to say it once," Garrett says carefully, wary of my trembling fists. "Repeating yourself is for people who get paid by the hour."

"Fuck you," I bite. I'd leave if my limbs would cooperate.

"Mean, but understandable." Garrett pushes the mixing bowl out of the way and leans forward. "I said tomorrow's challenge is a race, yeah? It's not identical to the one from my season—we've changed it up—but there's still a fork in the final road. Like I said, I told Carter to go right. But you? You go left."

"I'm sure you'd like that, asshole."

"I would. Because *left* is the quickest way to the finish line."

My next insult dies on my tongue. "Wait, what?"

"You weren't supposed to win—but I want you to." Garrett pushes himself away from the counter. "You're a fair player. Your mom was, too. I admire that. Jungeun never got a fair chance, so . . . I'm making sure you do."

He sighs and finally reaches underneath for a muffin pan to scoop the batter into. "I know the kid's my nephew, but Carter's sportsmanship leaves something to be desired. Besides, like I said, I think we're going to get funding for *Moxley to the Maximum* even if Carter loses, so no sweat off my back. If we don't, whatever. I'll milk the Moxley Merch cash cow a little longer."

I'm still stiff when Garrett loads the tray into the oven. He comes around the island and takes the list of questions from his pocket. "What you do with this information is up to you. Believe me or don't, I get paid the same. Muffins will be done in twenty-five. Do me a favor and go record your final interview question so Blake doesn't realize you've been missing this whole time."

Numbly, I shuffle out of Garrett's cabin and wait until he closes the door behind me before I unfold the list and carefully read the last question.

How do you want to be remembered?

CONFESSION TAPE, FINAL INTERVIEW—
Seyoon Shin, Contestant

Talking to a camera is really awkward, you know that? They never mention that part on TV. But I really have to get this off my chest. It may be my only chance to.

[She sighs and rubs her hands over her face.]

Vendredi. I'm *sorry*. I made you a promise I knew I couldn't keep because I was afraid of losing you. I should've been honest about how I felt, I know, but I'm always scared that if I let people see the weakest parts of me, they'll leave.

[She fidgets, dropping her eyes to her hands now.]

I did the same thing with another friend, too. Amelia. If . . . if you see this, I'm sorry. I promise to call and finally explain everything. We both know there's a lot to talk about.

I know I don't deserve it, but if you guys let me, I want to make things right. I want to be a better friend. I promise I can be.

[Her eyes get watery. She inconspicuously wipes them by rubbing them. She clears her throat.]

. . . And to my dad, who may or may not be watching. Whether I win this whole thing or not, it's not because of you *or* in spite of you. There's only one person I'm doing this for, and she's already proud of me.

[Seyoon pauses, then smiles at the camera.]

A smart woman once told me winning isn't the most important thing. I was too stubborn to believe her then, but I get it now.

I don't want to be remembered as a winner. I want to be remembered as a fair player, a good teammate, a better friend. I hope people see this and remember me for my efforts. I hope they see that I tried. I hope that counts.

40

SEYOON AND DEAN, SWINGING AROUND IN THE TREES

DEAN

On the morning of the last day of camp, the *Forest Feud* jingle blares at an ear-shattering volume from every speaker in the vicinity. I wake like I've been shot, jolting up so fast that I nearly fall off the bed. Luckily, I'm not in my top bunk—I faked a stomach bug yesterday evening so I could spend the night in the infirmary. Yes, *alright*, I'm hiding from Seyoon. Being around her is too painful right now. Besides . . . we have nothing left to say to each other.

"Wakey, wakey, campers! It's the moment you've all been waiting for, the final challenge!" Garrett's voice streams in surround sound. "You have an hour to get ready to head to set."

I linger in the nurse's office for as long as I can, then quickly scarf down breakfast and get dressed, hoping I don't run into Seyoon or Carter. Thankfully, the producers make it easy and chauffeur the three of us to the filming lot in separate cars.

We drive down the highway, pass the private property gates, and roll along a winding, gravelly road. I wonder what new section of the forest we're going to traverse today, but surprisingly, the bus rolls to a stop in front of a familiar clearing. A few weeks ago, I wouldn't have been able to tell you the difference between a maple tree and a pine, but after all this time out here, I instantly recognize this grouping of fir trees: It's the same location where the Trailside Treasure Hunt challenge was held. I look up, and my jaw drops. High off the ground are lines of rope intricately woven between the trees.

It's an obstacle course. Just like the one Dad competed in. Just like Carter said it'd be.

He wasn't lying.

The gravity of it all hits me: Garrett really *is* helping him cheat. Carter is trying to help *me* cheat too.

Am I going to let him?

I still haven't made up my mind by the time the crew start unloading. My stomach knots as we're brought over to the edge of the forest where the race begins. The area resembles a construction site more than an obstacle course, with all the scaffolds holding up wooden platforms and the countless support beams and wires keeping everything else suspended. How could they have set this up so quickly? It wasn't too long ago that we were here for the last challenge. Maybe it's like one of those pop-up carnivals with roller coasters that fold up into neat boxes. Hopefully, this is more stable than that.

While I inspect the course, a technician comes by and straps us into harnesses attached to an intricate mesh of cables and pulleys. Directly in front of us are three ropes spaced ten feet apart that I'm guessing we climb to reach the first wooden platform. Beyond that, the obstacle course is a mystery, meaning we have to think on our feet and be prepared for anything. Anticipation prickles at the base of my spine.

No, that's the feeling of eyes on me. I turn and see Seyoon staring, somewhat desperately.

"Dean, I—*oof!*" She tries walking forward, only to be yanked back in place by her harness. She swings around on the line before regaining her footing.

I try not to let my pursed lips wobble. There's no time to talk, or the privacy to. Even if there were—what would I say? Would I let her know what Carter told me? Would that change anything?

She made up her mind, I remind myself bitterly. *She doesn't need me to win. She doesn't want me.*

Carter, on the other side of Seyoon, leans back and watches our interaction carefully. He narrows his eyes at me, and I avoid looking at either of them for the rest of the time it takes Blake to send the huge crew into the forest to film us along the course. Once everyone's ready, Garrett turns on Dazzling Smile #5 for the cameras, and we begin filming our last-ever intro.

> Good morning, everyone! Thank you for joining me for the season finale of *Forest Feud*. It's been such a pleasure to be your host, and—wow, this will be my last spiel, won't it? Cue the waterworks.
>
> It's my greatest honor to introduce the final three: Carter Moxley, Seyoon Shin, and Dean Parker! Did someone say "legacy trio"? I did!

The cameras roll around, capturing the three of us. I think of how thrilled Dad and Meredith will be to see me in the finale, so I do my best to look happy to be here.

> Campers, get ready for Treetop Adventure—an homage to the final challenge from the original run of *Forest Feud*. It's everything you could ask for in a finale: an exhilarating race, daring obstacles, and the thrill of knowing you could die under a beautiful canopy of trees.

He pauses. "You all signed your safety waivers, right? It would be a PR nightmare if one of you actually fell to a painful death."

None of us laugh.

"I'm *joking*. Sheesh, I can't believe my best material is being wasted on this group."

> The rope course will begin here and spiral through the forest. Expect unfinished bridges, obstacles that will test your dexterity, and paths that could lead you astray if you're not careful.
>
> This isn't going to be easy. There's a million dollars on the line, after all.
>
> And only one of you can win.

Adrenaline kicks in. This is it. I can't resist the urge to peek over at Seyoon one last time.

She's already looking at me.

My affection for her returns with not just a wave but an ocean, threatening to pull me under.

Even if she didn't, doesn't, *won't* need me—I can't help but still want her. Because of everything.

"Good luck," Seyoon says, her brows pinched. She sounds sincere. I come up for air.

"You too."

It's too late. It's all I can say.

And then, as soon as Garrett gets beyond the edge of the forest, he blows his whistle.

The final challenge is on.

41

TEAMWORK MAKES THE DREAM WORK

SEYOON

I waste no time climbing up the rope. Sure, I may have realized there are—contrary to popular belief—more important things than winning, but that doesn't mean I'm not going to give it my all. I've never been good at holding back.

Hand over hand, I pull myself up, not thinking about the pain or the growing distance between me and the ground. The adrenaline helps. The thunderous cheering from the crew drowns out everything else until I'm on the first platform. It's more solid than I expected, thanks to the scaffold holding it up from below.

The next platform is about fifteen feet away, with two thick cables running between them. Carter's two seconds ahead of me and gets down on his knees next to the ledge. He holds tight to one of the cables, then lets his body fall, dangling midair with only his grip and harness to keep him tethered. As if he's on monkey bars, he swings and grabs a section farther away with one hand, then again with the other hand, then again. He's gaining the lead fast.

I only have one option to catch up, especially now that Dean's made it onto the platform.

"Garrett better not have been serious about those safety waivers," I mutter before running and leaping off the edge.

Gasps and shouts sound from below as I fly through the air—and latch onto the middle segment of the second cable with my whole body. I instantly flip upside down, still holding tight like a koala. Ow, *fuck*, that burned. But it worked. I've soared way past Carter.

Upside down, I keep my legs wrapped around the cable and pull myself across the rest of the distance. I accidentally glance down and see how high up I am. My breath stutters in my throat, but I just have to keep going. Umma's going to *kill me* when she watches this.

Garrett's moderation echoes from the speakers all around the forest.

> Bold and highly dangerous move from Seyoon! I like it, but our insurance won't! She's now in the lead and already up on the next platform!

I have a better view of the rest of the course from here. Across the maybe-two-hundred-meter distance are three smaller, standalone platforms, each about thirty feet up from the ground. Between them are different obstacles: The first is a suspended bridge of swinging logs, the second is a rope swing, and the third is a declining net wall.

Somebody whizzes past me and onto the first log in the split second I've taken to think.

"Get out of the way if you're just gonna stand around!" Carter yells, leaping from log to log, holding on to the handle strung parallel across. His steps send each of the logs rolling in place, bumping against one another.

"Motherfucker," I grunt, then jump onto the first log. It swings wildly, and I lose my balance, falling forward. Ow, my face. Ow, my *ego.* I try to stand back up, but it's impossible with how the bridge rolls under my feet. Every move I make sends the whole thing careening back and forth.

Dean catches up before I've found my footing. But instead of hurrying on, he stands back, analyzing with his hand on his chin. I'm still struggling to stand when he gets down onto the first log on his knees. Slowly, so he doesn't lose his balance or rock the bridge anymore, Dean reaches for the makeshift rope handle and pulls himself across, using the rolling logs to his advantage rather than fighting to stand on them.

Fuck . . . that's pretty smart.

I'm going to copy him.

By the time I make it to the rope swing, Carter's nowhere in sight, and Dean is already soaring across the huge distance. They're both so far ahead of me. What am I going to do?

Shit. *What am I going to do?!*

I'm going to stop thinking about it, that's what.

Dean lands on the other side and sends the rope back. Shifting control to the fibers in my muscles rather than my brain, I jump off the ledge without waiting for the rope to swing across entirely and—*oh fuck fuck fuck*—catch it in between the two platforms, thank God. Holy shit, adrenaline is a hell of a drug.

Dean lets out a worried, garbled shout. "What the *fuck*?!"

A nervous laugh bubbles from me as I careen over the distance. "We have these harnesses on for a reason, don't we?" I yell back.

I get to enjoy his panicked expression for another second before he snaps out of it and hurries to the third obstacle.

Not too long after, I land with an "*Oomph!*" on the platform. I scramble to peek over at the wide net wall. It slopes all the way down until it levels out onto a flat portion we have to crawl across to another platform. Dean hasn't gotten very far, but to my surprise, neither has Carter. The netting is probably hard to climb down at this angle. If it were more vertical, it'd be easier, like a ladder. But it's curved like a slide.

Wait . . .

> Carter is struggling with his footing there on the net wall, slowing down his lead and giving Dean and Seyoon the opportunity to catch up. Seyoon's getting ready to descend, but she'll have to hustle if she wants to—
>
> Oh?

"Watch out!" I yell as I toss my body sideways over the platform. I roll down the webbing as easily as I used to roll down grassy hills as a kid. Except, instead of getting grass stains and mud on my knees, I can already feel a pretty gnarly case of rope burn on my arms as I tumble down, down, down, until I roll to a stop on the flat part of the net.

I can't believe that actually worked.

God, I'm good.

> A genius strategy! Seyoon's in the lead again, with only two more obstacles before she reaches the end!

Carter and Dean gawk down at me, fifty feet ahead of them, then immediately follow my lead to roll down the rest. Ha. Suckers. It's too late though; I'm not letting go of the lead this time.

The next segment of the race is the easiest one by far, but also the longest. Dangling from a metal framework are large, square tiles of wood spaced a foot or so apart, stepping stones that weave and curve around tree trunks. Unlike the last bridge, this one has no handles. I have to pray I don't fall.

But of course, I don't.

As someone who's always loved running and never been religious, I thank both my cross-country coach and God as I sprint from tile to tile. *It's just a warm-up run,* I think as the path turns tightly around a tree. *Just a warm-up with long strides. I could do this in my sleep.*

But so could Carter, probably, who I sense is coming up fast.

When I leap off the last tile and onto another wooden platform, I have to take a moment to catch my breath. It's futile, because as soon as I look up and see what's next, all the air escapes from my lungs.

There are two bridges in front of me. The one on the right is made of logs tightly woven together, and the one on the left is constructed of rope.

This is my chance.

I could secure victory right now, provided that Garrett was telling me the truth. Something in my gut trusts him, and my gut's generally more reliable than my head. I know if I take the path on the left, I'll win. It's so tempting, it *burns.* I would show Blake and Appa how wrong they were for thinking I couldn't beat the odds.

I'd win the money and fix all of me and Umma's problems. I'd prove I'm a winner.

But that's not what I want to be remembered as.

Several seconds later, Carter jumps onto the platform, then Dean, and I hold my arm out to stop them both. "Wait," I say.

I have to brace my core against the painful knowledge that if I had just gone ahead, there would be no chance in hell either of them would ever catch up, even if they did take the correct path.

Carter tries to wriggle around me. "Seriously, hold on, you ass-cheek," I grunt. I don't have long to convince him; he's still moving as I speak. "Carter, Garrett lied to you. The path on the right *isn't* the fastest one. He told me that the left one is."

That gets Carter to freeze. Dean nearly snaps his neck from how fast he whips toward me. I squeeze my eyes shut and inhale through my nose. The crisp, pine air inflating my lungs slows the pounding of my heart and silences the chaos in my head.

When I exhale, it's like releasing a rubber band that's been stretched taut for far too long. The relief is instantaneous.

"Some things are more important than winning," I say. "No more tricks. This is our chance to play fair for once. What happened to our parents doesn't need to happen to us too."

Neither of them move yet. My hands shake at my side from the terrible anticipation: I could have just made the worst mistake of my life.

But then I catch the look on Dean's face and get to watch it transform from shock, to confusion, to glowing with devastating fondness. I think of Umma, and how she'd be proud of me. My fears ease. I'm sure I made the right choice.

Carter looks at me. The bridge on the left. The bridge on the right.

Then he throws his head back and laughs. "You must think I'm a fucking idiot. For the last time, get out of the way."

He shoulder-checks me on his way to the bridge on the right, cackling as he sprints easily over the wood. My eye twitches as I watch him go.

"Can't say you didn't try," Dean huffs, in a mixture of disbelief and amusement. He turns to me then, the smile on his face gentle and apologetic. "Lead the way."

We run stealthily but carefully across the suspended rope, holding on to our cables the whole time. The bridge goes up, until we're fighting through the foliage. Acid builds in my stomach as I pray Garrett was actually telling me the truth—that he actually wants to give us the fair chance he took from Umma and Dean's dad.

"What are we going to do when we get to the end?" Dean asks as we hurry.

I wince—both at the stitch starting to form in my side from all this running and the inevitability of the finish line approaching. I haven't thought through that part yet. Before I can answer, there it is: the end of the bridge.

It leads directly to a treehouse. But no, not any treehouse: the one from the Trailside Treasure Hunt.

Dean and I look at each other, then race to open the door, revealing the same three-sided interior as last time. Carter's not here. *Yet.* Garrett was telling the truth.

We hurry to the edge, where the walls open up to the forest. A net's been placed far below, suspended in the air. It's the finish line. We have to jump.

One of us does.

My thoughts race as fast as my beating heart. I wish I didn't have to choose. I wish I could have both, him and the prize, that *we* could have both—

Huh.

I have another idea.

"Let's jump at the same time," I rush out. The idea is settling in my bones now, and I'm energized by the potential of a *we* and an *us* again. "We'll split the prize. Let's do this together."

I get it. I *really* get it now.

There are a lot of things that are more important than winning.

Dean's eyebrows jump up beneath his curly bangs. I reach out and grab his hand to shake him out of his shock. His fingers clench over mine. Dean watches me like I'm the most precious thing in the world right now, even though a million dollars is three steps and a fall away.

"Why?" he asks.

His voice is flint against the fire steel of my heart, and it ignites everything I've been trying to choke out. "Same reason I gave you half my points, idiot!" I yell, face burning. "Because I want *you* more than I want to win. Do I have to say it out loud? Fine! I like you, Dean Parker, you—!"

He shoves me off the edge.

42

SEASON FINALE

DEAN

Seyoon's scream rings through the entire forest. I wait, watching as she flails through the air, falling, falling, *falling*—

Until she plummets into the net.

She won. Seyoon won.

I huff out a breath of laughter, my glee making me dizzy. I steel myself to jump after her when the door to the treehouse bursts open behind me—Carter. His pink face pales as soon as he spots me.

"How—" he sputters. "How did *you* beat me here?"

I'm reminded of how different the circumstances were the last time I met Carter in this treehouse. "Not just me." I gesture below, and I can practically hear his heart drop when he puts two and two together.

I step backward, one of my heels teetering off the edge. Carter is still frozen in place, his face slowly morphing from shock to fury. I grin, relishing the sight.

"Hey," I say, remembering what he told me yesterday. "Don't beat yourself up. Third place isn't *bad*."

Then I fall.

Carter's angry roar follows me all the way down. It's the most satisfying sound to ever grace my ears. The wind whizzes past me.

My stomach shoots into my throat. Then I land. Before I've finished gulping in a breath, fireworks go off. Like, actual fireworks. There is no way Garrett has a permit for that—but he might have a fantastic legal team.

His voice crackles to life over the speakers, ringing with pride.

> Ladies, gentlemen, and all the fine folk here, we have our winner of *Forest Feud*: Seyoon Shin!

Seyoon's still disoriented when I look over and find her a few feet away, bobbing on the wobbling net. It takes her another moment to regain her bearings and realize what's happened, and when she does, she crawls over. I sit back and don't bother wiping away the smug look on my face.

"What the hell?" she asks, shoving my shoulder. "We could have both won! This was important to you."

"It was important to you, too, and yet you still helped me." I brush my thumb over the corner of her mouth, thinking of how she's changed me. Turned me brave. Given me a reason to believe in myself and speak up. "Besides," I say, softer, "I *did* win."

She blinks at me. The chaos around us mutes to a dull hum. All I see is her, the smile starting to spread across her face. She laughs, first in disbelief, then with joy.

Not much comes naturally to me. But reaching for her, tugging her close, that feels like second nature. Like finally flipping the repelling pole of a magnet around. Seyoon leans in. I give in to my need, my want, without hesitation this time.

And Seyoon kisses me back.

43

NEXT ON . . .

SEYOON

No one ever talks about what happens after you accomplish your dreams.

I still don't believe it, no matter how many times I repeat it in my head. I won. *I won.* I mouth it again just to taste it on my tongue. Once Dean and I finish celebrating, I float through the immediate proceedings. My head is foggy from euphoria and my limbs are light as I'm helped off the net, posed before a camera, directed to say a few closing remarks, and a million other things that I barely recall until I'm finally staged next to Garrett, who's holding a comically large check for a million dollars. A check written out in *my name.*

My hands tremble as I grip the other side of the cardboard.

"This is just for the photo op," Garrett whispers through his toothy smile. "The real money will be transferred via electronic deposit."

"Right," I say, voice thin. "Real money."

Real money pays off debt. Real money can buy a home. Real money will keep the courts from splitting me and Umma up.

This is real.

Once they've gotten the shot, Garrett sets down the check and gestures for Dean—who's been watching from the sidelines with a soft smile—to join us. For a minute, I think Garrett's going to do something profound like shake our hands or tell us with bravado that we've done right by our parents, rewritten history, insert tear-jerking sentiment here, etcetera.

Instead, he gives us each a noogie.

"My hair!" I squawk, batting his hand away. Dean takes it with pursed lips, like he's used to this.

Garrett is smiling. It's kind of lopsided, and not a hint of teeth peeks out, so I think it's his real one.

"Not bad for a couple of brats," he says. "Nice job."

A few weeks ago, I wouldn't have been caught dead saying this—but Garrett's not *all* that bad, actually.

There's a disturbance in the air, and I look over to catch Blake glaring daggers at Garrett. She storms toward us, visibly twitching with rage.

"A moment?" she grits out, refusing to look at me or Dean. I smirk.

Garrett grimaces and slumps in on himself. I wouldn't want to be him right now. Or ever, actually.

He points at us. "Hey, give your parents my best, alright?"

Before he can leave, a promise I made long ago pops into the forefront of my mind. I groan. "Wait, Garrett?"

He stops. I trudge up to him and ask if he has a pen. Confused, he fishes one out of his pocket. I turn his palm over and write Umma's phone number. It takes him a moment before he realizes what it is.

"Is this you giving me your blessing?" he teases.

"Not by a long shot," I say, rolling my eyes. "This is your chance to make things right."

Not long after, Dean and I are ushered back to camp as the other crew members start tearing down the set. We ride in the same car this time. It's peaceful. Almost *too* peaceful.

"Hey, where'd Carter go?" I ask.

"He left when you were getting your photo taken," Dean answers. "He threw another tantrum and insisted on going home early. I don't think he's too happy about how things turned out." He grins. "You should've seen his face when he made it to the treehouse and realized he lost."

"God, I can't *wait* to watch his freak-out when this episode airs."

The adrenaline wears off after that, and I crash not even halfway through the ride, waking up only when it's time to hike back up the mountain and pack up. Camp is quiet and empty for once when we arrive, the ever-present buzz of a hundred production assistants and the glint of camera lenses in every corner noticeably absent.

It sets in slowly at first, then with finality. Filming has wrapped. The game is over. It's finally time to go home. I thought I'd be more relieved when this day came.

The first thing we do is exchange our mic packs for the phones we surrendered a few weeks ago, but I leave mine off, not ready to tune in to the real world yet. Dinner is a blur. After, Dean packs while I shower, and then we switch off. I'm alone in the cabin when it hits—that funny feeling. It settles in the pit of my stomach. I look at my hands. They're stiff, trembling from exertion. My skin is rubbed raw from the ropes and cables. Beneath the callouses, the scars I got on my first day are still visible. I'm here. This is real.

It's weird. I finally have what I wanted in the palms of my battered hands. And yet I can't get myself to really feel it. You spend so long chasing after something, it's hard to stop running. I just keep thinking about what comes next. I mean, I won—isn't that enough?

So, why does it feel like something's still missing?

By the time I've finished packing, it's beginning to get dark out. I stand by the dusty cabin window and watch the sunset bleed over the mountain. It's the last sunset I'll see here. By chance, it happens to be the most beautiful one yet.

When I step out, Dean's waiting for me on the porch with that god-awful, hideous neon-orange suitcase at his side.

"Keep that thing away from me," I say, closing the door. I let my palm linger on the doorknob, trying to commit to memory the feeling of the rusted metal.

Dean's cheeks burn. "I'm not going to drop it again."

Still, I stay wary of his death-machine-on-wheels as we venture across camp. We both linger at the entrance. The CAMP CLEARWATER sign arches over our heads. I take it all in one last time, like I did when we first arrived. The sounds of the forest have become background noise at this point, but I tune my attention back to them now. The rustling of pine needles in the wind. Water rolling gently onto a pebbled shore. A cricket humming in the grass. When the breeze settles, silence swallows up everything quickly. The quiet isn't an absence of sound but a sensation; I feel it wrap around me, hold me, pocketing me in this moment.

I don't want to leave.

The thought trickles into my head, surprising me. It's not that I'm not eager to see Umma again—I miss her more than words. But I'm . . .

I'm scared. I'm scared that I'll leave the girl I became here at camp, and as soon as Mount Rainier is out of sight, I'll step right back into the person I was before I got here. A million dollars may be following me home, but what if I come back empty-handed?

Dean has started walking away. He turns when he realizes I'm not following.

"You coming?"

It's hard leaving, but following Dean makes it a little easier.

We begin our trek down the hiking path to the parking lot. I clear my throat. "So," I say. "What are your plans for when you get back?"

Dean hums in thought. "Honestly? I want to go to Applebee's."

"*Applebee's?* What is wrong with you? You didn't get your fill of brown slop at the cafeteria?"

"It reminds me of home, okay? It's my sister's and dad's favorite restaurant—they share the same bad taste. I want to have dinner there as a family." Dean's voice takes on a fonder tone. "Usually when we have dinner all together, it ends in a fight or a lecture. But I think things are going to be better between us now."

"Yeah?"

"Yeah." Dean's smile is confident. "What about you?"

"What about me?"

"What comes next?"

My steps slow.

"Seyoon?"

"I . . ." My mouth goes dry. "I don't really know. I always knew—*hoped* I'd get this far, but I never thought about what comes afterward. What if . . ."

What if this prize money doesn't change anything? It's going to solve my immediate problems—it'll get me and Umma back on our feet—but what about after that? My parents are still divorced. I'm still not on speaking terms with one of my best friends. I still have problems that can't be solved with cash.

A gentle hand rubs my arm. Dean has stepped forward, a consoling turn to his lips.

"Hey, you don't have to have everything figured out all at once. Slow down. What's the *first* thing you're going to do?"

I take a deep breath. The air is thick with damp earth.

"I'm going to buy my mom a house," I say. I've known that since day one. "And help her pay off her bills. Then take her on a nice vacation." I bite my cheek. My phone burns a hole through my bag, still turned off. "But . . . actually, I have some apologies to make first."

Maybe that's why it was so hard to envision what comes next: I've changed too much during my time here to go back to the way things were. I can't pretend any longer that I'm okay with never having another sleepover with Amelia or that I'll be fine if I don't get to cheer on Vendredi when she inevitably makes it on the big screen.

That settles it: My first call will be to Amelia. Then to Vendredi—I'll look her up, I'll find her information. I will. I want to be there for them like they've been there for me. I want to make things right. I need to tell them I'm sorry, and that I miss them. That I'm ready to be a better friend.

I hope they give me a chance to prove it.

Dean bumps his shoulder into mine.

"I think it'll work out," he says. "You're kind of hard to stay mad at."

"Because of my charm, right?"

He rolls his eyes with a laugh. "Yeah. 'Cause of your charm."

Not long after that, the trees break and the trail ends. There are two cars in the lot, their engines running, parked on opposite ends: one to take me home and one to bring Dean to the airport.

"Um," Dean says. "I guess this is it."

The last rays of sun burn around the back of his hair in a blazing disk. Dean is a shocking kind of handsome. It always catches me off guard, no matter how ready for it I think I am.

I don't want to leave him.

When the thought pops into my head this time, it's not a surprise.

"Thank you," I rush out, like I won't ever get the chance to say it again. "For everything. For forgiving me. For being my friend. Thank you for being my partner."

He ducks his head, but I still catch his smile. "We're a team, aren't we?"

There's not a single camera in sight. We gave our clip-on mics back hours ago. There's no one here but me and him—for once, for the first time—and yet I've never felt more exposed.

Even after everything, when I step toward Dean, I hold my breath like I'm afraid he'll reject me. But of course, he doesn't push. He's been reaching out this whole time, waiting for me to do the same. I'm ready now. No more pretending, no more excuses.

Our lips slot together. Dean is fire in places I've only ever been warm. When we deepen the kiss, I focus on remembering how his skin feels against mine, the way he smells of citrus and wood. Even if I saw him every day for the rest of our lives, I'd remember this moment.

I always thought I needed to win. Before all of this, I *did* need it, more than I needed to know my own name. But Dean's helped me realize there's more important things than being a winner. He's helped me realize who I can be.

I want him to be part of everything that comes next.

When we eventually break away, Dean reaches into his back pocket and gives me a folded note.

"If this isn't a poem comparing my eyes to the night sky, I'm going to be really disappointed," I say. I shut up when I see he's written a phone number inside.

Dean wets his lips, staring at the trees instead of me. "I figured since, well, I'm moving to Portland next year for college, it might be nice to know someone in the area. A friendly face." He finally glances at me. "Plus, how else will I send you that poem when it's ready?"

I fold the note up, careful not to add any extra wrinkles, and tuck it into my bag. "Remember that promise I made you during the survival skills challenge? I said when I win, I'd fly you and your sister out to visit." I play with the ends of my hair, trying to act cool. "Offer's still on the table. You know . . . in case you want to come see me sooner. Or something."

I catch his eye then, and something tingles down my spine.

"Seyoon," Dean says around his grin, "if you wanted to go on a date, you could've just said that."

"Cockiness doesn't suit you."

"Then why are you blushing?"

I roll my eyes but drag him down for another kiss, so maybe it suits him a little. That funny feeling in my gut finally settles as soon as our lips meet again.

Right. *This* is what was missing.

I think I'm ready for what comes next.

ROLL CREDITS

ACKNOWLEDGMENTS

There's something writers warn each other about, whispered between inner circles in the same way campers tell ghost stories around a fire: *sophomore novel syndrome.* "Okay, sure," I had said when I heard about it. "Your second book is harder to write? Like, *really* hard to write? Yeah, whatever. Won't happen to me!"

It did happen to me.

If I could go back in time and throttle the Sujin who said that, I would. *Oh*, she was so young. So naive. So throttle-able. She had no idea of The Horrors that were to come. This book challenged me in ways previously thought unknown to man and pushed me to a brink I've never been to before. *However*, through the helping hands of so, so many people, this herculean task of writing a manuscript eventually morphed into a book that I'm really, really proud of. A story I love like a mother adores her problem child. It—and I—wouldn't be here without a dozen friends, families, and colleagues.

Thank you to my brilliant agent, Maeve MacLysaght, who none of this would be possible without. You're the best advocate an anxious writer could ask for, and I count myself lucky to have you in my corner to this day. A huge thank you to both my editors, Stefanie Chin and Abby Ranger, who sat with this book through its ugly, rebellious-teenager phase and helped shape it with patience and kindness. Thank you to Nathan Siegel, Chris Vaccari, and every person on the Union Square & Co. team who supported this project, whether through marketing, copy editing, and more. A big thank you to the talented creatives behind the cover: Marcie Lawrence, Sara Long, and Loz Ives.

To my parents—both sets of them. Mom and Dad, thank you for your continuous love, encouragement, and unwavering confidence in me as an author and person. To Ruthanna and Bill, some of my biggest supporters out there, thank you for being my second family, for your love and support always. I'm so lucky.

To my incredible partner, Ben Frizzell, who has more faith in me than most people have faith that the sun will rise. I'm not sure where it comes from, but if a person as good as you believes in me, it must mean something. Thank you for all you do and are. You're my peace, my favorite person, my best friend, and the reason I know how it feels to love and be loved so that I can write about it. This book wouldn't be here without you, because I wouldn't be here without you.

Writing may be a solitary action, but I was never alone. Thank you, Anahita Karthik, my first and best writing friend, who is so important to me that I can't imagine writing without you. You were the first person I trusted to read this book, and you were the first to make me believe it wasn't a flaming pile of garbage. Thank you to Elle Zi Dong, my favorite writing buddy and one of the most talented people I know, who always makes my day and listens to me vent about writing a million and one times. To all my friends in this industry, thank you: Steph, Zoe, Ash, Sydney, Briana, Chloe, Isa, Hali, Taylor, Nancy, Emma, Jude, Josh, the Magik Cabin group, my agent siblings, and countless others.

To my friends who aren't necessarily in the writing world but cheer me on and have been so excited for me regardless: thank you for everything, I'd be lost without you all. Kylina Nhem-Lim, Keyona Pine, Bella Zulueta, Alison Brashler, Kimmy Nguyen, Dawn Mai, Mia Johnson, Aman Thukral, and so many more.

Last, but definitely not least, thank you to everyone who picked up this book and my debut, *Bingsu for Two.* It's because of you that I'm able to do what I love. Thank you for reading and loving my stories like they're your own. Now, they are.

ABOUT THE AUTHOR

Sujin Witherspoon is a Korean American author, artist, and lover of words she can't pronounce. Her first novel, *Bingsu for Two*, was an Indie Bestseller in the Pacific Northwest. She earned her degree in English from the University of Washington and now spends her time writing, exploring Seattle, and going on very slow hikes. Find her online at sujinwitherspoon.com.